HOUSE OF EVIDENCE

Also by Viktor Arnar Ingolfsson
The Flatey Enigma
Daybreak (forthcoming)

HOUSE OF EVIDENCE

VIKTOR ARNAR INGOLFSSON

Translated by Björg Árnadóttir and Andrew Cauthery

Text copyright © 1998 by Viktor Arnar Ingolfsson
English translation copyright © 2012 by Björg Árnadóttir and Andrew Cauthery

House of Evidence was first published in 1998 by Forlagid as *Engin spor*. Translated from Icelandic by Björg Árnadóttir and Andrew Cauthery. Published in English by AmazonCrossing in 2012.

Published by AmazonCrossing
P.O. Box 400818
Las Vegas, NV 89140

ISBN-13: 9781611090994
ISBN-10: 1611090997
Library of Congress Control Number: 2012913725

This book is dedicated to the memory of my stepfather and friend, engineer Sigfús Örn Sigfússon, who practiced his profession on four continents.

Iceland's first and only railway was built in Reykjavik in 1913, with two locomotives running between Öskjuhlíd and the shore (a distance of two miles), conveying materials for construction projects at Reykjavik harbor from 1913 through 1917. It was decommissioned in 1928, and the last tracks were removed during the Second World War.

—*The Icelandic Encyclopedia*, Volume 2, page 199

FAMILY TREE AS RECORDED BY JACOB KIELER, HISTORIAN

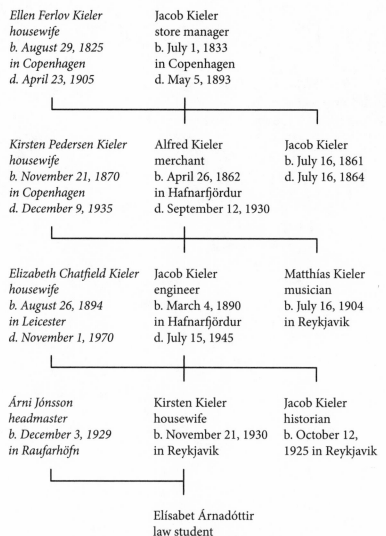

Ellen Ferlov Kieler
housewife
b. August 29, 1825
in Copenhagen
d. April 23, 1905

Jacob Kieler
store manager
b. July 1, 1833
in Copenhagen
d. May 5, 1893

Kirsten Pedersen Kieler
housewife
b. November 21, 1870
in Copenhagen
d. December 9, 1935

Alfred Kieler
merchant
b. April 26, 1862
in Hafnarfjördur
d. September 12, 1930

Jacob Kieler
b. July 16, 1861
d. July 16, 1864

Elizabeth Chatfield Kieler
housewife
b. August 26, 1894
in Leicester
d. November 1, 1970

Jacob Kieler
engineer
b. March 4, 1890
in Hafnarfjördur
d. July 15, 1945

Matthías Kieler
musician
b. July 16, 1904
in Reykjavik

Árni Jónsson
headmaster
b. December 3, 1929
in Raufarhöfn

Kirsten Kieler
housewife
b. November 21, 1930
in Reykjavik

Jacob Kieler
historian
b. October 12,
1925 in Reykjavik

Elísabet Árnadóttir
law student
b. August 8, 1951
in Akureyri

She took the diaries from the box and laid them out on her small desk. There were twelve old, worn books, varying somewhat in design but all of a similar size—four to five inches wide and around seven inches high. Each book contained at least two hundred pages, though the precise number varied. The paper was on the whole thick and of good quality, with well-spaced rulings; the bindings were superior, sturdy. Twelve books—and there were more, she knew that.

Most of the diary entries were short and mundane; descriptions of weather and the like, and she could skip these, but in between there were in-depth contemplations where one day might stretch over several pages. She would have to read these parts thoroughly. Perhaps she might find something that could give a clue to the reasons for the diarist's fate; it was a faint hope, but worth pursuing.

She picked up the first book. The handwriting was clear and easy to decipher.

She read well into the night that first day, and over the days that followed, she usually had two or three books in her bag, using every available moment to leaf through them.

Diary I

June 30, 1910. Today I graduated from high school. After the ceremony at the school, there was a coffee party on the lawn in front of the new house my father is having built on his lot next to Laufástún. Father gave me this book and suggested I should keep a diary. "There may come a time in your life when such a thing will prove very useful," he said in the speech he gave in my honor. I shall try and follow his advice, but I stared at this sheet for a long time before putting pen to paper. How am I going to approach this task? Each written word is there to stay and I must, therefore, think and plan the sentences well. Perhaps that is the first lesson he hopes this task will teach me...

CHAPTER 1

H e no longer felt pain.

Forty-eight-year-old Jacob Kieler Junior sat, legs outstretched, on the floor in the main parlor of Birkihlíd, leaning crookedly against the doorpost that led to the lobby. The wound in his chest bled incessantly. His gray knitted vest was soaked with the blood that poured down his body, forming a pool on the wood floor beneath him. When Jacob moved the hand he was leaning on and it landed in the blood, he looked down in surprise. His breath rattled, and bloodstained froth was forming at the corners of his mouth. His expressionless face had become white and his gray eyes were half-closed.

He had fallen off the chair when the shot hit him. The pain had been unbearable at first, but as he crawled toward the telephone in the lobby to call for help, he became numb and lost the power of his legs.

The parlor, where Jacob now found himself, was a large room, more than a thousand square feet, with a high ceiling. In the middle of the floor to his left were three large, heavy, leather settees; to his right a bay with tall French windows and long, heavy drapes. He examined the German chandelier as if seeing it for the first time. There were twenty-eight bulbs in all. They were arranged

1

in three wreaths, sixteen at the bottom, then eight, and finally four at the top. The light from each bulb was faint, allowing the chandelier's skillful craftsmanship and gilding to show through.

He noticed the open office door at the far end of the parlor. The light had not been switched on in there, and intricate silhouettes appeared on the walls where the light from streetlamps and the night's full moon shone through the windows between bare tree branches. Jacob could see the outline of the large desk in the pale light; it stood there, resolute, waiting patiently for a worthy master.

Through the office windows, he caught a glimpse of the house next door. It was completely dark and utterly silent.

Birkihlíd stands on a narrow street in Reykjavik's old district, to the east of Hljómskáli Park. Early in the century, well-to-do citizens had built their mansions at a polite distance from each other, but more recent residents had added garages and other extensions so now it was all much more cramped. The road, which had originally been intended for pedestrians and horse carriages, had been made into a one-way street with closely packed parking bays on both sides. Trees had been planted next to the houses soon after they were built; they had thrived, growing over many decades, and now towered above the streetlamps. In the summer their leafy crowns obscured the houses and gardens, but at this time of year they stood bare.

Jacob looked through the open door into the dining room. The light was on in there, and he saw eleven high-backed chairs around the large table in the center. The twelfth chair was in the parlor, lying on its side in the middle of the floor. This bothered him. The chair should be in its place. Jacob tried to get to his feet. He wanted to put the chair back where it should be, but he had no feeling below his chest, and the only movement he could manage was a feeble twitching of the shoulders. The large clock that hung from the dining room wall gave a single chime, indicating half past one.

There was a fireplace in the center of the wall to his left, its surround built of slabs of quarried dolerite, set into the wall. The hearth was large and deep, and the floor in front of it was tiled with the same stone as the surround. The fire had not been lit, and the ashes were cold.

A grand piano commanded the space to the left of the fireplace, while on the wall to the right was the portrait of his mother, painted when she was just eighteen years old. She sat straight as an arrow and gazed to one side, an inscrutable expression on her face. What would happen to this picture now, he suddenly wondered, but his thoughts came and went, and this one went without resolution.

He looked over his shoulder into the lobby. There was the telephone on the table, and a small calendar hanging on the wall above it. The year was 1973—Wednesday, January 17. Would anybody remember to change the date in the morning? No, it didn't matter anymore.

His attention was drawn to the chandelier again. Now all the bulbs shone as one light that dimmed and brightened and then dimmed again. In his mind's eye it changed into a globe that came closer and closer.

Outside it had begun to snow. The snowflakes were large and wet, and fell quickly to the ground in the still, dark night, as if the city was pulling a thick, white blanket over itself as it fell to sleep.

Diary I

June 30, 1910. While the visitors were staying with us, my father planted some birch trees along the boundary of the lot, and named the house Birkihlíd.

There are fifteen of us graduating from high school this time, the first ones under the new rules. Eight were external students...

July 1, 1910. The second day of this diary. I am still not sure how to proceed with making this record. It is probably best to let the mind decide, and write whatever is uppermost in my heart each time. I met with my fellow students and friends; we decided to take a trip north by boat to Akureyri, returning south by land...

July 2, 1910. Am getting used to the diary. It is probably best to write it while waiting for supper to be served. If something important happens after that, it can be added before retiring to bed. I cycled to Hafnarfjördur today...

July 4, 1910. I discussed my forthcoming studies with my father. He has not come to terms with my intention to become an engineer. I, on the other hand, am convinced that this is the right decision and am greatly looking forward to beginning my studies in Copenhagen this fall. I begin by reading propaedeutic at Copenhagen University while attending lessons in mathematics and physics at Polyteknisk Læreanstalt, and then start the engineering course the following fall, God willing...

July 5, 1910. Vestri set sail for Akureyri from the harbor at nine o'clock this morning with us companions on board. This is a decent boat, length 160 feet, beam 26 feet, and height 17 feet to the top deck. The first class has 40 passenger cabins, the second class 32. There is a lounge for ladies and a smoking salon for men on the top deck. 24 people can dine at the same time in the dining room. There are bathing cubicles and other amenities. Helgi is seasick...

CHAPTER 2

Jóhann Pálsson was woken at half past five in the morning by sounds of movement from the apartment above. He heard someone urinating, then flushing the toilet; a door closed, and whoever it was moved back across the creaky old timber floor. Then peace descended once more.

He lay still and tried to go back to sleep but his apartment was in a noisy old tenement in Hringbraut, where all sorts of sounds carried easily between floors and through walls. Jóhann began to turn things over in his mind, and this disturbed him. The task waiting for his attention at work had come into his thoughts and he tried without success to fix his mind on something else. It was no use; he was wide awake.

Jóhann sat up and switched on his bedside light. His double bed was in one corner of the bedroom, while an old desk occupied the rest of the available floor space. There was a large microscope in the center of the desk, which was otherwise covered in books, papers, and pieces of clothing.

It took him a while to get up, not because he was sleepy, but rather because his mind was elsewhere. Anyway, there was no hurry, he thought to himself. He washed his face with cold water and regarded himself in the mirror. His eyes were gray, his skin rather coarse following an adolescent spotty phase. He had a wide, slightly upturned nose and thick, unruly, mousy-colored hair. He stroked his cheek and decided to put off shaving. He planned to go to the baths at lunchtime anyway, where he liked getting into the hottest pool, submerging his head to soften the skin of his face, and then enjoying a good shave afterward.

Jóhann was in his early thirties, and worked in the detective division of the City Police in Reykjavik. By the time he was twenty-three years old, he had completed an intermediate degree in chemistry at the University of Iceland; the following fall he had traveled to America for graduate studies.

He settled down at the George Washington University campus in the center of Washington, DC, and started to prepare for his courses. While perusing the books at the university bookshop, he came across a thick book titled simply *Crime Investigation*. A textbook on scientific methods of police investigation, more than five hundred pages long, with innumerable pictures and drawings, *Crime Investigation* immediately captured Jóhann's interest. The description of how a burglar had been caught through the examination of traces left on the plastic shoehorn he had used to loosen a bolt from a door hinge absorbed Jóhann. Three hours later he stood up, walked to the counter, and bought the book, despite its high price. Then he went straight to the university office and asked where this subject was taught. He was directed to the Forensic Science Department, where he found a professor who was amused by this eager foreigner. Jóhann was given permission to take a look at the research laboratories and the various projects the students were working on.

The following night he couldn't sleep at all. This subject suited him to a T. He had never been interested in crime or the police—or even crime fiction—until now, but what this book revealed

7

about the research methods investigators used intrigued him. Scientific accuracy, patience, attention to detail, scrupulousness, and prolific imagination were required, and he had a feeling that these were attributes he might just possess.

By dawn he had made a decision, and the following day he put in an application to change departments. Three years later he had passed the exam, and when he needed to explain in his mother tongue what he had studied, he invented an Icelandic word, *réttarvísindi*, for forensic science.

At first he had worked for the police in Fairfax County, Virginia, but was soon offered his current job in Reykjavik. He had arrived here in spring 1971, and had been working as an investigator in the forensics department for a year and eight months.

Jóhann got dressed and went into the small kitchen. He was not hungry, but knew that would change as the morning wore on. He made three sandwiches with butter and a thick spread of liver pâté, wrapped them in plastic, and then rinsed the utensils and put them away. He had always lived in compact lodgings since he'd moved out of the family home in Akureyri in his early twenties, and had learned from experience that it was better to keep a tidy home. After all, there was nobody to clean up after him.

He put on a thick parka and crept soundlessly down the stairs, aware that most of the other residents of the building were probably still asleep. It was snowing, and he put on a woolen hat as soon as he got outside. His five-year-old Ford Cortina was parked nearby, and he carefully cleared the snow off it before driving away. The roads were slippery, so he drove slowly, first east along Hringbraut, then north along Snorrabraut toward Borgartún. He was in no hurry, and he found it comforting to be the only one up and about in the city so early in the morning.

The division's headquarters were situated on the top floor of an office building in Borgartún. Jóhann headed up the stairs and down a corridor to the laboratory. He started up the coffee machine before going to his desk and switching on his microscope.

A car had been stolen in Kópavogur, not really a story in itself, except that the thief had run over a pedestrian and then driven off. The pedestrian, a man in his seventies, had died in the hospital two days later. The car had been found abandoned a few hours after the incident, bearing clear evidence of the collision: a broken headlamp and various dents and scratches on the bumper and body of the car. An empty vodka bottle had been abandoned on the floor in the back of the car, and it was covered in the fingerprints of a well-known petty thief and all-around troublemaker. It didn't take long for the man to admit to having been in the car, and to identify a companion of his as the driver. The companion, on the other hand, denied everything, and now it was one man's word against the other's. The alleged driver had supposedly been wearing gloves, leaving no fingerprints in or on the car. Now it was Jóhann's task to find proof that this guy had actually been behind the wheel.

In Jóhann's experience it was highly likely that someone sitting in a car for any period of time would leave behind a few hairs. Human hair is complicated in structure, and while two hairs from the same person may not be identical, there is enough similarity to match them with some degree of confidence. And, in order to make this identification, various elements need to be examined, such as density, refraction, and so on.

Jóhann had vacuumed the car thoroughly using a machine with a special filter designed for forensic purposes. He had retrieved 374 hairs, discarding 220 of those that obviously belonged to the car owner's dog, and then sorted the human hairs according to type and color. He now compared them under the microscope with the hair of the car owner and of the two suspects. Various tests would then be carried out on these hairs, and when the tests were completed they might offer proof of the alleged driver's identity that would support the witness's testimony in court.

Jóhann was a scientist; he tackled this type of work objectively, dwelling on neither the tragedy that had taken place nor those involved. His job was to discover all the information that these physical pieces of evidence could provide. Either they would lead to acquittal or to conviction.

The building was quiet at this early hour. Now and again creaking and knocking noises from the central heating system could be heard, and outside the distant sounds of an occasional car driving past. There was a faint but distinct chemical smell in the room that was soon overpowered by the aroma of freshly brewed coffee.

Diary I

July 6, 1910. Woke up at seven on board Vestri.
Arrived at Hólmavík, docking at eight o'clock a.m.
There is still snow lying all the way down to the shore
in Steingrímsfjördur, it is cold and raining...

July 7, 1910. Saw Drangey Island. There were men
out there in boats, catching birds...

July 8, 1910. Arrived at Akureyri at four a.m.,
disembarked at six. Walked into town. Sunshine and
balmy weather, calm sea. On Oddeyrartangi there

were piles of small fish on the quaysides. Helgi and I walked to the church and back. The inhabitants of Akureyri are so wonderfully tasteful; they have beautiful gardens, with trees and flowers around the houses. In some places the trees are as tall as the houses...

July 9, 1910. We borrowed a boat and rowed across Eyjafjördur. We walked across Vadlaheidi to have a look at the new bridge that was built across the Fnjóská River in the summer of 1908. The bridge spans 55 meters from bank to bank, yet the thickness of the arch is only 50 centimeters at the top. Vigfús says that this is the longest arch bridge to have been built in the whole of Scandinavia. The woodland is fenced in, and the trees reach a height of 8 meters...

July 10, 1910. Set off on foot from Akureyri. Breeze from the north and rain showers. We have a picnic for the day...Öxnadalur valley is similar to Hörgárdalur except that it is narrower and there is less vegetation on the hillsides. Toward the mouth of the valley it is almost closed off by sand dunes partially covered by grass, "Hillocks high that half the valley fill," as poet Jónas Hallgrímsson put it; the farm, Hraun, where he was born, is there...Arriving at Bakkasel, where we shall overnight.

CHAPTER 3

It was almost eight o'clock, and *Morgunbladid* had still not been delivered. Halldór Benjamínsson opened the front door and looked around for the paperboy. He didn't want to start breakfast before the newspaper arrived. An eight-inch-thick blanket of snow had fallen during the night, greeting him at the threshold.

"Halldór, dear, your tea is getting cold," his wife, Stefanía, called from the kitchen.

He closed the door and went back inside. He was tall and slim, with a bit of a paunch. His gray hair, thinning a little, was carefully combed with a part on the right side. He wore spectacles with a thin gold frame. His face usually bore a benevolent expression, though this morning he was feeling grouchy.

"Can't you read yesterday's paper, dear?" asked Stefanía.

"I've already read it."

He looked at the kitchen table. There were two teacups and saucers, and plates with toast beside them. A fat teapot stood there, too, with red tea-bag labels dangling from underneath the lid.

He examined the pattern on the china as he bit into his toast. Gold wreaths and braids atop a white glaze—it had been a wedding present from nearly thirty-five years earlier; during the first years of their marriage, it had been used for best times only, but it had long since entered daily use, with another set reserved for special occasions. There were fewer cups than there used to be, though.

"Will you be working for long?" Stefanía asked.

"Probably not," Halldór replied, glancing at his wife. She was wearing a long bathrobe, but apart from that there was nothing to indicate that she had just woken up. Her blond hair was carefully combed and her modest makeup was in place.

"You remember we've got a bridge evening here," she reminded him.

"Yes," he lied.

"It's only once a month and there's no television tonight anyway," she said.

"I'll try and come home early."

"Since we're playing here, I must make a cake. What sort would you like?"

"Apple cake."

"I made apple cake last time. We can't serve it again."

"Make something else, then."

"I'll make apple cake if that's what you really want."

From the lobby came the snap of the lid of the mailbox and a faint thud as the paper landed on the floor inside.

"About time," he said, rising to get the paper.

He glanced over the front page as he came back into the kitchen.

"Vietnam: Peace Clearly in Sight but No Timeline Yet," the headline read. He turned the paper over. "Trawls Still Being Cut," read one headline under the fold, and another said, "Twenty-One Trawlers Out of Action if Strike Goes Ahead."

Halldór had been a policeman all his working life, and was now a senior officer at the detective division in Reykjavik, in spite of the fact that he had always found the job tedious, and in the beginning had only accepted it as a stopgap measure.

When he moved to the city with his elderly parents early on during the Depression, work had been scarce. He was a good prospect, however—a tall, polite young man. A member of parliament from his home district, who knew his father and knew that he had left behind many relatives in his constituency, had found Halldór a job with the police, where he had come to earn a reputation for conscientiousness and good handwriting. Halldór wrote better reports than almost anyone else, and this was one of the reasons he was offered a job in the detective division. He accepted it in order to get out of the uniform. Much later he had been given a promotion, when his turn came, on grounds of seniority.

When he was younger, he had sometimes thought about becoming a schoolmaster and teaching spelling, but then he had discovered that children scare him; he found it easier to deal with criminals. He had become used to this life, or else he lacked the courage to change it.

Halldór glanced at the clock and stood up. He took a thick gray overcoat from the closet in the lobby, along with a checkered scarf and a fur hat. At the front door he slipped into a pair of well-polished black leather winter boots. His wife handed him his briefcase and kissed him on the cheek.

"Bye, dear, and be careful; it's very slippery," she warned. He stopped for a moment on the steps. It was still snowing, and the branches on the big conifers sagged under the bulk of the snow that had piled upon them during the night. It was rare for this amount of snow to fall when it was so calm, and it rather reminded him of a Christmas card. The snow creaked as he carefully descended the steps.

Diary I

July 12, 1910. Skagafjördur. Woke early and crawled out of the tent. The fog had lifted and now there was a view all round. Hegranes is low-lying on the eastern side along the lagoons, but higher toward the west, where marshes alternate with gravel flats and steep cliffs...Crossing the western lagoons by an ancient rope ferry that is hauled by manpower with a winch, an antique if ever I saw one. The ferry carries 8 to 10 horses, and the tariff is 5 aurar per horse and 10 aurar per person. The ferryman is tall, with a full, strawberry-blond beard; a good-looking man, and likeable. He invited us to take a draught from his flask of brennivín after we had paid him a generous fare. He lives on his own in a hovel by the mouth of the lagoon. I felt dizzy during the ferry. Perhaps it was the brennivín. I am not used to it...

July 14, 1910. We set out over Holtavörduheidi. You are hardly aware of the escarpment, although the ground rises steadily. There are a number of watercourses and small rivers to wade across, with concrete arch bridges over the largest ones. In the middle of the heath, there are a number of small lakes with trout, and close by, on top of a prominence, there is a refuge hut; innermost it has a cabin intended for human habitation while the rest is for horses. There are two bunks in the cabin, a table and cooking utensils, kettles, jugs, a lamp, and other things. There are cribs along the walls in front, and in the loft there is hay. The house is built from turf and stone, with a metal roof and wooden gable...

CHAPTER 4

It was eleven o'clock in the morning, and Sveinborg Pétursdóttir, a stocky woman who was getting on in years, was on her way to work from her home in Ránargata, east through the Kvos then up toward Laufás. Day was just breaking, but the streetlights were still lit, casting an eerie glow over the snowflakes that drifted earthward in the stillness. There was not much traffic on the streets; most people were now at work and the new snow had already covered their footprints.

Sveinborg plodded on slowly but steadily. She was wearing woolen socks and a sensible pair of wellingtons that were covered by her heavy, long skirt. She wore a blue nylon parka and had a thick wool hat on her head.

This was the route she had walked most days for nigh on twenty-six years. Before that she had been a live-in housekeeper at her current place of employment, so altogether she had been at the house for forty-five years. It was her opinion that having a good employer and the ability to walk to work was life's greatest happiness.

She paused at a gap in the ice on the edge of Tjörnin Lake, took a paper bag out of her pocket, and picked out a few pieces of bread, throwing them one at a time to the hungry ducks paddling in the meager opening. She often stopped here in bad weather, knowing that there would be few people around to feed these poor creatures that she counted among her best friends. She watched the birds squabble over the crumbs, and tried on her next throw to divide the bread more evenly between them. One of the ducks seemed to be fighting a losing battle, so she threw the next bit in its direction.

"Here you are, ducky," she said softly, "there's a bit for you, and don't let those bullies take it, now."

When the bag was empty, she folded it up and tucked it into her pocket.

She crossed Fríkirkjuvegur, plowed through the snow diagonally across Hallargardur Park, and continued up Skothúsvegur. A few minutes later she paused for a moment on the sidewalk in front of her destination to catch her breath.

Birkihlíd was a handsome villa by Reykjavik standards, comprising a single main story with unusually tall windows, a large attic area under its steep roof, and a semi-sunken basement. The exterior walls were pale-gray roughcast and the roof was covered with red diamond-shaped tiles. A large bay window in the front, topped by a balcony leading to a large garret room, lent the house a distinguished appearance. The house name was displayed in relief lettering on the front of the bay, and below it the year it was built, 1910. Broad steps led to the front door on the home's left-hand gable, behind which was a later addition that, although quite tasteful, somewhat disturbed the balance of the whole.

The garden was enclosed by a tall stone wall topped with close-set metal railings between sturdy concrete posts. Flanking the garden were the majestic birch trees that had inspired the name of the house, their massive branches crowned with a thick layer of snow.

Sveinborg pushed open the heavy gate. Bypassing the front door, she headed toward the back of the house, where there was another, less imposing entrance. She took a large key from her bag and unlocked the door. Brushing off the worst of the snow, she took her coat off and hung it on a hook.

Entering the kitchen from the rear vestibule was like stepping back in time fifty years. Though the kitchen was nicely decorated and everything in it was spotless and perfect, there seemed to be nothing less than half a century old. The room was nearly three times as long as it was wide, and at the far end, just past the breakfast area, was a door leading to the dining room. Large worktables lined the outside wall, and along the inside wall stood a coal-fired range with a steam extractor above it. Antiquated kitchen utensils, pots, and pans hung from hooks everywhere.

Sveinborg looked into the kitchen sink and saw that it was empty. Her plump features registered surprise.

Jacob hasn't eaten anything, she thought, unless he's also cleaned the dishes, and it wouldn't be like him to do that.

On the inside wall, where the ceiling sloped down beneath the staircase to the second floor, there were some large cupboards, one of which she opened to reveal a newish refrigerator. There, on the shelf where she had left it, was a plate of carefully arranged cold cuts covered in plastic wrap.

"Oh, he hasn't touched his breakfast," she said out loud.

She looked up toward the ceiling and listened for a moment, but could hear no one moving about.

"Perhaps he's not up yet," she said, more quietly this time.

She went back toward the rear entry, turned, and ascended the narrow staircase to the attic rooms. There she came to a wide corridor that stretched the length of the upper floor. A little farther along the corridor was the head of another, much wider, staircase leading down to the main lobby. She continued along the corridor and looked into one of the rooms on the left. There was a made-up bed, a bedside table, a large clothes closet, and a chair. This was a relatively comfortable room, somewhat more modern than the other living quarters in the house.

He was not there. Sveinborg was becoming anxious now, and felt a strange premonition. She went downstairs using the main staircase, and it was when she reached the middle landing, where the stairs turned a full ninety degrees, that she saw him. Jacob Junior was sprawled, legs outstretched, against a pair of double doors that opened into the parlor. His legs pointed toward the parlor and his head hung limply on his chest. Beneath him lay a pool of congealed blood.

Sveinborg felt a chill seize her heart and creep up her neck to the roots of her hair. She made her way down the stairs step by step, leaning on the massive carved-oak handrail for support. When she reached the bottom she hesitated for a moment, as if she dared not let go of the rail, but then moved toward him and tentatively touched his forehead. It was ice-cold.

She pulled her hand back, turned, and ran to the front door.

"Help, help," she called faintly from the front steps, but there was nobody to hear her cry.

She retreated to the lobby, stumbling toward the old telephone by the window. She retrieved the directory from a low shelf and quickly leafed through it with trembling hands.

"Police, police," she repeated frantically, paging back and forth until she at last found the number she was looking for, and then shakily dialed 1 11 66.

Diary I

July 16, 1910. Started the day early at Reykholt. Wonderful weather, sunshine and clear skies. Had salmon to eat, with melted butter and bread to accompany. Before setting off today we had coffee and sandwiches with all kinds of fillings, meat, sausage, etc. The pastor refused to accept any money for the accommodation, but we were allowed to pay for the picnic. Traveled diagonally across Reykholtsdalur valley by Kópareykir. Here there were young women washing clothes in a hot spring...

July 17, 1910. As we arrived at Svínadalur, we met a man who told us that a motorboat would be sailing that evening from Saurbær to Reykjavik, carrying passengers. We hastened our journey and managed to arrive in time to be ferried on board...

July 18, 1910. Arrived Reykjavik at six a.m. after a difficult sea crossing. Everybody was up by the time I got home, cold and tired. Slept for the better part of the day...

CHAPTER 5

Halldór was standing by the north window, looking out. There was a good view to both the north and south from the detective division's floor, though people working on the south side of the building often complained about the heat when it was sunny. Reykjavik's Criminal Court headquarters was on the floor below, and Halldór knew that despite the good views, the building was cramped and in many ways unsuitable for so many staff.

It had finally stopped snowing, and by now was quite bright, though the wind was kicking up. Halldór could see north across the bay to Engey Island, and in the distance, snow-covered Mount Akrafjall, the dark-blue sea separating the two. The harbor was to the west, and a Coast Guard boat was just putting out to sea; Halldór thought it might be the *Thór*. The Coast Guard had plenty to do now, defending the new fifty-mile fishing limits.

It was a quiet morning in the detective division. One man had been arrested for alleged assault, and interviews in a rape case had been completed. Apart from that, two men had been taken into custody and charged with car theft and driving under the influence that had resulted in a fatal accident.

Halldór picked up binoculars that lay on the windowsill and followed the Coast Guard boat as it turned out into the bay and headed into the north wind. From the back of the room came a series of rhythmic clicks and squeaks; a man was talking on the phone at his desk, squeezing a small fitness tool with his free hand.

"But he was totally unmanageable!" the man exclaimed.

Halldór put the binoculars down, turned his gaze back to the room, and looked sadly at Egill Ingólfsson, his subordinate. He knew what the case was about. Egill had supervised an arrest the previous Tuesday that had resulted in a confrontation and now complaints were being made.

Egill was tan and semi-bald, with snow-white, close-cut hair and a long pointed nose. His tight white short-sleeved shirt showed off an athletic chest.

"He already had the mark on his face when we arrested him," Egill said, frowning and squeezing the fitness tool even harder.

The room contained three old desks, a few filing cabinets, and two typewriters. Innermost was Halldór's small office.

At the other end of the room, Erlendur Haraldsson, another colleague, was trying on some ski boots and had scattered the packaging all over the floor. He had rolled his trousers up above his knees, displaying his hairy legs, and now crouched, rocking back and forth to test the fit of the boots. He was a little over six feet tall, with a slender frame that got wider the farther down you went.

"You have to break new ski boots in before using them for the first time," he replied to Halldór's unasked question.

Halldór simply nodded, feigning only minimal interest. Erlendur was about to take a winter vacation, going with his family on a long-planned ski trip to Austria the coming Saturday. They had been saving up for two years, and Erlendur hardly talked about anything else.

"Is Halli looking forward to it?" Halldór asked in order to say something. Halli was Erlendur's younger child, a lad of seventeen, loved by everybody but educationally impaired and hard of hearing. He was good at math but challenged in other areas.

"I'll say," Erlendur replied. "He has become very good at skiing. He goes to Skálafell on his own by bus, and was working for his uncle in the Kerlingafjöll mountains all summer."

"Now, you listen to me," Egill barked angrily into the phone, "we arrested the guy; he resisted and got a few scrapes. I got some scrapes as well." He put the fitness tool down and examined the back of his slightly scraped hand.

"Bloody rude of the lad to chew your knuckles," Erlendur interjected.

"Oh yeah, is that what she says?" Egill spat into the phone, shooting an annoyed glance at Erlendur. He covered the mouthpiece and explained to Halldór, "It was the *girl* who complained."

Halldór knew that Egill meant Hrefna Hilmarsdóttir, their colleague. They had been working together that week and it had apparently not been altogether peaceful.

Erlendur continued to offer his opinion: "Typical of these broads. Nothing but trouble." He shook his head, pretending to be terribly shocked.

Halldór sat down and leafed through some reports that were ready for the prosecutor. He was irritated by the style of Egill's writing about the assault and the report's many spelling errors. He pushed the papers to one side, planning on correcting it later. He glanced at a report on an alleged rape that Hrefna had written; it was tidy and well written, but it was obvious where the writer's sympathies lay. Hrefna occasionally forgot that everyone is innocent until proven guilty, but there was nothing in this report that actually overstepped the mark so Halldór approved it.

Just then his telephone rang.

"Detective division, Halldór speaking," he answered and then grabbed a pad and began jotting down some notes. "We'll be there immediately," he said and hung up.

"A man's been found dead," he announced as he stood up. "The guys at the downtown station need help. They say there are signs of assault."

Egill brightened, and then turned back to his phone call. "Look, I don't have time for this; we've got work to do here." He slammed the phone down, and called to Halldór, "I'll get the car."

Halldór turned to Erlendur. "Get Hrefna and follow us. Tell forensics too, and remember to change your footwear. Here's the address."

He tore a page from his pocket diary and passed it to Erlendur before walking out.

Diary I

July 21, 1910. Have at long last got rid of the fatigue from our journey, but am still suffering from a cold. Young Matthías has contracted scarlet fever and has to be in isolation in his room...

July 25, 1910. Went to watch a 500-meter running race at Melarnir. Ólafur came first. Not many spectators, only two to three hundred people...

August 2, 1910. My journey abroad is in preparation...

CHAPTER 6

Hrefna lay awake in her bed gazing up at the white ceiling. In spite of having worked long into the night, she had woken early, around ten o'clock, unable to sleep any more, and now she had been just lying there for an hour.

I'm a detective, she thought. Once upon a time that had seemed a big word to her. Two years ago she was just a cop, a woman in an ill-fitting uniform that had been designed with a man's body in mind. It had been a relief to not have to wear that outfit anymore. Now, however, she was thinking about her plans for the future. She knew she had abilities that were not being exploited in this job. The only thing she lacked was self-confidence, but that had grown as she had gotten older. At thirty-three years old, she was ready to tackle something new, which is why the resignation letter was in her handbag.

Hrefna missed those lazy mornings long ago when she had been able to sleep in. That had all changed when Elsa was born. She had been only eighteen years old at the time, and now Elsa was fifteen. Elsa was going to be okay—indeed, Hrefna felt at times that her daughter was the more mature of the two of them. In a way, they had grown up together, but Elsa was quicker and more successful at exploiting the talents she possessed.

Hrefna sat up on the side of the bed and shivered. The window was open and a cold breeze was blowing in; she was wearing only panties and her yellow-and-red Led Zeppelin T-shirt. She reached for her thick bathrobe that lay under a pile of clothes on the chair next to the bed, and, after putting it on, went into the bathroom.

Her blond hair was far too long, she thought, as she looked at herself in the mirror over the sink. She brushed her teeth carefully, noticing the front tooth that was crooked and overlapped its neighbor. Her dentist had tried to convince her that she should have it fixed, but she didn't want to; someone had once told her that it made her look aggressive and she liked that.

Elsa was already at school and Hrefna was on call that day after four long shifts in a row. Perhaps she would have the day off and could use the time to do some long-overdue tidying of the apartment. The last few days had been grueling.

A young woman in her twenties had brought forth a charge of rape, and she had taken the victim's statement. This was her usual role in the detective division and probably the only reason she had been recruited there. They felt they needed a woman for such interviews, and she was good at it. She knew that in order for a case to hold up in court, the victim would need to know exactly what had happened, and Hrefna was adept at getting the women to express themselves. The victims often had problems finding the right words to describe what had happened to them, and she was able to help them by showing them previous reports. For while each crime was unique, the language for these crimes had long since been standardized.

In this particular case, the young woman had reported the rape on Monday morning. She was an air hostess, and had been alone at home in her apartment on Sunday evening when an old boyfriend of hers had phoned, asking if he could come over. She agreed, since they had parted on friendly terms and she could hear that he was feeling miserable. Although he had been under the influence of alcohol when he arrived, she had offered him a beer. He talked and she listened, and finally she asked him to leave, as she had a flight the following morning and needed to get up early. But he didn't leave. And not wanting to argue with him, she climbed into bed fully dressed and fell asleep. She woke later in the night, took off her jeans, and fell back to sleep.

The next thing she knew he had slid naked under her duvet.

She told him to get out, but he got on top of her, and when she tried to scream, he covered her mouth. Then he was inside her. She couldn't breathe and when she had at last managed to free herself from his grip, she screamed and cried. He stopped then, got up, dressed, and left. She had lain, curled up and shaking, for several hours before daring to move. Then came uncertainty: Would this count as rape? Did she want to charge him? She phoned a girlfriend and, in tears, told her what had happened; her girlfriend came over immediately and they went together to the police station, where they were sent to see Hrefna.

After the victim had made her statement, Hrefna sent her to the hospital for an examination, and the subsequent medical report stated that the capillaries in her eyes evidenced temporary oxygen deprivation and the skin around her lips was reddened from when his hand had covered her mouth; a bruise was evident on the inside of her thigh; and no semen was found in her vagina.

The accused was arrested and brought in for questioning. The man did not acknowledge rape of any kind. He said he had had sexual intercourse with this woman many times, and they had for a time been going steady.

"What is a guy to think when a woman he's visiting goes to bed?" he had smirked.

He did admit that the woman had started crying and screaming, which was why he had stopped immediately. He said he hadn't even had an orgasm.

Hrefna was convinced that the man would be found guilty. The doctor's note supported the woman's testimony, and the guy was stupid. He had confessed too much. He was dumb enough to think that the woman's behavior indicated consent.

Hrefna was in the shower when the phone rang. It was Erlendur. He would pick her up in ten minutes.

Diary I

August 5, 1910. On board Sterling. *Second day at sea. Vestmannaeyjar in sight. Played bridge and read from* Hjemmet *and* Familie Journal *magazines to practice my Danish...*

August 6, 1910. Third day at sea. Sat up on deck and thought. I sense clearly that I am at the beginning of a new and important period in my life. I shall spend a long time in distant lands...

August 12, 1910. We sailed into Øresund early this morning. There were forests of ships' masts and land visible on both sides as we progressed, with thick-trunked trees and stately farms. Soon the skyline was broken by towers; the big city was upon us.

On tying up at the quayside, one could see wide, cobbled streets and many-storied houses. Everywhere multitudes of people and a variety of vehicles. I find the trams most remarkable... We students are received at the Customs Wharf and escorted to a hall of residence...

August 13, 1910. Walked about the city with my companions and looked at places of significance. I became separated from the rest of the group at the train station. The station building is enormous and has an arched roof. There are four tracks beneath the roof. I am told that an even larger train station is being built here in the city. I spent most of the day in the station, watching the trains come and go. People streamed in, ready to travel, and disappeared into the passenger cars. Whistles were blown and the trains ground into motion amid much discharge of steam and smoke...

September 3, 1910. Studies begin at the School of Engineering. The president gave a speech outlining the school's history. It was founded through the agency of the famous physician H. C. Ørsted, in accordance with royal decree, on January 27, 1829. In his speech the president gave a detailed account of the enormous importance all natural sciences *have, together with mathematics, for the physical and cultural development of all nations... This winter I shall prepare for the engineering entrance examination by attending classes in mathematics and physics. I shall also read philosophy at Copenhagen University...*

CHAPTER 7

Halldór had noted the time of the call in the pocket diary lying open on his desk: 11:27 a.m. Now, as he got into the car, it was 11:35.

He directed Egill to one of the older areas of the city; a neighborhood where Halldór and his wife often went for walks. The house in question was one he was familiar with, and although it had an address, it was usually referred to simply as Birkihlíd.

As they drove, he read to Egill what he had noted during the phone call: "Male aged about fifty, dead for several hours, clear signs of violence, no one else in the house, lives alone, the house-keeper found him."

Egill drove fast and the car slid about in the snow but Halldór didn't protest, he just held on tightly. As they arrived at Birkihlíd, Halldór noted the time: 11:46.

A large police car was parked outside the house, and next to it stood two women chatting. A small boy wearing waterproof pants and mittens that were too big for him came shuffling along the sidewalk dragging a toboggan.

The detectives paused at the gate, peering into the garden.

"This snow might prove useful," Halldór remarked.

Clear sets of footprints were visible, and it was obvious they belonged to at least three different people. Egill nodded, and they both looked down at the sidewalk in front of the gate. Many feet had already trampled a deep track through the snow. Nothing to be gained there.

They passed through the gate and made their way toward the house, keeping well to one side of any visible footprints. As they came up the steps, the front door opened and a young police officer looked out.

"You had, of course, to walk all over any footprints," Egill barked without further greeting.

The young man squirmed. "We had no idea what had happened." Then he added, a bit more confidently, "But we've taken care not to touch anything inside."

"Including the doorknob you're clutching at the moment," Egill replied.

The policeman yanked his hand from the knob as if it were red-hot.

"Go and get some people to close the area off," Halldór ordered. "Cordon off the whole garden apart from the track we took. There's yellow plastic tape in our car in case you haven't got any. Follow our tracks and make sure that anybody else who comes near the house does the same."

The two detectives then stepped inside the lobby. Directly opposite the front door was the entrance to a larger, inner vestibule, with a window to one side that allowed sunlight in. To the right of where they stood was a large space for hanging coats, and to the left a closet for footwear and a small chair.

Once inside the inner vestibule, they saw the lifeless body of the victim on the floor. He was slumped against the doorpost of the parlor. Another police officer, an older man, approached. He had taken off his uniform cap and was clutching it between his hands. Halldór wondered if this was a sign of respect for the dead or just an indication that the officer was too hot.

"The lady who found him is in the kitchen," the policeman remarked by way of a greeting.

They didn't need to talk to her just yet, Halldór decided; Hrefna would do it when she arrived.

"Go to her. Make sure you don't touch anything, but you can give her some water to drink," he told the policeman.

Halldór and Egill moved toward the body. The man did look to be about fifty years old, though it was difficult to tell for sure from his now snow-white face. The man's eyes were half-open, dull. He was dressed neatly, in dark gray, well-pressed trousers, a white shirt, a blue bow tie, and a light-gray knitted vest. A hole in one of the shirt elbows had been mended. On his feet he had well-worn slippers made of black leather.

To the left of his chest, beneath his heart, was a black hole in the vest with a dark stain trailing down to the floor, where it ended in a pool of congealed blood. Halldór bent down and examined the hole carefully. Tiny black specks were visible on the vest around the hole.

"Gunshot wound from close range," he said, straightening up.

"Looks like he bled to death," Egill added.

Halldór followed the trail of blood across the parlor floor with his eyes. Egill did the same and then exclaimed, "Fancy parlor or what!"

Halldór contemplated the furniture: three heavy leather sofas, two three-seaters and a two-seater, formed a wide U in the center of the floor in front of the fireplace, with a pair of low coffee tables between them. Beautiful woven rugs lay on the shiny, varnished floor. While the furniture was clearly all quite old, it was remarkably unworn. One of the dining chairs lay on its side between the leather sofas, and it was there that the trail of blood ended.

He turned back to the body. There was blood on the knees of the trousers and the toes of the slippers, and the trail on the floor showed signs of smudging.

"Looks like he crawled here himself," Halldór said. "I doubt he's been dragged here."

Egill returned to the lobby, where there was a low table made of dark wood. An old black telephone with a steel dial rested on it, and underneath it had a shelf containing some newspapers and a telephone directory. Beside the table was a matching chair with an embroidered cushion and an upholstered back.

"This is odd. It looks as if he's tried to get help, but gave up just before reaching the phone," Egill said, coming back into the parlor.

"That's true," Halldór replied. "Maybe he just couldn't manage to get any farther."

Egill was not satisfied with this explanation.

"But he could have written some clue on the floor, in blood. There's plenty of it."

"He was probably thinking about something else," Halldór answered, looking at the chair lying on the parlor floor. It had been removed from the dining room and placed there. That must mean something. The chair was the only thing out of place in the room. "It's not easy to pin down the direction of the shot," he continued. "It looks as if he was by the chair, probably sitting on it, and then knocked it over when he was hit."

Halldór removed a small flashlight from his coat pocket and knelt down, shining the light underneath the chair.

"Well, there's no gun here," he said. "So he didn't shoot himself."

He examined the dining chair a bit more carefully. Based on its current position, it had most likely been facing into the parlor, in which case the shot would have come from the bay window. It could, of course, have come from a different direction, but nevertheless he checked the thick drapes that covered the windows. They seemed intact. He drew them slightly apart, letting daylight into the room.

The windows were also undamaged. Halldór could see the street from where he now stood, and he noticed that Jóhann from forensics had just arrived.

"Go and tell Jóhann to start by checking the footprints in the snow," he told Egill, before turning his attention back to the chair. Why had it been moved over there? Maybe the housekeeper could explain it. He hoped that Hrefna and Erlendur would arrive soon.

Diary I

October 24, 1910. My studies are progressing well and I lead an orderly life. Not something that can be said of all my fellow students. Minerva, goddess of wisdom, and Bacchus, god of wine, fight for their souls. It is mainly my visits to the train station that affect my studies. I was tested in front of the class today and gained a "meget godt," a merit grade...

November 2, 1910. I and seven of my fellow students have established a Rise-and-Shine Club among ourselves. Members of the club are obligated to meet at seven o'clock each morning except Sundays. I was voted treasurer, and have to note down the names of those who do not attend, and they must pay a fine. The funds thus accrued are to be used to pay for a celebration for the club members. This is an attempt to keep us comrades focused on our studies...

November 4, 1910. I like the mathematics and physics very much. Philosophy, however, I find tedious, though I do try to pay just as much attention to it as to the other subjects, in order to get good marks. I am now convinced that I have chosen the right course of study, and am very happy to have followed my instinct. In my work as an engineer I shall have to deal with a great number of problems posed for me by life and nature. These I shall solve with a scientifically disciplined mind...

December 5, 1910. The Rise-and-Shine Club has been disbanded. Helgi did not once show up, he always oversleeps. Others owe less. Little of the amount due has been paid...

CHAPTER 8

Hrefna had just started dressing when Erlendur rang the outside bell. She answered the intercom and told him she'd be down in a moment, knowing that he would get back into the car and wait patiently. Erlendur did not get unnecessarily stressed.

She slipped on a pair of jeans, a T-shirt, and a light-colored pullover. It looked cold outside, so she decided on her thick parka, too. She stuffed a hat and some gloves into her pockets and pulled on a pair of thick woolen socks and her sturdy winter boots.

As she ran down the stairs, Hrefna noticed the worn linoleum floor, which, though clean, had seen better days; the potted plants on the landing were slowly being killed off by the cold that penetrated easily through the single-pane windows, and now the wind had kicked up, making the front door difficult to close.

Hrefna's apartment building was conveniently located in the Hlídar district, but the building was showing its age both inside and out. Hrefna noticed the building's yellow exterior paint was patchy and dirty as she climbed into Erlendur's car.

"What's happening?" she asked, as she closed the passenger door.

Erlendur told her he wasn't exactly sure, but it seemed to be serious, perhaps even a murder. They drove in silence the rest of the way, in the direction of the city center, listening to the chatter on the police radio.

The road the house stood on had been closed off, with a police car parked right across the carriageway and a wide yellow ribbon strung between the lampposts bearing the words "Police—No Admittance—Police."

Erlendur parked the car as close as possible, and they walked the last stretch. The weather was not too bad—though getting colder. For now it was bright and quite still, and they were temporarily sheltered from the strong north wind.

A wide zone of the garden leading up to Birkihlíd had been cordoned off with yellow tape, and Jóhann was sticking labels in the footprints.

"Have we got four suspects?" Erlendur asked, noting the four differently colored labels he was planting.

"Probably two cops, the housekeeper, and one other," answered Jóhann, greeting Hrefna with a nod and a smile. He was wearing a blue snowsuit and a burgundy-and-gold knitted hat.

A tall, blond young man named Marteinn followed them into the garden, carrying a small yellow gas cylinder. He was a new recruit to the department, an enthusiastic athlete who was always asking for time off to train, here to assist Jóhann.

Hrefna and Erlendur met Egill in the outer lobby. "You're not exactly supportive of your colleagues," Egill said sharply, fixing Hrefna with a cold stare. "I've had the Super bending my ear all morning over one of your complaints."

Hrefna remained silent. The previous Tuesday she had been sent with Egill to pick up a man for questioning, a seaman they were acquainted with. He was usually a gentle soul, though apt to get in fights when he'd been drinking. He had knocked someone's tooth out, and they needed to take a statement. The man had been sober when they arrived at his home and seemed willing to go with them to the department, but Egill had in no time at all managed to aggravate him to such an extent that the man jabbed at Egill, who immediately responded in kind. Then all hell had broken loose, and in the end, Hrefna had to help Egill cuff the outraged man's hands and feet and then get assistance in transporting him to the cells. Hrefna had, naturally, filed a report on Egill's conduct, which she had found intolerable: an otherwise under-control situation had escalated to an all-out brawl because of the idiocy of people, at least one person, who should know better.

Her spat with Egill was forgotten as soon as she saw the man lying on the floor in a pool of blood. Halldór approached, explained briefly what had happened, and then asked Hrefna to speak to the housekeeper, showing her the way to the kitchen.

The old woman sat at the kitchen table with one hand covering her eyes; on the table in front of her was a glass of water, half full. A uniformed officer stood in the middle of the room, turning his cap back and forth in his hands.

"You can take a seat," Hrefna said to the policeman, as she sat down in front of the old woman.

"My name is Hrefna. I'm from the police. Do you feel ready to answer a few questions?"

The woman looked up and nodded. Her eyes were red.

"I was told it was you who called the police," Hrefna began gently.

"Yes," replied the woman softly.

"What is your name?"

"Sveinborg Pétursdóttir."

Hrefna wrote the name on a piece of paper in front of her. "I understand you are the housekeeper here."

The woman nodded.

"And the man lying out there, who is he?" asked Hrefna.

"It's Jacob—Jacob Kieler Junior. I suppose he is dead, isn't he?"

"Yes, that's right, he is dead."

Sveinborg bowed her head and wiped a tear from her eye.

"Did he live alone here?" Hrefna asked.

"Yes."

There was a short silence.

"Have you any idea what happened?" Hrefna asked.

"No, not at all," the woman answered.

"Please tell me about this morning, when you arrived," Hrefna continued.

Taking a sip from her glass, Sveinborg began her slow and tentative account. She described how she had entered the house and then gone into the kitchen, where she had noticed right away that things were not as usual. Jacob was in the habit of having his breakfast, and then leaving the crockery in the kitchen sink. She would assemble some cold meats and other things each evening, and leave them for him in the refrigerator. They hadn't been touched. She described how she had searched the house and then where she had found him.

Her account was disturbed by Jóhann, who wanted to check the soles of Sveinborg's shoes in order to compare them with the footsteps in the snow. She pointed him toward the shoes in the rear vestibule. He also asked to check the shoes of the police officer still sitting with them in the kitchen.

"What was Jacob's occupation?" Hrefna asked after Jóhann had left.

"He had an office job in a bank. He had been with them for over twenty years," Sveinborg answered, adding apprehensively, "They must be wondering where he is. Can you let them know what's happened?"

"Yes, we'll do that," Hrefna replied, catching the policeman's eye and nodding.

"And Matthías. He must also be told straightaway," Sveinborg added.

"Who is he?" Hrefna asked.

"Matthías Kieler. He is Jacob Junior's uncle. He is staying in an apartment not far from here."

"We will see to that," reassured Hrefna, writing down the address Sveinborg gave her. "I shall need a good deal more information from you, but I don't want you to have to stay any longer in this house. Wouldn't you feel a bit better in your own home?" Hrefna asked kindly.

The old woman nodded with relief.

Diary I

March 4, 1911. My birthday. I am 21 years old and life is very good. I celebrated the day by taking a train to Roskilde and back again. This is the route of the first railroad here in Denmark, opened in 1847. I have never before traveled by train, and I was shaking with enthusiasm as the train set off. It felt as if the platform was beginning to move while the train remained stationary, just as when a ship moves off from the jetty...

March 5, 1911. I am still reflecting on my railway journey yesterday. It is utterly astonishing that no railway has yet been built in Iceland. I know that the

Government Chief Engineer has been campaigning for us to build a railroad, but the voices of dissent are always strong. There is an ample sufficiency of arable land in Iceland, but lack of transport has been a hindrance to agriculture. Product sales are held up in winter, efficient feed transport is impracticable, and there are shortages of fertilizer and fuel. If we are to harness the power of waterfalls, there is no question that we must also build a railroad. I have been contemplating whether to focus my studies on building power plants or railroads. I shall probably choose the latter, since they must take precedence over power plants, besides which they interest me far more...

June 5, 1911. Was awarded "udmærked godt" (excellent) in philosophy. Went to the Tivoli amusement park and stayed well into the evening. The fireworks are my favorite feature...

July 10, 1911. Entrance exams finished today. Professor Christiansen bade me welcome to the engineering course this fall...

CHAPTER 9

Jóhann was nearly done examining the footprints, and Marteinn followed him around, carrying a small pocket book into which he jotted down the observations that Jóhann dictated, stamping his feet in between notations to keep warm.

All the footprints had been identified, apart from one trail that led to the front door of the house and back again. The person who made these prints must have been there either early in the morning or during the night, as a considerable amount of snow had subsequently fallen on them. It was possible, by carefully heating the snow with a gas burner, to melt away what had fallen into the footprints, since the snow underneath was packed more densely and could take more heat without melting. Jóhann had thus managed to retrieve good samples of the prints of both the left and right feet. He arranged his camera on a tripod and pointed it down directly above the right footprint, then set a fifty-centimeter ruler, marked alternately black and white at each centimeter, next to the print before taking a picture. He photographed the left shoe print in the same way.

An overview picture was taken of the area and the footprints were measured carefully. The feet were twenty-three centimeters long, with an average stride length of forty-five centimeters. This could not be a tall man, and the shoe size was too small for an adult man at all, so Jóhann guessed that the prints belonged to either a woman with small feet or an adolescent.

Lastly, he set about taking an impression of the shoe print. He mixed hardener with some liquid plastic and poured it into the print, placing a fine wire net on top to reinforce it. The plastic hardened in no time, and the result was a reasonable, if not perfect, reproduction of the print. They would probably be able to discover the size and make of the footwear using the photograph and the plastic cast, but it was not likely that it would suffice to distinguish one particular pair of shoes from another of the same type and size—the prints were not so well defined that any distinctive feature could be made out.

The final task was to carefully melt all the snow from a selected area in front of the house and around the back door, in case this should reveal prints formed just after it started snowing; that night's snow had fallen on bare ground, so if there were any prints, they would be fresh ones.

Jóhann found no further prints, however, so they could assume that nobody else had come to the house during this time.

Egill emerged from the house with his coat on; he was to organize a search of the garden and its surroundings. A team of officers were to comb the snow with garden rakes to see if anything lay hidden there. It was possible the gun might have been thrown into the garden, in which case it would be preferable to discover it now rather than waiting for the spring thaw.

Some of the snow that had piled up on the roof of the house broke away and slid down the slope, falling from the eaves with a substantial thud. Jóhann glanced up. The roof looked wet where the snow had been. That meant the insulation was poor and the snow had no doubt been melted by the heat coming from the house. It must be an expensive house to run, he thought to himself.

Jóhann saw Hrefna coming down the path beside the house with an older woman on her arm. Hrefna smiled to him as they walked carefully past. Watching the women go out into the street, Marteinn asked Jóhann, "Is she married?"

"No."

"Seeing someone?"

"No."

Marteinn sniffed. "So one could ask her out."

"No," answered Jóhann, "I've tried. She says she doesn't want to date colleagues."

"Oh, well. Of course, she's much older than me," Marteinn said.

She would only laugh at you, thought Jóhann, but sympathizing, said instead, "Yes, she is too old for you."

Diary I

September 17, 1911. We are now well into the university term. During the first semester we study principally mathematics, physics, thermodynamics, and structural engineering. The practical projects will be in the second semester. I have, out of interest, taken note of the senior students' projects…

November 21, 1911. It is my mother's birthday today. She is 41. It is now well over a year since I have seen my parents, and it will probably be a long time before I return to Iceland. But I write home frequently, so they know that I am prospering in all respects...

November 30, 1911. The new train station, Københavns Hovedbanegård, was inaugurated today. This is an impressive construction. The main entrance faces Vesterbrogade near Rådhuspladsen. Over the entrance is a square tower with pinnacles on the top and all four corners. Inside is an enormous ticket hall, with steps leading down from it to the platforms. They are 6 in all, which means that 12! trains can be dispatched simultaneously. The tracks run under the station...

February 10, 1912. I have visited the train station frequently this winter. I have been examining both the buildings and the railway itself. I intend to study railway engineering for my master's degree. I think it must be a most rewarding occupation to build a new railroad. I have been thinking about all the potential back in Iceland. The trip I took to Akureyri the year before last would have been so much quicker by railroad. I can visualize a train speeding through the Öxnadalur valley with people looking up from haymaking to wave to the engineer...

February 17, 1912. Had an interview with Professor Christiansen this morning. He thought well of my idea of studying railway engineering. He recommends that I should complete my Bachelor of Science degree here at the engineering college in the spring of 1913, and go from there to the Technische Hochschule in Berlin. I can use the time to study German. The professor knows a German lady who might be able to give me lessons...

February 23, 1912. Went for my first German lesson to Mrs. Sabine Heger. She is in her thirties, a widow of a Danish professor of law. We agreed that I should begin by reading the works of Goethe, starting with Die Leiden des jungen Werthers. *She had a used copy, which she sold to me...I have now come to the end of the last page in this, my first diary, which I started writing on June 30, 1910. I have already purchased another book, similar to this one, which I shall commence to write tomorrow.*

CHAPTER 10

Through the parlor window, Halldór watched Hrefna walking Sveinborg to the street. It was quite sensible of Hrefna to take the old woman back to her own home and continue talking to her there. It must have been a difficult experience, and she would probably feel better in more familiar surroundings.

Erlendur had gone to report the death to the uncle, and Egill had begun the search of the garden, so Halldór was now alone in the parlor. Putting on a pair of fine white cotton gloves that he kept in his pocket, he walked back to the lobby. He found the number of the bank in the telephone directory on the shelf under the telephone and then picked up the receiver, holding it by the bottom of the mouthpiece to avoid destroying any fingerprints that might be on the handle. Using his pen, he dialed the number of the bank, and when the receptionist answered, he was put through to Jacob's superior.

Yes, it was true, they were beginning to wonder about Jacob's absence; he always let them know if he was unable to come to work. This was, of course, dreadful news. The bank would assist them in every possible way.

Halldór hung up the phone and looked again at the body lying untouched in the doorway. A cold chill ran down his spine.

He was expecting the pathologist, who would arrange the post-mortem and should be able to give an estimate of time of death.

Halldór passed through each room, noting down which lights were on and which drapes had been closed, in case they should later need to stage a reconstruction of the crime scene. He noticed that the doors leading to the main parlor from the dining room, the office, and the lobby were all the same: double doors, painted white, with eight glass panes to each door. They all stood wide-open, folded back against the walls.

The floors were of dark wood, and the lower parts of the walls, up to chest height, were paneled in the same wood, with the upper parts and ceilings painted pale yellow.

The main feature of the parlor was the fireplace. Halldór knelt down and looked into the grate. The bottom was covered in ash from its last use, and everything was black with soot. There were a few pieces of wood in a basket next to the fireplace, but they were bits of broken-up boxes and scrap timber, not at all in harmony with the rest of the room.

Three pictures hung on the parlor walls: to the right of the fireplace was a painting of a young woman in a blue dress; to the left, slightly smaller, a photograph of an older couple; and on the north wall, a large painting, obviously a foreign one, depicting a handsome country house in forested surroundings. Initially Halldór thought it might be a reproduction, but on closer examination he saw some fine brush marks on the canvas. He tried without success to make out the artist's name.

Halldór entered the office in the southwest corner of the house. It featured a window on either outside wall, hung with net curtains and thick drapes, the latter drawn back, making it relatively bright in the room, even without the lights on. In the middle of the floor stood a large, heavy desk made of dark wood, with turned feet and carved molding around the top. There was a matching office chair, upholstered in brown leather, and, opposite the desk, two deeper chairs on either side of a small table that held a large ashtray.

On the gleaming desktop lay five frames containing postage stamps, which Halldór examined without touching. They were old stamps from various countries, with pictures of railway locomotives and carriages, carefully arranged on a black background and covered with glass.

On the south wall was a locked glass-fronted cabinet containing various firearms, while directly opposite it stood a low table against the wall, with an old model of a railroad station and train.

The inner wall behind the desk was lined with bookshelves from floor to ceiling. The books were all old, many of them with English titles. There were also some photo albums, one of which Halldór carefully extracted from the shelf and opened. It contained some old photographs of Reykjavik, including one of Birkihlíd being built. The next album contained old family photographs, while the third had pictures of the interior of the house, showing furniture and fittings, with neatly written captions under each photo. He found a picture of the desk and read the accompanying caption: "Desk in library. Design Philip Burden. Made in his workshop at Red Lion Square, London, 1898. Alfred Kieler bought it new that year and had it shipped to Iceland in 1899."

It dawned on Halldór that this house functioned as a kind of museum, containing all available source material on the life of an upper-class Reykjavik family during the first part of the century. It contained better preservation and documentation than many museums he had visited; a great attention to detail lay behind this. He looked at the next caption: "Electric chandelier in parlor.

51

Purchased by Alfred Kieler in Stettin 1922. Made in Beringer's workshop in that city. This type is attributed to him."

Halldór flipped to another page: "Porcelain chamber pot. Purchased in Copenhagen 1895."

He smiled, closed the album, and put it back in its place.

On the shelf next to the albums was a row of diaries. The period covered by each book was inscribed in black lettering on each book's spine. There were twelve in all, the first labeled "June 30, 1910–February 23, 1912," and the last "March 1, 1931–January 10, 1932." Halldór picked out the first book and examined its title page.

Diary started in the spring of 1910. Jacob Kieler student, born March 4, 1890.

Halldór looked at the dead man in the parlor. His name was the same, but he was known as Jacob Junior, so he was probably the son of the Jacob who had written the diaries. Halldór looked up the first entry. The handwriting was clear and very legible:

June 30, 1910. Today I graduated from high school. After the ceremony at the school, there was a coffee party on the lawn in front of the new house my father is having built on his lot next to Laufástún. Father gave me this book and suggested I should keep a diary.

Hearing a noise, Halldór quickly put the diary away and went out into the parlor. He found Jóhann and Marteinn carrying in some bags and Fridrik Leifsson, the pathologist, following close behind. Halldór and Fridrik had served together on the parish council and were friends.

"Sorry to be so late," Fridrik said, as they shook hands. He squatted awkwardly by the body, examined it carefully, and then stood up.

"It would be very good to have an estimated time of death," Halldór said.

"I'll try and work something out," replied Fridrik. He waited until Jóhann had taken a few photographs, then laid the body carefully on its back on the floor and loosened the clothes in front, before taking some instruments from his case.

Halldór retreated to one of the many windows and looked out at the snow-covered lawn. He knew that Fridrik was going to stick a thermometer into the body's abdominal cavity and measure the temperature of the liver, enabling him to estimate time of death. Halldór preferred not to watch.

He spotted Erlendur accompanied by a man wearing a long black overcoat and black hat out on the street in front of the house. They had arrived at the yellow tape cordoning off the road, and he watched as Erlendur ducked underneath it.

They were met by a police officer, and the man in the black overcoat said something, pointing at the yellow tape with the walking stick he carried. The officer removed the tape from the fence and the man proceeded, following Erlendur through the gate and toward the house.

Halldór turned back around. Fridrik had covered the body with a green sheet and was scrutinizing his notebook. "If the parlor was this cold all night, then he must have died at one thirty, give or take an hour."

Diary II

April 10, 1912. Snitkræfter og deformationer i statiken (stress and distortion in load-bearing structures) this morning. My calculations were correct. A German lesson with Mrs. Heger in the afternoon. Remained there well into the evening...

April 25, 1912. My mother and father arrived here in Copenhagen this morning from Hamburg. My father is on a business trip and they used the opportunity to visit me and celebrate my father's birthday. I showed them the city today. They think that I have become very sophisticated. My father gave me the money I needed, and agreed to the plan I have made for the next four years. I am extremely grateful that my parents are able to support me financially, because I have watched some very talented young men being driven from their studies by lack of funds...My father has a significant birthday today, he is 50...

May 13, 1912. My fellow student Jørgen Renstrup asked me if I would like to travel with him to Tirol and Salzkammergut in Austria this summer for some hiking in the mountains. He had heard my accounts of my travels in Iceland, and is also a keen hiker. This will be a good opportunity to exercise my knowledge of German...

May 15, 1912. It is being reported in the city that King Frederik VIII died suddenly yesterday while traveling in Hamburg...

June 28, 1912. Jørgen Renstrup and I are setting off on a three-week journey to Austria. We shall have a sleeper cabin on the train...

CHAPTER 11

Hrefna had led the old woman gently out of the house via the back door, past some uniformed officers searching the garden with rakes.

"What are these men doing?" Sveinborg had asked.

"They are checking to see if there's anything lying in the garden that might help us solve this case," Hrefna explained.

"The garden is very messy just now. Jacob Junior has tried to keep it tidy, but the wind blows garbage into it all the time. I really don't know where it comes from," she remarked.

It will probably get cleared properly this time, Hrefna had thought, but said nothing.

They were silent on the drive to Ránargata. The apartment was small but cozy: a living room, a small kitchen, and a bathroom. The furniture was old and didn't match, but everything was very clean. The only bed was a sofa bed, with its mattress folded away. Embroidered cushions lay on top, and above it was a large wall hanging decorated with matching embroidery.

Sveinborg immediately began to make coffee; she seemed to feel better when she was doing something. Hrefna sat down on a bench by the small kitchen table and took out her notebook and pen.

"Has Jacob lived alone for long?"

"Mrs. Kieler, Jacob Junior's mother, lived in the house, of course, while she was alive," the old woman replied. "It was first and foremost her home. She died two years ago, bless her soul."

"Are there any other relatives?"

"There is Kirsten, of course, Jacob's sister. She lives up north, married to a headmaster. They have a daughter, Elísabet, named for old Mrs. Kieler. She is presently at the university here, studying law. She is lovely, but a little bit unsettled, as the young often are. Kirsten wanted Elísabet to live in Birkihlíd with Jacob Junior when she came south to go to school, but that came to nothing. She does pop in to see me now and again for afternoon coffee."

Hrefna jotted the names down.

"Why did she end up not living in the house? There must have been plenty of space."

Sveinborg shifted uneasily. "It wasn't easy to live with Jacob Junior. He was, of course, very kind to me, but it wasn't easy for a modern young girl to put up with him."

"How did that manifest?"

"Oh..." Sveinborg hesitated. "It's just that he was rather domineering."

Hrefna understood that the old woman didn't want to talk about this anymore, so she changed course. "Are there any other relatives?"

"There's Matthías, of course," Sveinborg continued. "Matthías Kieler, a cellist. At the moment he is visiting Iceland for a few months. He's renting an apartment not far from Birkihlíd, and lives there with his manservant."

"His manservant?"

"Yes, well, Klemenz has his own apartment, I think, in Austria, where they live. They are only here on a visit. The family is settling old inheritance matters."

Sveinborg had misunderstood Hrefna's surprise.

"It's a bit unusual for people to have servants," Hrefna clarified. "Is he in full employment as Matthías's manservant...this Klemenz?"

"Yes, of course," Sveinborg replied. It seemed perfectly natural to her that people should employ servants. "Klemenz has been with Matthías for many years, ever since he went to live in Germany. Matthías is a well-known musician, you see, who has worked abroad ever since he completed his studies. As he never married, he has always needed a servant. Klemenz has stood by him all this time; he's been very loyal and devoted."

Diary II

June 30, 1912. Arrived in Tirol and stayed the first night in Kitzbühel. The proprietor of the bed and breakfast informed us that local people were now encouraging tourists to come to the town in winter to pursue the sport of skiing. When he heard that we were "ingenieurstudenten," he said that constructing cable cars in the local mountains would be a worthwhile project for us. The proprietor tries to speak High German to us, since it is impossible for us to understand the local dialect...

July 4, 1912. We set off on foot early in the morning from St. Johann. Our route followed excellent footpaths that farmers have used throughout the centuries to reach their shielings high up in the mountains, to which they move their cattle in summer...At noon we overtook a group of young people sitting on the slope having their picnic. These people were not dressed like the locals, so we took them to be tourists like us. We didn't want to disturb them at their meal so we just greeted them with a "Grüss Gott," and continued on our way. I couldn't take my eyes off a girl who was standing by the path, and she boldly returned my gaze until I became embarrassed and looked away. Her image has been in my mind all day...

July 5, 1912. It is many years since I have walked such a long distance. The muscles in my thighs and buttocks are sore; the locals call this phenomenon "Muskelkater." We both had "Tirola Gröstl" for supper. As we were sitting in the drinking parlor afterwards, I saw again the girl whose eyes I had gazed into when we met on the mountain path yesterday. Her name is Elizabeth Chatfield and she is of English nationality. She is nearly eighteen years of age...

July 6, 1912. We met the group from the English school at breakfast, and their tutor, who is their guide, invited us to walk with them today. This makes a pleasant change and it is fun to practice one's English. Elizabeth asks whether I would like to correspond with her. She says she has a few pen pals, albeit mainly female ones...

CHAPTER 12

Marteinn was in the outer lobby when Erlendur entered with his new companion.

"Good morning to you," the man in the black overcoat said to Marteinn, taking off his hat and offering him his hand. "My name is Matthías Kieler."

"Um…Marteinn Karlsson," the young detective replied, removing the rubber glove he was wearing and taking the man's outstretched hand.

"You would perhaps be so kind as to hang this up for me," Matthías said, handing his hat and walking stick to the young man. Marteinn cast a surprised look at Erlendur, who just nodded discreetly.

"Yes, of course," Marteinn said, taking the hat and walking stick.

Halldór, observing this exchange from the inner lobby, imagined that Matthías was probably around seventy. He was rather portly and sported a substantial double chin. The old gentleman removed his hat, revealing a bald head fringed round with white hair, combed straight back. He was clean-shaven and very neatly dressed.

"It was not necessary for you to come here, sir," Halldór said, striding toward Matthías and introducing himself.

Matthías's hand was thick and soft, yet the handshake was firm. "I preferred it. I hope I do not disturb," he replied solemnly.

"No, not at all," Halldór reassured him.

Matthías entered the inner lobby and approached the body, now lying next to the doorway to the parlor and covered with a green sheet. He bent down with some difficulty and lifted the sheet from the face; then he stood up again and looked down in silence. No one said a word.

Halldór watched as Matthías's face turned grave and seemed to age by many years as he gazed at the snow-white, lifeless face of his nephew. It was impossible to work out what he was thinking, but this sight clearly affected him. He finally bent down again, made a small sign of the cross with his hand over the body, and covered it gently with the sheet.

"Have you found any clues yet?" he asked Halldór.

Halldór shook his head. "Not so far."

"You will keep me informed of the progress of the investigation," Matthías said.

Halldór was not sure whether this was a question or a statement, and decided not to reply, asking instead, "Do you feel able to answer a few questions at this stage, sir?"

"Yes, but I should prefer to sit down. Perhaps you would have someone bring me a glass of water…with a little lemon."

"I'll do that," Erlendur offered.

"My investigators have not finished checking the main rooms. Is there somewhere upstairs where we can sit down?" Halldór asked.

"Yes, there is a small sitting room," Matthías replied.

Halldór followed Matthías upstairs to a wide, white-painted corridor that stretched the length of the house. A dormer window at each end made the space reasonably bright. There were three doors on each side of the corridor, and beautifully framed, colored drawings of old steam locomotives adorned the walls between.

At the far end of the corridor on the left-hand side was a small parlor, containing modest but comfortable contemporary furniture and a television set. The room was under the slope of the roof, with a large dormer window. A small writing desk stood by the inner wall, and above it were family photographs in frames of all types and sizes. Above the television hung a sizable painting of a small white house with a red roof in an Icelandic landscape, a lake in the foreground; the painting was neat but rather amateurish.

This room is obviously not part of the museum, thought Halldór. He looked around, but saw nothing to suggest there might be clues here that would be compromised if they sat down.

"Jacob and his mother used this room as a day parlor," Matthías explained. He noticed Halldór examining the painting and added, "That picture was painted by my niece Kirsten in her youth. It shows a summerhouse at Lake Hafravatn that belonged to the family"

They sat down, and Halldór asked, "Are there any valuables here in the house that thieves might be interested in?"

"No more so than in any other house," Matthías replied. "The contents of the library are, of course, of value, as is the furniture, but there is no one specific item here that is particularly precious. I understand that the stamp collection has been returned from the exhibition; it might be worth something."

"There are a few frames of old stamps on the desk downstairs," Halldór said, taking out his notebook and a pen.

"If they are untouched, then the motive for this atrocious act can hardly have been robbery," Matthías concluded.

Erlendur arrived with the glass of water, handed it to Matthías, and perched himself on the edge of the little desk.

"This is a quaint home," Halldór remarked, deciding to change the subject a bit. "Some sort of a museum, isn't it?"

"Yes, this house and its furnishings have been preserved in the condition they were at the end of the war, and most of the pieces of furniture are quite a bit older; some date from the previous century. My brother's family attempted to keep it that way." Matthías took a sip from the water.

"Why did they do that?" Halldór asked.

"My late sister-in-law was very sensitive about my brother Jacob's memory, and wanted to keep everything as it had been while he lived. Jacob Junior followed suit, continuing the tradition. Perhaps he took it too seriously, though; it became a bit of an obsession with him in later years."

"Who owns the house?"

Matthías hesitated briefly, then said, "Jacob Junior was considered the owner of the house."

"Was it an inheritance?" Halldór asked.

"No, he purchased shares belonging to other heirs a few weeks ago."

"Who were they?"

"Half of the house belonged to me, inherited from my father. Jacob Junior and his sister Kirsten owned a quarter each, inherited from their parents."

"So Jacob Junior bought your share and that of his sister?"

"Yes, contracts were exchanged, and he paid the deposit."

"When was this sale arranged?" Halldór asked.

"After Elizabeth died, two years ago," Matthías replied, using the English pronunciation of his sister-in-law's name. "At that point Kirsten and I felt it was time to put the house on the market."

"Was Jacob Junior unhappy about this decision?"

"Understandably he was not keen on it. This was his childhood home and he had been assiduous in maintaining it," Matthías replied.

"So the decision to sell the house was made two years ago."

"Yes, discussions regarding the sale began two years ago."

"Was the delay at that time due to Jacob Junior's resistance?" Halldór asked.

"You could say that. He was looking for ways to avoid selling the house," Matthías replied.

"When did he decide to buy the house himself?"

"I arrived here in Iceland from Austria just under two months ago with the intention of finalizing this matter, and I have since pursued that aim in collaboration with Kirsten and our lawyer. Jacob Junior finally realized that neither I nor his sister wished to retain our shares, and as a result began to look at the possibility of acquiring sole ownership of the house."

"How was the purchase price agreed upon?" Halldór asked.

"The house and its furnishings were assessed by experienced appraisers. He agreed to pay the price thus determined."

"Do you know how Jacob was planning to finance this purchase?"

"He obtained a mortgage for part of the sum. But it was nothing to do with me. It is my understanding, however, that he had plans in place to raise the rest of the money," Matthías replied.

"Do you think that he already had this money?"

"I have no idea," Matthías said wearily. "I only know what Kirsten has told me, that when their mother died and her estate was settled, she was as good as penniless apart from her share of the house. So there was certainly no cash for him to inherit."

"You are telling me, sir, that half of the house has belonged to you since your father died. Why wasn't the estate divided earlier?" Halldór asked.

"Alfred, my father, died in the fall of 1930 when I was studying in Berlin, and at that time my brother Jacob Senior agreed to look after my affairs. My brother and I had a close relationship, and he looked after me very well. We agreed that he would carry on living in the house for the foreseeable future, but that I always had a home here."

Matthías paused briefly, glancing down thoughtfully.

"When Jacob Senior died I had already decided to live abroad and practice my art," he continued. "I knew how important this home was to Elizabeth, and I promised her that as far as I was concerned she could live in the house for the rest of her life."

There was another silence, before Matthías added, "I felt this was a good offer and I was not expecting the division of the estate to be delayed after her death."

Halldór decided to change the subject. "Are there many visitors here?" he asked.

"No, not at all," Matthías replied. "Jacob Junior has always led a very quiet life. Only his family and a few friends ever visit as far as I know."

"So Jacob Junior has never married?"

"No. We in the family were expecting him to start looking around after his mother died, but that did not happen."

"After his mother died. But then he must have been..." Halldór did some mental calculations, "forty-six years old?"

"Yes?" It didn't sound as if Matthías considered that an odd age to be getting married for the first time.

Halldór turned to a fresh page in his notebook and asked about Jacob Junior's friends.

"It's mainly a few men who are fellow members of some Christian society."

"Was he a great believer?" Halldór asked.

"Nothing more than the usual. But it provided good companionship, and that's what he sought more than the praying, I think. His childhood friend, Reverend Ingimar, is chairman of the society. You will, of course, speak with him."

"Who inherits from Jacob Junior?" Halldór asked, returning to the previous line of questioning.

"I am not familiar with the contents of the will," replied Matthías. "His sister Kirsten would be the principal heir, and I suspect that young Elísabet will inherit something. She is the only descendant of the family. Sveinborg the housekeeper also deserves to be remembered. She has probably not been paid much in recent years, poor woman."

Halldór leafed back through his notebook and examined the notes he had made.

"You say you live in Austria, sir," he said.

"Yes," Matthías replied. "I have been a member of a string quartet in Salzburg for many years. I retired this fall as I have not been very well, and am, consequently, sorting out my financial affairs."

"Are you planning to live here in Iceland?" Halldór asked.

"No. I rented a furnished apartment for a few weeks while these matters are being settled. Then I shall return home. I have lived in Europe since I was twenty-five years old and the climate here does not suit me."

Halldór pondered how to proceed. There was an awkward silence, and then Erlendur, still sitting on the little desk, cleared his throat and said, "I happen to be going to Austria this Saturday, on a ski trip with the family."

"Where will you be going?" Matthías asked.

"A place called Zell am See."

"A lovely town. Admittedly I have only been there in summer, but I understand that the valley and the lake are just as beautiful in winter. I know nothing about skiing, however. You should try and spend a day in Salzburg; it's not far from there."

Jóhann stuck his head in the door. "Halldór," he said, interrupting them, "it's Hrefna on the phone for you. She wants to speak to you. It's important."

Halldór stood up and joined Jóhann in the corridor, leaving Erlendur alone with Matthías. Halldór had the feeling Erlendur would use this opportunity to find out more about Salzburg and Austria.

Diary II

January 27, 1913. Went by myself to Thorvaldsens Museum, where I remained the best part of the day. In my life's work I must remember that structures should above all enhance the environment and reflect favorably on the designer. It is not enough to build robustly if the result offends one's fellow citizens' sense of beauty. Studying such works of art as are here on display must increase one's feeling for the form and balance of objects, small and large...

March 5, 1913. Had a letter from Elizabeth to which I shall reply immediately. Mrs. Heger does not approve of this correspondence; she maintains that the English will muddle my German...

March 21, 1913. Had a letter from my father. He says a railway is being laid in connection with the building of the harbor in Reykjavik, to transport stone from Öskjuhlíd down to the shore. I am writing back to ask him for further information on this railway and the locomotives...

April 2, 1913. Went with Helgi to the pawn shop to redeem his best trousers for him. He promises to pay me back when the residence grant is paid out...

May 17, 1913. Elizabeth writes and welcomes my idea of visiting her in my summer vacation...

June 5, 1913. A letter arrives from my father with information on the railway in Reykjavik. There are two locomotives: Pionér, built by Arnold Jung in Germany in 1892; and Minør, built by Jungenthal in Bei Kirchen in Germany the same year. The gauge is 90 cm...

June 6, 1913. The final BSc examinations are imminent. I shall miss this college, but I nevertheless feel certain that my decision to go to Berlin is the right one...

CHAPTER 13

"Have you worked for these people for long?" Hrefna had resumed her questioning of Sveinborg, wanting to find out more about the family that had lived at Birkihlíd.

"Yes, forty-five years this coming spring," Sveinborg replied, as she poured coffee for the two of them and sat down opposite Hrefna. "I began working for the family in May 1928."

"That's a long time. You must have been happy there."

"Yes, the family has always treated me well."

"Can you describe the household for me?"

"When I started out, there were four of us in service," Sveinborg replied. She stopped briefly to think before continuing. "There was an older woman, Mrs. Elínborg, who looked after the kitchen and did the cooking. Her husband was called Hjörleifur, and he did outside work and managed supplies. Then there were the two of us maids, me and Magga; I mainly looked after the children, who were lovely. We domestics lived in the two basement rooms." Sveinborg smiled faintly at the memory, and went on, "At that time it was very much an upper-class establishment. Merchant Alfred had actually retired, and old Mrs. Kirsten was in poor health. Jacob Senior, the engineer, was, on the other hand, highly regarded in town, and Elizabeth was a real lady; visitors were constantly coming and going, and there were wonderful parties. What with everything, we domestics were kept very busy during those years."

"What sort of a man was Jacob Senior?"

"Jacob Senior was an extremely handsome man. He was polite and considerate, and everybody felt comfortable in his presence. He inspired confidence, if I may put it like that. He had very elevated ideas on many things, and it was interesting to listen to him when he sat at table with important people and bombarded them with his ideas on all kinds of projects."

"And Elizabeth?"

"She was a good mistress; somewhat dictatorial, it is true, but that was the norm in those times. It was sometimes difficult to please her because, in the beginning, my understanding of English was limited. The mistress never spoke Icelandic, but she understood it well enough. Occasionally Jacob had to interpret when he came home in the evenings, and it irritated her having to involve him in the running of the house. But he didn't mind."

"What has the household been like in recent years?"

"Everything changed when Jacob Senior passed away. The mistress stopped holding receptions, and the domestic staff was given notice. I stayed on because I had gained a reasonable understanding of English. Later my duties were reduced as well, as Jacob Junior was studying abroad and Kirsten had gotten married, so I moved into my own apartment and worked only half a day. Naturally the mistress had to reduce her outgoings."

"What has your job consisted of lately?" Hrefna asked.

"I would usually go there around eleven in the morning and prepare lunch. Jacob Junior used to come home at lunchtime to eat with his mother, and he kept up the habit after she died. When I had cleared up after lunch, I would do the cleaning. The mistress used to give me instructions of what to do, and I have maintained her routine ever since she passed away. I always go over all the main rooms once a week; she was very firm about that. Round six o'clock I would start to prepare supper, which I served at seven o'clock sharp. Jacob and his mother always used the dining room in the evenings, but recently Jacob Junior had taken his meals in the kitchen with me, both at lunchtime and in the evening. When I'd cleared up after supper and prepared breakfast, I would go home."

"And what is your salary?"

Sveinborg looked away. "It would not be considered generous today," she demurred. "The house is very expensive to run, and Jacob Junior is not a high earner. But I get my pension and I own my apartment outright."

"Can you describe your day yesterday in Birkihlíd?" Hrefna asked.

"Yesterday was a Wednesday, when I usually clean the main rooms and wash the floors. They are not used much, but there is always a bit of dust. The stamp collection came back from the exhibition over the weekend, and the frames were very smudgy, so I gave them a good polish. Jacob was going to put them into the safe."

"There's a safe in the home?"

"Yes." Sveinborg thought for a bit, and then whispered, "It's under the desk in the office."

"Do you know what is in it?"

"Jacob keeps his stamps in it, and some of the diaries are kept there."

"What diaries?"

"Jacob Senior's diaries. He kept a diary throughout his entire adult life."

"Do you know where the key to this safe is kept?"

"No, I didn't need to. I would never open the safe."

Hrefna didn't doubt her. She dropped the subject of the safe, and asked to hear more about her routine yesterday.

"I always putter about in the kitchen while the afternoon serial is on the radio; they are reading Jón Gerreksson's biography right now. The serial finishes at three o'clock, and after that I went out shopping, as I usually do on Mondays, Wednesdays, and Fridays. I always go to the same neighborhood store; Jacob has an account there that he settles every month. An old friend of mine lives next door to it, and I always visit her; she is now in terribly poor health, so I also do some shopping for her as well."

"When did you get back to Birkihlíd?"

"Before five o'clock."

"What did you do then?"

"I'd finished in the main rooms, so I stayed in the kitchen. I cleaned the floor and put potatoes on to boil. I was going to cook haddock fillet; it's usually fish on Wednesdays."

"When did Jacob get home?"

"It must have been after six. He went straight to his study upstairs. He usually worked there until I told him supper was ready."

"When did you go home?"

"As soon as I had cleared up after dinner."

"What time was it then?"

"Sometime after eight, I think. I don't know the exact time; I don't wear a watch. I just hear on the radio what time it is," Sveinborg said apologetically.

Hrefna smiled. "Approximately is good enough for me. Was Jacob at home when you left?"

"Yes, he rarely went out in the evening." Sveinborg thought it over. "He usually watched the news on the television after supper, but when I went into the television room to say good-bye, he wasn't there. I found him downstairs in the office. I thought perhaps he was putting his stamps away."

"What did you say to him?"

"I just sort of said good-bye. I told him that there were milk and cookies if he wanted a snack later in the evening, and that everything was ready for breakfast."

"What was his reply?"

"He just said thank you."

"Did you know if he was expecting visitors that evening?"

"No, if so, I would, of course, have stayed longer and served coffee to the guests."

Hrefna looked at the cup in front of her. This seemed to be Sveinborg's favorite occupation, supplying people with good, strong coffee.

"Er…" Sveinborg suddenly began, hesitantly, "do you think that Jacob Junior was…shot with a gun?"

Hrefna put away her pen and looked at the older woman. "Yes, that is what it looks like."

Sveinborg shook her head. "This is a dreadful notion," she said.

"Yes?" Hrefna waited for further explanation.

"Yes, well, it's like this," Sveinborg replied. "Jacob Senior also died in the parlor in Birkihlíd, almost thirty years ago. He was also shot with a gun. Thank goodness the mistress did not have to relive this."

"Who shot him?" asked Hrefna.

"Nobody knows; they never found him."

Diary II

July 10, 1913. Elizabeth and her friend Miss Annie Barker met me at the quay in London. They have organized a ten-day hike round northern England with three of their friends...

July 20, 1913. We struck camp and set off on the last leg of our journey at dawn. We walked all day. We are now proceeding along the Scottish border. We men carry the best part of the burden in our knapsacks, but the girls carry small knapsacks as well. Elizabeth's energy amazes me. I lead the walk but she is always right behind me; she is enjoying the trip even though we are all exhausted...

July 25, 1913. Elizabeth invited me to dinner at her parents' home along with Miss Annie. The Chatfields are extremely formal and polite. Afterwards we attended a concert given by a large orchestra. A work by the Czech composer Antonín Dvořák, the New World Symphony, was the one that will stay in my memory. He was born in 1841 and died in 1904, according to the program. This is the last evening of my visit...

CHAPTER 14

Jóhann and Marteinn had brought some bags into the parlor, one including a camera and various accessories; another, equipment to collect fingerprints; and a third holding containers for the samples they hoped to collect. They then set up powerful spotlights on tall tripods around the parlor, leaving the windows covered.

While Fridrik waited to supervise the removal of the body, Jóhann began taking photographs of it, first full-body shots from several angles, and then close-ups of the entry wound, outside as well as inside the clothing.

Jóhann got Fridrik's permission to take samples of the deceased's fingerprints right away, rather than leaving it for the postmortem, which he was relieved not to have to attend. He drew from one of his bags a metal horseshoe-shaped tool, which somewhat resembled a shoehorn, that he used for fingerprinting. It had slots through which he could thread paper tape printed with five squares. He also withdrew a small inkpad containing special fingerprinting ink and, grasping one of the deceased's hands, pressed each finger onto the inkpad and then onto the paper in the tool, whose horseshoe shape ensured that the impression of the whole fingertip was clearly reproduced on the paper. Jóhann processed both hands, and then covered them with plastic bags, securing them with rubber bands around the wrists.

He would have liked to check if the deceased had fired a gun recently, but it was not possible. He did have equipment back at the lab for doing a so-called paraffin test, where warm paraffin wax was applied to the hands to see if they revealed nitrates left by a gunshot, but recent research had shown this method to be very inaccurate so Jóhann had stopped running these tests. There were new methods involving expensive chemical tests, but he did not possess that equipment. In any case, a positive result would not have shown whether the deceased had fired the gun himself or had used his hands to protect himself from a shot fired from very close range.

Finally, he took out a clear plastic box from the samples bag and, with a small pair of scissors, cut a lock of hair from the victim's head and placed it in the box. He wrote the name, place, and time on a sticky label, and affixed it to the lid of the box.

Two officers had brought in a modest aluminum coffin, and after Marteinn helped Jóhann put the body into a large plastic zippered bag, it was set in the coffin and taken away. A postmortem would soon take place to establish cause of death, and Jóhann would have the clothes sent to the lab, each garment individually wrapped in plastic.

With the deceased no longer present, the atmosphere at the house changed considerably, and all unconsciously heaved a sigh of relief. Their next task was to examine the scene; if there was the smallest crumb of evidence that could point to the perpetrator, it was Jóhann's job to find it.

Marteinn was given the task of vacuuming. He used an ordinary vacuum cleaner, but with a specially made nozzle into which a very fine filter could be slotted; anything the cleaner picked up would get caught by the filter, and could be extracted easily and examined under a microscope if necessary.

Marteinn was to clean the floors and furniture in stages, replacing the filter each time and placing the used filter into a labeled plastic container. This way, they would be able to identify exactly where in the parlor they had found a particular piece of evidence—a hair, for example, or some cloth fibers.

Meanwhile Jóhann examined the trail of blood. It seemed to indicate that the man had dragged himself across the floor, but Jóhann wondered if there were any other imprints in the blood. There didn't appear to be, but nevertheless he took photos of the whole trail. The spot where the man had been shot was, of course, of particular interest; there was a lot of blood in a small area here, but also droplets dispersed over a wider area, and it was these droplets that caught Jóhann's attention. He placed a numbered label next to every drop and took a photograph of the whole area, and then set the camera above each drop to take an accurate close-up that included the numbered label and a millimeter-scale ruler. He could use this to help determine the angle and range of the shot.

He then examined the fruits of Marteinn's work; the filters were remarkably clear. There had hardly been any dust on the floors and furniture—the parlor had obviously been recently cleaned, though there was a bit of soot on the floor next to the fireplace.

Finally Jóhann turned his attention to fingerprints. He pulled on a pair of white cotton gloves and surveyed the room for drinking glasses or similar objects that somebody was likely to have touched, but there was nothing of that kind here. The dining chair looked like the only thing that had been recently moved, so Jóhann photographed it where it lay, then moved it carefully onto a white cloth that he spread out on the floor.

Jóhann chose a gray powder from his bag that would not cling to the varnish on the chair. Fingerprint powder works by sticking to traces of grease left behind when a finger touches an object; the grease carries the same pattern as the finger itself, and the powder therefore displays an accurate copy of it. The trick was to use the right powder for the circumstances. It must not cling to the surface bearing the fingerprint, and it must be the correct color: black powder was used on light surfaces, gray powder on dark ones. Different methods were applied depending on whether the fingerprints were old or recent.

This powder was designed to show up on only recent prints, those containing grease and moisture, and not old prints, which consist mainly of salts. Jóhann applied the powder to the chair with a soft brush. He then carefully blew the dust off the surface, revealing prints left there by hands that had held the chair and probably moved it; there was also a single handprint on top of the chair back. Jóhann photographed all these prints with a special lens, before transferring each print to a card by carefully placing adhesive tape over the print, peeling it off again, and sticking it to the card to produce a clear reproduction of the original fingerprint.

Jóhann had a good impression of a right-hand thumbprint from the chair that he now compared with the samples he'd taken from the deceased. It was the same fingerprint; there was no doubt about it. The victim had carried the chair to the place where it had lain—a conclusion that would no doubt cause some disappointment, but that was not Jóhann's concern. He was just pleased to have an answer. His task was simply to establish facts; other people had to interpret them to find the perpetrator.

As he was brushing some gray powder onto the telephone receiver in the lobby, it rang. Jóhann was so startled that he nearly dropped the vial of fingerprint powder. He blew the powder off and picked up the receiver, holding it by the bottom of the mouthpiece.

"Hello?"

"Jóhann, this is Hrefna. Sveinborg, the housekeeper, just told me that this isn't the first time murder has been committed in Birkihlíd. The father of the deceased was fatally shot in that parlor in 1945. Let me talk to Halldór."

Jóhann fetched Halldór from upstairs, reminding him to put on gloves before handing him the telephone.

Halldór listened with interest to Hrefna, saying little. When the conversation came to an end, Jóhann asked for the phone again.

"Hrefna," he said, "I need to get the housekeeper's finger-prints for comparison. Can I pop in on you in a little while?"

"Yes, I'll prepare her for it. She'll probably offer you coffee," Hrefna replied with a smile.

"Sounds good to me," Jóhann said, putting the phone down.

He needed fingerprints from both Sveinborg and Matthías to compare with other samples. Matthías was still in the house, so that was easy, but he would need to pay a visit to Ránargata later, on his way to the lab. It might have made more sense to send Marteinn on such an errand, but Jóhann wanted to do it himself; after all, Hrefna was there.

Jóhann had been attracted to Hrefna from the moment he began working for the detective division. His attempts at chatting her up had not produced any results though.

"I really don't want to have a relationship of that kind with a colleague," Hrefna had said good-naturedly when he tried to invite her out to the cinema on one occasion.

Nevertheless they had a good working relationship, and often had coffee together in the lab. Jóhann, Erlendur, and Halli,

Erlendur's son, had even helped Hrefna and Elsa move into their new apartment.

When Jóhann finished his work in the lobby, he turned his attention to the office.

Diary II

August 20, 1913. Arrived in Berlin this morning. I rented a room in a cheap hotel for one night...

August 21, 1913. Took a tram to Steglitz and paid a visit to a lady who rents out cheap rooms to students. She will accept me if I pay the rent in advance...

August 22, 1913. Sightseeing in the city. Pictures of Kaiser Wilhelm in every shop window. Most of the houses look similar, like boxes with flamboyant decorations in the front. Everything is very clean here, as all the streets are washed during the night. There are policemen on every corner...

September 6, 1913. College begins...

September 9, 1913. Professor Schmidt revises the history of the railways. I have to make a great effort to understand the German language. He details some experiments in building locomotives early last century. He mentions the Englishman George Stephenson in particular as one of the pioneers who built practical steam locomotives during the years prior to 1830. He describes the first German railroad, which was built between Nürnberg and Fürth in 1835...A bit of vocabulary I need to master: Rails = Schiene, Sleepers = Schwelle, Gravel = Schotter...I must practice pronouncing the voiced sch-sound...

October 2, 1913. The landlady has assisted me with a number of small things in the last few weeks, but when I paid the rent this morning she presented me with a bill. Every single little favor is detailed and priced, for instance three schillings for fastening a trouser button, 27 schillings in total.

October 12, 1913. Draftsmanship lessons all day. Drawings of road cross-sections (Ger. Querschnitt), ditch and fill...

October 19, 1913. A college friend, Helmut Klee, invited me to supper in his parents' home on Akazienallee. They are excellent people. Helmut has a younger brother named Björn. He did not know that his name means bear (Ger. Bär) in Scandinavian languages, and was thrilled when I told him that. I must remember to write to Matthías...

CHAPTER 15

"Your older brother, Jacob Senior," Halldór said, returning to the room where Matthías and Erlendur were waiting, "he was also murdered here in this house, in 1945."

"Yes, clearly, you recall the tragedy," Matthías replied.

"No, I don't actually remember it. It's come up in our investigations," Halldór said.

"Well, there was not much talk about it at the time," Matthías remarked by way of explanation. "People used their influence to prevent the press from making a big thing of it."

This did not surprise Halldór; he could well believe that friends of the family that had lived in this house at that time would have had enough influence to control the newspapers. Would the same apply today? He doubted it. If nothing else of note happened in the next few days, this case would be news fodder for weeks to come. He dreaded the inevitable battle with reporters.

"Would you be so kind as to describe that incident for me, sir?" Halldór asked.

Matthías thought for a moment. "There is not much to say about it. Mrs. Kieler and the children were at the summerhouse, and the domestics had been given time off. It appeared as if someone had broken into the house and my brother Jacob had woken up and gone downstairs. He probably surprised the intruder and was shot as a result."

"Were there signs of a break-in?"

"Yes, a pane in the front door had been broken and it was possible to reach the lock through the broken pane. The police assumed that the burglar had watched the family set off on their trip and had not expected Jacob Senior to return to Reykjavik so soon."

"Was nobody arrested?"

"There was actually a man in custody for some weeks, but I cannot recollect on what grounds. There were all manner of speculations flying around; my late sister-in-law was, for instance, always convinced that the murder was a communist conspiracy," Matthías said, smiling sadly.

"Did she have any reason to believe that?"

"No, it was all in her imagination. She was a good person but very conservative, and saw communists in every corner. I expect that her upbringing is to blame for that; her father was an industrialist in England."

"Did you have an opinion about who might have murdered your brother?"

"As I said, the police assumed it was a burglary that had gone wrong. There were a number of firearms in circulation in town after the wartime occupation, so I think it was a reasonable assumption."

Halldór had been jotting all this down in his notebook, and now there was a short silence while he finished writing. "Why did the widow not move back to England?"

"That never seemed to be in the cards," Matthías replied. "Birkihlíd was her home. My brother had taken out a life insurance policy with an English company, as her family had made that a condition of their marriage. The policy proceeds she received after his death were considerable, and she was able to keep her home without any other financial help; but she had no pension, so there was not much left of the money when she died."

"What was your brother's profession when he was alive?" Halldór asked.

"He studied railway engineering, and his intention was to pursue that profession here in Iceland. That type of operation never took off here, but he carried out a number of different research projects in the field, both for the public sector and for his own company."

"What company was this?"

"When my brother realized that political agreement to build a national railway would never be reached, he took things into his own hands and set up business with a group of Icelandic and foreign backers. It was called the Iceland Railroad Company."

"Did it carry out any business operations?"

"No, but it invested a good deal in research and design. Jacob Senior did not manage to acquire sufficient capital stock to go into production until it was too late, due to the war."

"So the investments were written off?"

"Yes. Jacob Senior had considerable income during the war years, when he worked for the British and American forces, and that went a long way to pay off the company's debts. After he died, the widow used a part of the insurance proceeds to put the company into liquidation and close it down."

Halldór got up and went over to the writing desk, which was small and neat, with a number of little drawers. There was nothing on it apart from a few papers, marked at the top with the name "Elizabeth Chatfield Kieler" in gold lettering.

"Was this where the lady of the house worked?" he asked.

"Yes." Matthías got up. "She often sat here and wrote. She kept up a lively correspondence with her relatives and friends in England."

Halldór examined the photographs on the wall.

"The family, I assume," he said.

Matthías came closer and examined the photos in question. "Yes, she has arranged them so that the Icelandic half of the family is to the left on the wall and the English half to the right. The largest picture is of my brother."

Halldór examined this photograph. It showed a good-looking man in middle age, with a high forehead and dark, wavy hair, combed back. His eyes were dark and intelligent, the nose straight and delicate, his well-shaped mouth lightly smiling.

"My brother was a handsome man. Here is a picture of him and his wife on their wedding day," said Matthías, pointing to a picture of a young couple posing by a church door. Elizabeth was wearing a white wedding gown with a long train, artistically arranged at her feet, and Jacob was in a morning coat and striped trousers, holding a top hat under his arm.

"They were married in her hometown in England." He pointed at another picture. "These are the children, Jacob Junior and Kirsten. This was taken at a photographic studio in England when they all went to visit her family, in 1934. Jacob Junior was nine years old at the time and Kirsten four."

The photograph had been carefully posed. The boy wore short trousers and sat bolt upright on an upholstered chair, and the girl stood beside him wearing a long, full dress. His clothes were dark in color, hers were light; the background was tastefully draped with cloth, and there was a rocking horse and a leather ball in front of them. Brother and sister bore similar expressions—somewhat arrogant, thought Halldór.

Matthías pointed at a picture of an older man with white hair and a full beard. "This is old Jacob Kieler, my grandfather. He was born and brought up in the province of Schleswig, which at different times has belonged to both Denmark and Germany. He arrived in Iceland in 1857 to work as a shop assistant for a fellow countryman of his. This, on the other hand," he said, pointing to a picture of a young man sporting a generous mustache, "is my father, Alfred. He ran a store, first in Hafnarfjördur and later here in Reykjavik. He built this house. And this is my mother, Kirsten." Matthías pointed at a picture of a plump older woman wearing Danish ceremonial clothes and decked with jewelry. She reminded Halldór of Queen Victoria of England.

"My niece, Kirsten, was of course named for her. This is the old house in Hafnarfjördur, taken in 1901." Matthías pointed at a picture of an old two-story wooden house. A young boy wearing shorts was standing in front of it. "This is my brother Jacob. He must have been eleven years old at the time. I think the photo was taken by a foreign friend of my father's."

Matthías pointed at another picture, this one of Birkihlíd under construction; the main walls of the house had been set up, and the builders were working on the roof. In front of the house was a small hayfield, where a cow and a few sheep were grazing.

"This picture was taken in 1910, when Birkihlíd was being built," he said.

"Is this a picture of you?" Halldór asked, pointing at a photo of a slim young man with a dapper mustache, playing the cello.

"Yes, the picture was taken in Berlin in the spring of 1932, the day I gave my first solo concert."

"I assume these are your niece and nephew with their mother," Halldór said, referring to an enlarged color snapshot of an older woman with a young woman and a man. Though he had only seen Jacob Junior after his death, he recognized him immediately. The decorations in the background indicated that the picture had been taken during Christmas celebrations.

"Yes," Matthías replied, "Elizabeth and Jacob Junior went up north every other year to celebrate Christmas with the family there, and in alternate years Kirsten and her husband Árni came south. I understand that after Elizabeth's death, Jacob Junior used to celebrate Christmas at the home of his friend Reverend Ingimar."

"May I interrupt?" Jóhann said, appearing at the door of the sitting room carrying a cardboard box.

"Oh, yes, of course," Halldór said, and turned to Matthías. "This young man needs to take your fingerprints, sir, to compare with the ones found here in the house. We're assuming, of course, that you were a frequent visitor here, so that many of the prints found will be yours, and we can then exclude them from further investigation."

"Yes, well, I suppose so," Matthías said, wrinkling his nose.

Jóhann took a card out of the box and set it on the desk; it had a series of printed squares on it and some markings in English. He then produced an ink pad.

"This is just ordinary printing ink. It washes off easily," Jóhann said. "It would be better if I might take your hand myself, sir. That's the best way."

Matthías held out his hand, and Jóhann carefully took one finger after another, pressing each onto the ink pad before rolling it across one of the squares on the card. Having done this with all the fingers of both hands individually, he then took each thumb, pressing it directly onto a square on the card, and finally, the other four fingers of each hand together, onto the largest squares.

"Thank you," he said, making notes on the card.

Matthías glanced awkwardly at his blackened hands and then at Halldór. "Perhaps you wouldn't mind escorting me to the bathroom. I can't touch a thing."

Holding his hands up in the air, he followed Halldór to the end of the corridor. The bathroom suite was clearly very old and worn after decades of use, but it was obvious from the quality fixtures that no expense had been spared when the bathroom had originally been installed.

"Thank you," Matthías said, and then added, "Perhaps you would be so kind as to fill the sink with water?"

Diary III

January 12, 1914. Professor Schmidt talks about the variety of railroad gauges that have been employed. He firmly recommends the use of standard gauge, which is 4 feet 8½ inches, i.e. 1.435 meters. I asked him if it would not make sense to use a narrower gauge in Iceland in order to save on infrastructure. He said that would be reasonable, since Iceland would not be connecting directly with other railroad systems. Once a decision on gauge had been made, however, Icelanders would have to apply it throughout the country...

January 15, 1914. Today Herr Lautmann, an agent from the Association of Railroad Companies in the United States, paid a visit to the college. He is German by birth but has lived in North America for 20 years. He urged us to seek employment in the United States after graduation; he says they offer great prospects and generous salaries. He received mixed reactions from my college friends, but I wrote down his name and address in Chicago...

January 24, 1914. Calculating curves between two straight sections. The radius of curvature may not be sharper than 300 meters. The professor shows me how to make use of books of tables...

May 2, 1914. My father sends me Ísafold magazine, with articles arguing about the cost of building a railroad in Iceland. There is much disagreement: those in favor put a figure of 27,000 krónur per kilometer for standard gauge track, while opponents say 49,000 krónur. Both sides quote experience from abroad, but I feel that it is impossible to price accurately the construction of a railroad until it has been designed and surveyed. On can invite bids for materials from many countries, and who can say in advance what that would bring. With careful planning and preparation it should be possible to build an inexpensive, fully budgeted railroad...

June 10, 1914. I shall not take a vacation this summer; instead I plan to devote myself to college studies in order to shorten the duration of my course.

If all goes well, I shall have finished by next spring, and then I can turn to real projects. I am writing to Elizabeth to tell her that I shall not be able to pay her a visit this summer. I don't feel I can suggest that she comes here to Berlin, which would of course be my dearest wish...

June 28, 1914. News arrived from Sarajevo in Bosnia that Archduke Franz Ferdinand and his wife had been fatally shot as they drove through the city. People here in Berlin are dismayed: Franz Ferdinand was heir-presumptive to the Emperor of Austria and considered a good friend of Kaiser Wilhelm...

CHAPTER 16

Egill set himself up in one of the police cars, while officers in thick overcoats and fur hats fine-combed the snow with garden rakes, bringing him any objects they found. These he examined carefully, recorded, and wrapped in individual plastic bags.

Found in the garden of Birkihlíd, January 18, 1973, recorded by E.G.

One child's mitten, frozen, red
An empty spirits bottle (Tindavodka)
Empty milk carton
Dead mouse (half-eaten, probably by a cat)
Burned-out firecracker

Other items he put in one bag and labeled them "Junk." When his men had completed the search of the Birkihlíd grounds, he had them check the neighboring gardens, but nothing remarkable was found, apart from some rusty tree clippers, which he examined with particular care. After that the men searched all the neighborhood trash cans in case the weapon had been dumped in one of them; by now dusk was falling and the men had to use flashlights.

It remained for Egill to talk to the neighbors. He took along one of the older policemen whom he knew well from his own uniform days; he liked to demonstrate his authority when he spoke to people, and a small identity card was not as effective as a uniform.

The house just to the south of Birkihlíd had been built for a single family, but now contained three apartments. Its white exterior paint was flaking.

Egill knocked on the door of the basement apartment first. A young woman with a small child on her arm opened the door, but didn't invite them in, so they had to ask their questions from the steps outside.

No, she hadn't been aware of anything unusual until all the policemen appeared that morning. No, she had not heard a gunshot during the night.

On the floor above, an old, bent-backed woman with a cane invited them into the parlor, where an old man sat in a deep armchair, a blanket over his knees and knitted mittens on his hands. He was listening to *Children's Hour* on the radio. The light was off so it was rather dark.

The old woman offered the visitors a seat on the couch, but she remained standing beside them, rocking to and fro.

"We are investigating a death in the house next door. Are you familiar with the people who live there?" Egill asked, raising his voice in order to be heard over the radio.

"What?" the old man said.

"Familiar and not familiar," the woman said. "The Kielers don't pretend to be familiar with just anybody. Who is dead?"

"His name is Jacob Kieler."

"What?" the old man said.

"Well," said the woman, "that's good news."

"Excuse me?" Egill said. "That's good news?"

"Yes, he was a stuck-up so-and-so."

"Had you any complaints about him?"

"What?" said the old man, turning to the woman. "What's that man saying?"

"Might it be a good idea to turn down the radio?" Egill asked.

"Complaints about him!" the woman said, ignoring both the old man and the radio. "He's done nothing but grouch, ever since he was a boy. He says that trash comes blowing over from our garden, but he burns scrap wood in the fireplace and doesn't give a damn about the smoke drifting over our way. He was on the roof the day before yesterday, pretending to fix the chimney."

"What, doing what?" asked the old man.

Egill tried to write but couldn't see anything in the gloom.

"He also complains about our tenants. Says they park in the spot in front of his house," the old woman continued. "It's not as if he even owns a car himself."

"Would it be possible to put the light on in here?" Egill asked.

The woman pretended not to hear, and continued, "That lot thought highly enough of themselves, and then the master himself ends up shot like a dog."

"How do you know he was shot?" Egill asked suspiciously.

"Yes, well, they thought they could keep things under wraps, but there's more to life than meets the eye."

Egill wasn't sure what to make of this reply; he found it difficult to think in this darkness and noise, so he just wrote *SUSPICIOUS* in large letters in his notebook.

"Did you see anyone out and about near Birkihlíd last night? At around midnight, say?" he asked.

"Around midnight? No, we go to bed at nine thirty on the dot. We won't have any noise in the house after that," the old woman said.

Egill gave up, but he underlined *SUSPICIOUS* twice, and he and the policeman took their leave.

"What did that man want?" he heard the old man say as the door closed behind them.

The top-floor apartment was accessed from inside the house. They were received by a man in his fifties who did not invite them in, but came out onto the landing and closed the door behind him. He wore a thick sweater with a jacket on top, and Egill noticed that he was not wearing shoes, just socks with a hole in one heel. He told the man who they were, and that they were investigating a death.

"Did you notice anything unusual last night?" he asked.

"Maybe, maybe not," the man replied.

"Which means?" Egill asked, opening his notebook.

"What is unusual and what is not unusual?"

"Anything that's not usual," replied Egill impatiently.

"I see," said the man.

"What happened yesterday that was unusual?" Egill said more firmly, moving to the side so that his uniformed colleague could be better seen.

"I went for a walk during the night, and the lights were on in the downstairs rooms in Birkihlíð."

Egill brightened. "Is that unusual?"

"It is certainly not usual," the man replied.

"Why were you going for a walk at that time?"

"I work as a night security guard at the docks. I sometimes find it difficult to get my sleep patterns back on my days off. So I go for walks."

"How frequently does this happen?" Egill asked.

"It varies. Sometimes every night but then not for weeks. The landlady complains if I move about in the apartment at night."

"So you noticed that the lights were on?"

"Yes, because it's very rare that the lights are on in the reception rooms in that house. They seem to mainly live upstairs," the man said.

"What time was this exactly?" Egill said.

"I walked round the neighborhood in a big loop, but returned home when it began snowing, just after one thirty. That's when I saw the lights on."

"Did you see anybody else during your walk?"

"Not here in the street, no."

Very suspicious, Egill wrote in his notebook.

Diary III

July 25, 1914. The newspapers report disputes between the Austrians and the Serbs. People seem to think it will end in armed conflict. I am designing a 20-meter-long railroad bridge with two parallel tracks...

July 27, 1914. It is being reported that hostilities have broken out between Austria and Serbia. Kaiser Wilhelm is hurrying back to Germany from Norway. People here in Berlin are very worried about an impending war...

August 2, 1914. Germany has declared war on Russia. Naval battle in the Baltic...

August 4, 1914. All-out war between Germany and Austria on the one hand, and England, Russia, and

France on the other. Prices of goods rising here in Berlin...

August 15, 1914. Fighting on the German-French border. Neither side prevailing. A war has begun that has no end in sight. I fear that the fighting will continue for many months...

September 4, 1914. College begins. Some of my classmates have registered for military service, while others want to complete their studies before joining the military. Our professors urge us to focus on our studies in spite of the hostilities...

November 1, 1914. Instruction in mechanics begins. We begin by studying basic steam engines, and the professor shows us calculations on energy efficiency for railway trains powered by steam. Apparently only 6% efficiency is achieved. I am looking forward to learning about locomotives powered by electricity. The professor says that such a train was first demonstrated here in the city in 1879, and the first extensive electric railroad, between Bitterfeld and Dessau, was opened in 1911 (15 kV, 16.7 Hz). An engine that Rudolf Diesel had completed before his death last year is also thought to be very promising. It is powered by oil...

November 15, 1914. I do not allow the war to interfere with my studies. The worst thing is not being able to write to Elizabeth. Only letters written in German or Danish are permitted, and they are read before they leave the country...

January 12, 1915. Structural engineering. Dr. Hagendorf showed us a photograph of the Firth of Forth railroad bridge in Scotland, which was opened in 1890. It is 2,530 meters in length overall and constructed mostly of steel. A true feat of engineering, says the doctor. Gerhard Grau asks about the best places to set explosives to destroy the bridge. He is very keen to complete his exams as soon as possible and begin military service. Dr. Hagendorf did not reply to his question...

CHAPTER 17

Halldór waited out in the corridor while Matthías Kieler scrubbed his hands clean. Erlendur had gone to see to a number of things, including a visit to Jacob Junior's long-standing friend the Reverend Ingimar Thorsteinsson.

"Most things in here have not changed at all since the house was built," Matthías observed, as he dried his hands. "My father had the whole house plumbed, which was very rare in those days. Allow me now to show you round the rest of the house."

The master bedroom was in the center of the house facing the street, with a balcony in front. In the middle of the floor stood a large double bed, covered with a beautifully woven bedspread, and on each side of it a small bedside table with turned feet, covered with a white crocheted cloth. On one of the tables was a pocket watch, a small box, and some old spectacles. The walls were decorated with tasteful, old-fashioned wallpaper.

"This was my parents' bedroom and, later, that of Jacob Senior and Elizabeth. After Jacob died, Elizabeth moved to another room on the other side of the corridor. This bedspread is considered a great treasure, and was Elizabeth's wedding present from her parents in Leicester."

He opened the large closet, which contained old clothes, packed in plastic bags.

"This is Jacob Senior's wardrobe," Matthías continued. "Everything here is as it was when he died."

Halldór took a bowler hat down from one of the shelves, removed it from its bag, and examined it. He had once dreamed of owning a hat like that.

"I hope someone will be able to make use of these clothes now, perhaps a museum or even a theater," Matthías remarked wistfully. "They are clothes of quality."

Opposite the television room was Jacob Junior's study, with shelves bearing large numbers of books, ring binders, and stacks of papers.

"I assume you will need to look through Jacob Junior's papers. Everything is on hand here. My nephew was very organized. All the account books for the running of the house will be found somewhere here."

Elizabeth's bedroom was directly opposite the bathroom. It had been arranged in the same manner as the master bedroom, with clothing packed in plastic bags in the closet, and everything kept clean and tidy. There were a few personal effects on the bedside table; some simple pieces of jewelry, a comb, and a Bible in English.

The last room upstairs was Jacob Junior's bedroom. It contained a neatly made single bed and, on the bedside table, an alarm clock and a copy of Goethe's *Die Leiden des jungen Werthers*, with a bookmark tucked toward the back of the book.

"Did Jacob read German?" Halldór asked.

"Yes, he was a good linguist; he spoke English like a native, of course, but also had a good command of German. His father encouraged this."

Halldór examined the book. It was dog-eared and worn.

"This is a much-read book," he said.

Matthías took it and looked at the title. "Yes, my brother Jacob was fond of quoting *Werther*. A wise man once said that if a book was not worth reading twice it was not worth reading once."

Halldór opened the closet. The clothes were somewhat shabby, though they had been neatly hung up or arranged on shelves.

As they walked back along the corridor, Halldór pointed at a trapdoor in the ceiling.

"What is up there?" he asked.

"A storage loft; among other things, it contains odds and ends from when the children were young. Nothing was ever thrown away in this house."

"How do you get up there?"

"There is a ladder attached to the trapdoor that slides down when the trap is opened. You can also get out onto the roof through a skylight up there."

They went back down to the ground floor. By now, Jóhann had left, and the two men found themselves alone in the house. A green sheet covered the largest bloodstain on the floor. Halldór could see that Matthías was not comfortable here in the parlor: he wrung his hands repeatedly and didn't seem to know where to turn.

"This is an unusually large parlor," Halldór said.

"Yes, it is spacious. My parents often invited guests here to listen to music. They would move in the chairs from the dining room, though the men usually remained standing. I can remember around eighty people attending a concert here. As I progressed with my music studies, I would sometimes play at these concerts, but otherwise the performers would be the very best instrumentalists or singers the town could offer."

"Who is this woman?" Halldór asked, pointing at the painting on the wall to the side of the fireplace.

"That is my sister-in-law, Elizabeth Chatfield Kieler. The picture was painted at her home when she was in her late teens."

It was undeniably a fine painting, and the sitter clearly exuded considerable character in spite of her tender years, Halldór mused.

"Can you describe her to me?" Halldór asked.

"Elizabeth was a grand woman. She was exceedingly intelligent and well educated, as well as being very determined and strong willed. She proved a very good wife to my brother and the best possible mother to the children." Matthías moved closer to the painting and continued, "I remember very well the first time I saw Elizabeth. She and my brother arrived here in Iceland on board the *Gullfoss*, and my father and I went down to the quay to meet them.

"I had only just turned sixteen, and I hadn't seen my older brother for ten years. He had written numerous letters to me, but when it came right down to it, I had no idea how to behave toward this sophisticated man. I was even less sure about how to greet his foreign wife, and when Jacob Senior and Elizabeth came down the gangway toward us, the words froze in my mouth; but to my great joy Elizabeth shook my hand and greeted me in Icelandic. Jacob Senior had taught her that on board the ship.

"Though the words were correct, the pronunciation was, of course, not perfect. Two daughters of a friend of my father's, teenage girls, had joined us on the quayside while we waited, and when they heard what Elizabeth said they started giggling like idiots. I caught a flash of anger in my sister-in-law's eyes, and she never again spoke a single word of Icelandic. She learned very quickly to understand the language, and she enjoyed reading books in Icelandic, but she never again tried to speak it. Elizabeth was not a person you mocked."

Halldór led the way into the office. There was gray fingerprint powder on the desk and on the stamp frames.

"I do apologize for this mess," Halldór said, as he examined the stamps. "These must be worth quite a bit."

"I don't think they're worth a fortune, but they are attractive and neatly displayed. Jacob Junior inherited a large stamp collection from his father, but I gather he had sold everything apart from these here."

Halldór selected the latest diary from the bookshelf. "I assume that Jacob Senior continued to keep a diary after he completed this one at the beginning of 1932."

"That's right. He kept a diary until his death."

"Do you know where the more recent books are?"

"No."

Halldór turned to the gun cabinet. It seemed quite sturdy, with the guns securely locked behind an iron grill. There were two shotguns, three rifles of various sizes, and one pistol, all clean and shiny—it looked as if they had recently been polished.

"Who owned these weapons?" Halldór asked.

"Jacob Senior was a great shooting enthusiast; they were his," Matthías replied. "Jacob Junior also went shooting with his father, and was a reasonable shot."

"Is there ammunition here for the guns?"

"I expect so, but Jacob Junior probably kept it in a safe place."

"Can you tell me why one of the dining chairs has been moved into the parlor?" Halldór asked, as the two men made their way through the parlor toward the dining room.

"No," Matthías declared, shaking his head.

In the dining room was a large sideboard for china; some of the doors were glazed, revealing the collection of beautiful plates inside. There was a small trolley in one corner of the room.

They passed through the door that led from the dining room into the kitchen. And Matthías paused, looking around the room. "Jacob and his mother showed great persistence in putting up with this turn-of-the-century kitchen all these years. The refrigerator was the only thing that was bought new, but it was hidden inside one of the cupboards. There is also an electric stove."

Halldór examined the utensils hanging on the walls. "Has this stuff been in use here all the time?" he asked.

"No, hardly," Matthías replied. "I assume that Sveinborg has cooking equipment that she keeps somewhere. These things are more museum items. Jacob Junior even collected old kitchen equipment from other houses to display here."

"There is a coal-fired range here; is it in working order?" Halldór asked.

"Yes, it is connected to the house's main chimney stack, which has three flues. There is also a fireplace in the laundry room in the basement. Come, I'll show you all this on the plan of the house that is kept in the studio."

To the right of the house's main entrance was a door leading to the extension. "Jacob Senior had this studio built in 1935 to provide a work space for himself and his assistants," explained Matthías.

It was a spacious room, about twelve by twenty-six feet, containing a large drafting table with a complicated wrought-iron support that allowed one to adjust the table's height and position. A heavy counterweight made it easy to set the angle of the table, and a drafting machine with two long rulers was attached to its top edge. There was a chair with a screw thread so it could be made higher or lower by turning the seat. Halldór's eye was caught by the large framed drawings, white lines on a dark blue base, hanging on the walls. He examined the one nearest to him. "Reykjavik Station, Scale 1:2000, 1923." The drawing was a rough sketch of Reykjavik city center, showing the outlines of the principal buildings and Tjörnin Lake, but also incorporating a railroad station and train tracks.

The railroad station had been drawn on the corner of Skothús-vegur and Sóleyjargata, where the Hljómskáli building had later been built; Birkihlíd could also be seen nearby. The tracks were shown running southbound along Sóleyjargata, and northbound along Lækjargata toward the harbor. There was a legend with explanations and references by letter or number to the various features of the drawing: station building, office and heated warehouse, freight shed, freight-loading bay, weighbridge, workshop and locomotive shed, turntable, ash hopper, water tank, main running tracks, passenger sidings, freight sidings, freight yard, harbor yard, locomotive sidings.

"So they must have done a great deal of the planning for this railroad," Halldór said.

"Yes, there was a lot of work behind this. Jacob Senior was very proud of these drawings," Matthías said.

"These are photocopies of the originals, aren't they?"

"Yes, that is correct. The originals are somewhere in safekeeping. I remember helping my brother Jacob make this copy."

"How was that done?"

"The original was fastened into a frame over a sheet of paper that had been treated with chemicals, ammonia among other things; the stench was dreadful. The frame was then held in a window, and the part of the copy exposed to daylight turned blue, while those parts under the pen markings remained white."

Halldór moved to the next drawing. It showed a railroad track leading eastward from Reykjavik over Mosfellsheidi, north beyond Lake Thingvallavatn, and from there south toward Ölfusá River, and east to Thjórsá River.

"Is this not an odd route for a railroad?" Halldór asked.

"It seems like it today, but at the time that they were planning the railroad, the heath over Hellisheidi was considered too high and steep to be crossed. Mosfellsheidi was much flatter. Later on, the route through Threngsli was discovered, and subsequently all plans were based on that one."

There was a large bookcase on the inner wall of the room, all but one of whose shelves was filled with old ring binders and books.

"Here you can find all the data relating to the railroad," Matthías said, "in case anyone should be interested in it."

On one shelf were two old surveying instruments, and Halldór picked one of them up and peered into its eyepiece.

"That is a theodolite; the other is a leveling instrument. You'll probably see everything upside down."

"I don't really see anything at all," Halldór said.

"The lenses need to be focused," Matthías said, taking the instrument from Halldór. He held it briefly up to his eye before replacing it on the shelf. "I helped Jacob Senior with some of the surveying in the summers before I emigrated; for instance, I helped with the route east through the Threngsli Pass."

There was a rack on the wall in which a number of thin plywood curves of different radii were arranged.

"What is that?" Halldór asked.

"When they were designing railroad tracks or roads, they used these curves to plot the shape of bends," Matthías replied. He pointed to some thick books with German titles in the bookcase. "These are tables of coordinates for shapes like these, and were used to calculate transition curves." He took out one of the books and flipped through it, revealing pages covered in columns of numbers printed in tiny characters.

"And this is where the drawings are kept," Matthías said, pointing to a three-foot-high cabinet with wide, shallow drawers, standing on an eight-inch-high plinth to make it a comfortable level to work at. Matthías opened a drawer labeled "Birkihlíd and other houses" and took out a large drawing, placing it on top of the cabinet. "This is a ground plan of the main floor of the house. There are also drawings of the other floors with all the elevations."

"We might perhaps borrow them at a later date to copy them. It could be useful for the investigation to have an overview like this," Halldór suggested. "Now let's see the basement."

The basement was reached by a staircase from the kitchen, leading to a short corridor, which, unlike that in the upper floor, was dark, cold, and dirty. Since the house was built on a slope, the basement extended only under the front half of the home.

"Jacob Junior had completely given up trying to keep the basement clean," Matthías said. "Dear old Sveinborg couldn't manage any more than what she did upstairs."

He opened the door into a small bathroom that stunk of sewage.

"The trap has dried up; it is never used and thus the unpleasant smell," he said, flushing the toilet before shutting the door again. "It would have been a really good idea to make a cozy apartment here for Sveinborg, but nothing was allowed to be changed, and she was supposedly only working half a day anyway."

Along the corridor were two small rooms, mainly empty and smelling of damp.

"These were staff living quarters in earlier days; they were a bit more comfortable then," Matthías said, apologetically.

At the end of the corridor was the entrance to a large laundry room, where there were big wooden tubs, drying racks and clotheslines, and a large open fireplace.

"Jacob Senior had this fireplace bricked up a little while before he died. He probably wanted to modernize the laundry room. On the other hand, Jacob Junior had it opened up again after his mother died, using it to store some old housekeeping tools he had collected. The idea was to show what laundry facilities were like in an affluent home at the turn of the century."

At the far end of the laundry room, a door led to the boiler room. "This is where the coal was shoveled in," Matthías said, pointing to a hatch covering an opening on the outside wall next to a coal store containing a few remnants of fuel. The majority of the space was dominated by a massive old boiler. "The house was connected to the hot-water main in 1943, but there is still some coal here, even so."

They returned to the corridor through the laundry room. There was yet another door into an empty larder, beyond which was a room that Matthías said was a wine cellar.

"My father was a very moderate user of alcohol, but he enjoyed being a generous host. Before prohibition took effect in 1915, he filled this room with bottles of wine, which lasted throughout the prohibition years. Now it is a very meager cellar."

The main floor, while chilly, felt rather pleasant to Halldór after their visit to the basement.

"We have finished here for today, sir," Halldór said, "but we might need to talk a bit more to you later."

Matthías nodded, put on his overcoat and hat, and Halldór escorted him out, asking an officer to drive the gentleman home.

Diary III

February 23, 1915. Life continues as usual here in Berlin in spite of the war. There is, however, much unemployment, and business is generally stagnant. At college the students do their best to concentrate on their studies...Military processions march through the streets to the beat of drums. They are all dressed in gray uniforms with either beribboned caps or spiked helmets...

April 25, 1915. The final examinations are imminent, but the war eclipses everything. My college friends intend military service after graduation. Some are eager, others anxious. What is certain is that there will be a multitude of railroad projects because of the war. They are now attaching huge cannons on to railroad wagons...

May 8, 1915. Newspapers here in Berlin report that a German submarine U-20 sunk the giant ocean liner Lusitania *south of Ireland yesterday. Kapitän Schwieger has received much praise for this act here in Germany. The German Ambassador in the United States had warned tourists against taking passage with the ship. I doubt whether this will prove to have been a judicious move for the Germans in their conduct of the war... The newspapers have not reported this, but rumor is flying round here in college that several hundred passengers died on the* Lusitania, *including many Americans. It is said that women and children were among those who perished...*

May 12, 1915. The woman with whom I take meals wishes fervently for peace, as supplies are continually dwindling. Now you may no longer serve meat on Tuesdays and Fridays. Occasionally there is fish instead and then nobody notices it, but on some meatless days, the shops have no fish either. The cabbage does not taste of anything, and the soups are insubstantial. The bread is good, but the worst thing is when there is no butter or margarine available. Then we have jam or honey on our bread...

June 4, 1915. The final exams are over. Celebrations here are muted because of the war. I have said good-bye to those professors and college friends I was able to get hold of. I am going to haste my way to Denmark. Probably best to go overland through Jutland...

CHAPTER 18

Erlendur telephoned Reverend Ingimar. The pastor had been audibly shocked by the news of his friend's death, but seemed to recover enough for Erlendur to ask if he could come by later that day. The reverend agreed and said he'd let their other friends know what had happened. Then Erlendur spoke to Jacob's sister Kirsten in Akureyri, who, after a short silence, said she would come south to Reykjavik at the first available opportunity.

Erlendur was frequently given the task of bringing bad news to relatives. He had a way of doing it that was both considerate and calming, which surprised those who didn't know him well. Erlendur had a reputation as something of a joker, and while he liked to laugh and tease, he was also quick to sense when it was appropriate to be serious.

He would be working on the case for the rest of this day and the following one, and then heading off on holiday. He was looking forward to the trip, but was now feeling a bit apprehensive about being away from the investigation. He had a feeling he would be needed over the next few days. Halldór always relied on having someone to discuss things with, and that was usually him. There would be difficult decisions to make in this case, and Halldór didn't really trust his colleagues: Egill was not good at giving appropriate advice, Jóhann never took a stand on anything, and Marteinn was new to the job. That left only Hrefna, but Halldór was not in the habit of turning to her.

Reverend Ingimar was tall and slim, though slightly stooped; he had dark hair and graying sideburns.

"It is incomprehensible how something like this can happen," he said, inviting Erlendur into his home. "Here you are, this is my office, please take a seat. My wife will bring us coffee in a minute."

They sat down, and Erlendur got out his notebook and a pen. "I understand that you and the late Jacob Kieler were good friends."

"Yes, we met in the first year of high school and immediately became good companions," Ingimar replied.

"So perhaps you can tell me a bit about him, what sort of a person he was?"

"Yes," the pastor cleared his throat, "I was indeed thinking back to our school years when you arrived. I'm rather expecting the family to come to me about the funeral, and I shall begin working on the eulogy presently."

He leafed through some papers on the desk in front of him.

"Jacob Junior was the son of Jacob Kieler, engineer, and his wife, Elizabeth. The Kieler name stems from Jacob Junior's great-grandfather, who emigrated from Denmark to Iceland in the middle part of the last century. His name was Jacob as well. His son, Jacob Junior's grandfather, was called Alfred. They were both killed in accidents while still full of life; Jacob the elder fell off a horse, whereas Alfred died in a car accident many years later."

Reverend Ingimar was interrupted by his wife, a pale, thin woman, bearing a tray of coffee. She had overheard this last sentence and said portentously, "The Kieler males do not perish from old age. The legend does not lie."

The pastor glared at his wife but said nothing.

"What legend would that be?" Erlendur asked.

"There was once a loathsome and unchristian calumny told about the Kieler family," replied the pastor. "It will not be repeated in this house, and I had hoped that it had been forgotten," he added, directing these words toward his wife.

As soon as she had put out their cups and poured the coffee, his wife left the room, allowing the pastor to continue. "Merchant Jacob Kieler made his money in trade during the second half of the last century, and his son, Alfred, took over when his father died. He built Birkihlíd in 1910. He had two sons, Jacob the engineer and Matthías the musician." The pastor consulted his notes. "There was a bit of an age gap between the brothers. Jacob Senior was born in 1890 and Matthías in 1904. Jacob went abroad to study in 1910, first to Denmark and then to Germany, where he took a course in railway engineering in Berlin. After completing his studies, he worked for a while in the United States. He was married in the summer of 1919, and he and his wife moved back to Iceland in 1920."

The pastor paused again to check his papers.

"Jacob Senior worked on a variety of engineering projects over the years that followed. His main interest was, of course, railways, and he devoted a great deal of his time and his own resources to traveling round the country to survey routes for the railroad, and designing station facilities and bridges. But these projects never came to anything."

Reverend Ingimar took a sip of his coffee, crunching a lump of sugar between his teeth before continuing. "Well, the war began and the British army occupied the country.

Naturally Jacob Senior acquired an important role then. His knowledge of English and his education made him a vital link between the occupying forces and the locals, and construction works for the military were, to a great extent, under his supervision. He very much came into his own, and was highly regarded by everyone."

The pastor was quiet for a while, and when he continued his tone of voice had changed. "It was in the summer of 1945 that the terrible tragedy occurred. I assume you have familiarized yourselves with the case, which naturally affected the family greatly. Mrs. Elizabeth had put down roots here, and she continued to live at Birkihlíd, but she felt the loss sorely. It was very hard for Jacob Junior to lose his father and witness his mother's grief. He tried to be a good son in every way, and was her support and her rock until the day she died. Mrs. Elizabeth died two years ago, a venerable old lady. I conducted the funeral at the cathedral, and some of her relatives came over from England to attend; I had to deliver the address in English, of course..."

"What can you tell me about Jacob Junior?"

"Yes, Jacob Junior. Well, we met at high school. He was quiet and aloof, and did not have much in common with many of our classmates. I myself came from out of town, from Snæfellsnes, where my father was a pastor. I was a shy youth and unsophisticated, and so tried to pick a friend who was not particularly conspicuous. During my two last years at school, the Kielers allowed me to live in a room in the basement of Birkihlíd. For board, however, I used to go to an aunt of mine who lived in Vesturgata, a very nice woman who took in people for meals, mainly students. She and my father were cousins—"

Erlendur interrupted him. "What about Jacob Junior, what did he study?"

"Well…Mrs. Elizabeth always kept in good contact with her relatives in Leicester and frequently visited them in the summer. Jacob Junior always accompanied her, and when the time came for him to go to university, the Chatfield family helped him get into Cambridge, where he studied history and philosophy. During our high school years, I had thought he would study theology with me at the university here in Iceland, but that's not the way it turned out. I became a theologian and the following year I was ordained to the north to—"

"What did Jacob Junior do after completing his studies?" Erlendur asked, interrupting him again.

"When he returned home he was appointed history teacher at our old school, but unfortunately teaching did not suit him and he left after the first term."

"Isn't it rather unusual," Erlendur asked, "for teachers to leave in the middle of the school year?"

Reverend Ingimar was quiet for a while before continuing. "As I said, teaching did not suit him; he did not manage to connect with the students, and there were some disciplinary issues. He was extremely upset about this, and in the end had a bit of a nervous breakdown. He was in the hospital for a while, but his mother nursed him back to health and he recovered very well in the end. After completing his university degree, he had planned to write a doctoral thesis on the adoption of Christianity in Iceland and the adaptation of heathen philosophy to Christian society. I think he sought financial support from his mother's family in order to focus on these studies, but was declined. They were practical folk who were not very impressed with his choice of study. Then he took a job at the bank, initially for the short term only, but he settled there."

The pastor stopped, and seemed to be waiting for the next question.

"What did he do apart from this?" Erlendur asked.

"He attended to his hobbies. He read history and, from time to time, wrote articles for various periodicals. He was very meticulous, and as a result probably undertook fewer things than he would otherwise have done. Always when he completed a project, he felt he could have done better."

He took another sip of coffee before continuing. "He was also very fond of Birkihlíd and was extremely diligent in maintaining both house and garden."

"Who were his friends?"

"He was not gregarious by nature, and after the setback at the school, he became very isolated for a while. But he always took part in the fraternity's activities."

"The fraternity?"

"Yes, when we were at high school, we and some other friends founded a fraternity named Gethsemane, whose objectives were Bible readings, prayers, and fellowship, besides which we went on outings together. It has, of course, always been within the framework of the established church. I have been the fraternity's chairman for twenty years, and Jacob became treasurer seven years ago when the previous treasurer fell ill. The operations of the fraternity have always been blessed with success. One of the older brothers who passed away without offspring bequeathed his estate to the fraternity, and we have been fortunate in our investments ever since. Of course, some money is donated to charity each year, but we have amassed considerable capital, some of which we now plan to use to add an extension to our meetinghouse. The membership may remain unchanged, but it will be beneficial to have more space. We have been freeing up assets recently in order to get started."

"Whom did Jacob Junior mainly associate with?" Erlendur asked.

"He and I always kept in good touch; we have, for instance, continued to play chess together once a week, regularly. Our companions on these chess evenings were my brother Steindór and Sveinbjörn, a primary-school teacher."

"Did Jacob have any enemies?"

The pastor smiled faintly and shook his head.

"No, my friend Jacob had no enemies. I think that most people will at some time, intentionally or unintentionally, do something to offend others, and so generate enmity. But Jacob was someone who tried to be kind to everybody he met. He never engaged in any kind of business activities, he did not push to get promoted at the bank, and on the whole, he never competed with a soul. I even think that he was happiest when we, his chess companions, checkmated him."

Reverend Ingimar smiled at the thought, but immediately grew solemn again.

"Were any valuables kept at Birkihlíd?"

"No, definitely not. Contrary to what many people think, Jacob and his mother were not wealthy. I understand that Jacob Senior had taken out a life insurance policy that provided a reasonable living for Mrs. Elizabeth, but they did not accumulate any wealth. There are, of course, various objects in the house that are quite valuable, but hardly enough for dishonest people to want to try to acquire them, never mind kill for them. Their value lay above all in the memories the family associated with them, and in their historical worth."

"Did Jacob's circumstances alter when his mother died?"

"Yes, everything to do with maintaining the home at Birkihlíd changed, of course. The estate had to be divided between the heirs, forcing them to sell the house. I do, actually, know that Jacob Junior was having talks with the municipal authorities about the city buying the house and its contents to turn it into a museum—it is, of course, a unique record of what a well-to-do family home in the early part of the century was like."

"Do you know who will inherit Jacob's share?" Erlendur inquired.

"I believe that his sister Kirsten is the legal heir, though I am sure he will have bequeathed a sum of money to the fraternity."

"Were you and Jacob Junior close friends?"

"Yes, of course," replied the pastor. "Naturally, we discussed our hopes and feelings more when we were younger, but I always had my friend's full confidence."

"Did you notice any changes in Jacob's behavior in recent weeks?"

"No."

"Did you meet frequently…that is to say since the New Year?"

"We played chess last Friday."

"Did anything unusual happen then?"

"No."

"Did you not meet him after that?"

"No."

Diary III

June 7, 1915. Have now crossed the border and am sitting in the train on my way to Copenhagen. I feel as if I am back home. I would never have believed that I would be so happy to hear Danish spoken. The German border guards were very strict. They examined my books thoroughly. Fortunately they were all in German, apart of course from my diaries, which I was very relieved that they did not examine thoroughly. They were among my workbooks in my trunk...

June 8, 1915. I am going to stay here in Copenhagen for a few days, rest and decide what to do next...

June 10, 1915. I am thinking of going to England to visit Elizabeth. The crossing is dangerous, of course, yet I must not be afraid of undertaking this journey but once, when the sailors are doing it all the time. I read in a newspaper that 1,382 steamships sailed in and out of British seaports in one week and that 8 of these had been sunk. That is just over half of one percent. The Danish ships are, of course, neutral and they fly the Danish flag...

June 11, 1915. I visited the office of the British Embassy this morning to apply for a visa. The purpose I gave for my visit was that I wanted to look up some friends of mine with whom I had lost touch. I had to give a thorough account of my stay in Berlin. In the end I got my visa on condition that during my stay I present myself each week at the office of the Immigration Authority...

June 12, 1915. The old railway station here in Copenhagen has been turned into a cinema. I went to a film show, but could think of nothing but my recollection of the day, five years ago, when I first came here and saw the trains. I feel as if a whole lifetime has gone by since then. I do remember the arched roof, though; otherwise it all seems a lot smaller than it was in my memory...

June 15, 1915. I heard that the Icelandic Steamship Company's brand new ship the Godafoss *is to embark on its first journey to Iceland on the 19th of this month. The ship stops en route in Leith, so it seems an excellent idea to try and get a passage on it...*

June 19, 1915. It was a festive occasion when the Godafoss *set off from the dock in Copenhagen. The ship is 70 meters long and 1,374 tonnes. It has a crew of 31 and accommodation for 56 passengers. Everything here on board is new and splendid. The only thing I do not like is that the ship has two Danish flags and the word "Danmark" in large white letters painted on each side, but this is of course necessary because of the war. It must be clear that the ship comes from a neutral country. The captain told me that they had painted over these markings on the* Gullfoss *before it entered the port of*

Reykjavik this spring... The Godafoss *is, apparently, the first Icelandic ship with radiotelegraphic equipment, and through this, we heard that the Danish government had today approved a new constitution for Iceland and also agreed on a new Icelandic national flag, which will have an ultramarine field with a red cross superimposed upon a white cross. The blue color is lighter than, for instance, the blue of the French, Norwegian, and English flags...*

CHAPTER 19

Jóhann had a visitor at the lab that afternoon; Erlendur's son, Halli, had come to the office, as he occasionally did, to get a lift home with his father. Erlendur couldn't always leave on time, and on those occasions Halli would seek refuge in the lab with Jóhann. He would sit in a corner drawing with a pencil on squared paper, always starting his pictures in the top left-hand corner and working systematically down the sheet. His illustrations depicted things from daily life: cars, roads, houses, or people skiing. Each drawing was careful and exact, though completely devoid of any sense of perspective.

Blue-eyed Halli was tanned and handsome, with blond hair cut straight across his forehead. His right ear was slightly deformed, and his long hair concealed the hearing aid he wore there. Halli usually had a smile on his face that highlighted his straight white teeth, but when he was busy drawing, as he was now, his expression became serious as he frowned in concentration.

Jóhann had arrived at the lab just after five o'clock with all the data he had collected at Birkihlíd. He arranged the cards with the known fingerprints in a semicircle on the table in front of him, and began sorting the unknown prints he had retrieved at the scene. Marteinn had taken the film to be developed, before heading to the hospital for the postmortem. When Fridrik had extracted the bullet, Marteinn was to bring it to Jóhann for examination.

It didn't take Jóhann long to recognize and put aside the prints that matched those of the dead man and of Sveinborg, the housekeeper. One print lifted from the telephone table obviously belonged to his colleague Egill; not an unusual occurrence in cases like this. The detectives were not always quick enough in donning their gloves, leaving fingerprints in unhelpful places, but Jóhann could recognize most of them by sight. It was an unusual talent, one that he developed at college in the States. He remembered fingerprints almost as well as faces, and if a print was clean, he could often tell immediately whether he had examined it before.

In the end, there were only two samples left that he had no match for, but they seemed to belong to the same person. Someone had opened the lid to the keyboard of the grand piano in the parlor, and also picked up one of the stamp frames from the desk. He knew that Sveinborg had polished the frames the previous day, so her prints would be on them, but the frames had been picked up again after that. To his surprise, he recognized these prints.

Some weeks before, a building that housed one of the city's best music studios had been broken into; many valuable instruments and pieces of equipment had been stolen, and damage had been done. Jóhann had carried out the fingerprint examination, acquiring some exemplar prints from the staff and all the musicians who had been there recently. One set of prints in particular had attracted his attention; their owner was a guitar player, so his fingertips were unusually calloused. He had also been left-handed, and the fingerprints on the stamp frame at Birkihlíd matched those of a left-handed guitar player. Though he had taken the man's fingerprints himself, he did not recall his face well, but he did remember the prints, and these were the same.

Now he needed to find the paperwork for the burglary and hope that those prints were still on file; privacy rights required that prints taken from innocent people during the course of a criminal investigation be destroyed as soon as the investigation was completed, but there was sometimes a bit of a delay in the process. Even if the prints had been destroyed, it would be easy enough to find the man and get some new prints. But that, Jóhann thought, would be for someone else to worry about.

Jóhann checked his notes on the shoe print that he had taken in the garden, wondering if it could possibly belong to the same man as the fingerprints on the frame. It seemed unlikely; the guitar player had not been a very large man as he could remember, but even so, the footprint they found was very small.

He was reasonably pleased with the results of his day's work, which had established that two people had arrived at the house in the hours around the time of death—the person with the small footprint, and the left-handed guitarist. Whether these visits had anything to do with the death was another matter, and again not for him to investigate.

"That was disgusting," Marteinn exclaimed, entering the lab and handing Jóhann a clear plastic bag containing a bloody bullet. He was short of breath from his run up the stairs to the fourth floor, a common practice of his—part of his training regimen, he claimed.

Jóhann opened the bag to examine its content. "What was disgusting?"

"The autopsy."

"You didn't stand over them while they were cutting?"

"Yes, wasn't I supposed to?"

"No, not necessarily," Jóhann said, smiling. "I always wait outside." Moistening a cloth with denatured alcohol, he tipped the bullet from the bag onto the cloth and wiped the blood away.

"Can you find out what sort of a gun was used?"

"I'll try," said Jóhann, "but I'm no firearms expert. At college they told us if you are going to be any good at ballistics, you have to be crazy about guns; you can't learn it from a book. I've only ever fired a gun in the lab, so my knowledge of this stuff is limited."

He measured the diameter of the bullet with calipers.

"9.6 or 9.7 millimeters," he said, getting up and going to the corner where Halli was working on his drawing. Jóhann put a hand on his shoulder and the boy looked up.

"Halli! We need to calculate," Jóhann said in a loud, clear voice.

Halli looked up and smiled broadly. "Calculate, yes, I like calculating. Absolutely."

He happily followed Jóhann to the workbench.

"First, we'll convert to inches. What is 97 divided by 254?" Jóhann asked in a loud tone, and making sure to look Halli straight in the eye.

"What is 97 divided by 254?" Halli repeated, closing his eyes and bobbing his head up and down.

Jóhann took out a slide rule and moved the slide back and forth.

"Why do you speak so loudly to him?" Marteinn whispered.

"He's hard of hearing," Jóhann replied.

"I know; 97 divided by 254 is 0.3819. Absolutely," Halli said.

Jóhann had also completed his calculations. "That's right, 97 divided by 254 is approximately 0.38 inches, or .38 caliber."

"That narrows the field," Jóhann explained, turning to Marteinn. "That's the way ballistics investigations usually work, through elimination, but if we wanted to rely on this sort of thing in court, I would send the stuff to a lab abroad for confirmation."

He then got a small pair of scales along with a box of small weights down from a shelf; on one of its trays he placed the bullet, on the other a ten-gram weight. The side with the bullet swung down, so he kept adding one-gram weights until the scales balanced.

"Thirteen grams," he said, looking at Halli, who had been waiting patiently. "How many grains is that? Thirteen times 15.4."

"What is 13 times 15.4?" he repeated, closing his eyes and bobbing his head once again.

Jóhann began again to calculate with his slide rule.

"I know; 13 times 15.4 is 200.2. Absolutely," Halli said.

"That's right; it is…about 200 grains. Now you can finish your picture," he said kindly, dismissing the boy.

"Finish the picture, absolutely," Halli said, scurrying happily back to his corner.

"About 200…I'm beginning to get some ideas," Jóhann said. He took out an American ballistics manual and leafed through some tables.

"I know the type of gun this might come from. It was often called the 38/200. Smith and Wesson in the United States started to produce these for the British army in 1940, and a few of them remained in circulation here in Iceland after the war, left behind by British officers, but it was difficult to get ammunition for them after the British army left."

Jóhann read from the manual: "*Rifling: Five-groove right-hand.* I think that means that there are five grooves in the bore that spiral around to the right." He looked at Marteinn. "Do you know what that is for?"

"So that the bullet spins as it flies, then it goes straight and doesn't tumble. I learned that at Police College," Marteinn replied, clearly pleased with himself.

"That's right," Jóhann said, examining the bullet under a magnifying glass. "One, two, three, four, five grooves turned to the right. It figures." He put the magnifying glass down and added, "The parts of the bore between the grooves are called the lands. When the bullet is fired, it gets hot and expands into the grooves as it goes down the barrel, so the lands leave marks on it. There are five such marks on this bullet."

Jóhann retrieved a wooden box from the bottom of a closet in one corner of the lab. "I brought this back from the States," he said, placing the heavy box on the table. It had several labeled, shallow drawers, and Jóhann opened the second to last drawer, marked *Smith & Wesson etc.* The drawer was divided into many compartments, each containing one unused cartridge and one used bullet, along with an information sheet.

"This box contains samples of the most common ammo used in the States," Jóhann said. "I'm sure there is a 38/200 here somewhere." He ran his finger across the compartments as he read the information. "Yes, it's here." He took the used bullet and compared it with the bullet that had killed Jacob Junior. The color finish was slightly different but the shape was identical.

"That's the one," he said, flipping through the manual to the index. He turned to the relevant page and found some good color photographs of the gun from both sides, together with a comprehensive description. "*Repeating handgun with revolving cartridge cylinder.*" On the left side of the barrel was the maker's name, SMITH & WESSON; on the left side of the butt the trademark; and, attached beneath the butt, a lanyard loop.

Jóhann read out some numerical information, writing it down as he did: "*Length 10 inches or 254 millimeters. Weight 29 ounces or 820 grams. Length of barrel 5 inches or 127 millimeters. Six rounds fully loaded. Muzzle velocity 198 meters per second."*

He referred to a table listing the muzzle energy and velocity of handguns.

"This gun seems to me to have been rather underpowered compared with other types of the same caliber," he said after comparing some numbers.

Just then Hrefna entered the lab and sneezed; her face was gray with fine dust. "I went to the document store and finally managed to find the file on the death of Jacob Senior," she announced, then sneezed again and blew her nose into a tissue. "I must be allergic to this stupid dust," she said. "Here's the bullet." She handed Jóhann a brown transparent paper envelope, its glue long since dried out. Jóhann took out the bullet and examined it.

"This is interesting. Another 38/200, as far as I can see." He told Hrefna what he had discovered about the other bullet as he marked each one on its flat end with a felt-tip pen, *A* on the new bullet and *B* on the old one.

"Now let's check to see if this could be the same weapon," he said. "We'll use the comparison microscope."

This was the largest piece of equipment in the lab, and it was composed of two gray-colored microscopes linked by a white crossbar, with lenses for both eyes. Jóhann carefully clamped the bullets in place, one under each microscope. The clamps were designed so that objects under observation could be aligned in any direction, and miniature lamps enabled Jóhann to illuminate both bullets from exactly the same angle.

"The light sharpens the marks," he said, peering into the microscope. It took a moment for him to synchronize the focus, and then he slowly revolved bullet A to find the deepest mark. He repeated the process with bullet B, turning a fine adjusting screw back and forth until he was finally satisfied.

"Here, take a look at this," he said.

Marteinn and Hrefna took turns examining the bullets through the microscope. "That's very interesting," said Marteinn tentatively.

"What am I supposed to be seeing?" Hrefna asked impatiently. Neither of them had been able to discern anything aside from a mass of horizontal marks bisected by a central black vertical line.

"The horizontal marks fit perfectly together," Jóhann explained. "You are looking at the two bullets on either side of the black vertical line."

Hrefna peered into the microscope again. It was true; the marks were unbroken across the whole image.

"Does this mean that the same gun was used to fire both shots?" she asked.

"Probably," Jóhann replied. He looked again into the microscope and slowly turned both bullets a full 360 degrees. They had been distorted on contact with their targets, but it was very clear that the pattern was the same all the way round.

"Very probably the same gun," Jóhann repeated.

Diary III

June 22, 1915. Elizabeth met me on my arrival at Leicester and introduced me to her fiancé, Mr. Peter Faidley, a lieutenant in the army. I was, naturally, deeply disappointed but I was also happy for them. They certainly make a handsome couple. I had never asked for Elizabeth's hand in marriage, nor indicated that I had any intentions of that nature.

And she heard nothing from me for two years. I can only blame myself that I have lost her. They plan to marry when Mr. Faidley has completed his military service...

June 23, 1915. Everything in England is much duller than when I was here before. This is of course due to the war. It feels odd to have dwelt among two warring nations in the same summer. In truth, the feeling is very similar for both places...
There is nothing for me here as things stand, and I must make a decision as to what to do next. I sent a telegram to Herr Lautmann in Chicago asking about employment prospects in railway engineering in North America. I need to gain practical experience...

June 26, 1915. Received a telegram from Herr Lautmann. He has engaged me as a railway engineer with the Chicago & North Western Railway. He requests me to come as soon as possible...

June 29, 1915. On board the Cunard liner Pannonia. *We sailed from London about midnight and are heading, without navigation lights, north of the British Isles.* Pannonia *is 9,851 tons; she was built in Glasgow in 1902, and can accommodate 90 passengers in first class and 70 in second class. We have no idea when we shall reach New York...*

CHAPTER 20

Hrefna sat opposite Halldór, absentmindedly chewing on her Biro pen, while he talked on the phone.

"Yes, I'll be there soon," he said, unsuccessfully trying to end the call. Halldór listened on wearily, and finally said, "No, no, I won't be too late."

Halldór and Hrefna had been looking through the files she had found on the investigation into the death of Jacob Kieler Senior before the phone rang.

After hanging up, Halldór turned glumly to the pile of documents between them. First was a report by a Detective Constable Andrés Hjörleifsson, who had been called to the scene in the summer of 1945; Hrefna read it aloud, skipping the less important bits:

> "Today, July 15, 1945, constables N.L. and
> O.A. were called to the house named Birkihlíd.
> Household servant H.J. had found his employer,
> Jacob Kieler Senior, deceased in the main parlor
> of the house, with a large wound to the right eye.
> I, the undersigned Detective Constable A.H.,
> was called to the scene and investigated the

*situation. My examinations and conversation
with household servant H.J. revealed the following:*

"*A glass pane in the main door had been
broken from the outside, making it possible to
unlock the door by extending an arm through
the broken pane. The deceased was alone in the
house during the night, as his wife and two children were out of town, and the staff, who live in
the basement of the house, were absent, having
been given leave for that weekend. The deceased
was dressed in pajamas and dressing gown,
and seems to have gotten out of bed during the
night when he heard a noise, and encountered
his killer in the parlor. No valuables are missing
from the house, so it appears that the burglar
was discouraged. It was not possible to take
fingerprints from the door handle, as several
people had passed through and touched it before
I arrived at the scene.*

"*Search for clues outside the house was
unsuccessful. Inquiries have found no evidence of
dispute initiated by or against the deceased.*"

Several black-and-white photographs accompanied the
report; the overview pictures of the parlor showed where Jacob
Senior's body lay between the large leather sofas.

"He seems to have been standing in a similar spot as Jacob
Junior when he was hit," Halldór remarked. "This is getting
stranger by the minute."

A close-up of the head of the deceased showed that the shot had hit him directly in his right eye. Hrefna was grateful that the picture was not in color, it was gruesome enough as is. The left eye had remained open, and when she covered the right eye with her finger, it looked as if he were still alive.

Next in the pile of documents was the report of the pathologist who had carried out the postmortem. Hrefna read aloud again:

> *"The body is that of a 169-cm tall male. It presents dressed in pajamas and a dressing gown. Much loss of blood from the head, which displays evidence of a gunshot wound. Clothing is removed, and the body shows no other signs of injury apart from the aforementioned.*
>
> *"Examination of the right eye reveals a gunshot wound in the center of the socket. There is a 1-mm powder ring round the entry wound, which measures 1.0 cm in diameter. The wound and surrounding tissue is excised and placed in a glass.*
>
> *"On opening the skull and removing the brain, it transpires that the bullet has passed through the eye, fundus oculi, and right-brain hemisphere, stopping at and fracturing the occipital bone. The bullet was retrieved with minimum handling, and measured at approximately 1.0 cm. The brain weighed 1,470 grams.*
>
> *"The man would have died instantly from this injury. No other pathology was found."*

Hrefna continued to leaf through the file, coming to a document written in English on FBI letterhead and translated into Icelandic by a state-registered translator on the reverse side:

"September 23, 1945
Att. Chief of Police

Dear Sir,

"This examination has been conducted on
the understanding that the findings are related
to an official criminal investigation and that this
ballistics report is to be used solely for official
purposes in connection with inquiries into, or
later prosecution of, a criminal case. No permission is hereby granted for the ballistics report to
be used in civil court actions.
"(Signed) David Gray, Superintendent.
"Ref: Jacob Kieler, deceased, murder.
"Requested investigation: bullet Q1. Arrived
sealed in government mail September 20, 1945.
"Investigation findings: The sample Q1 was
shot from a weapon with five lands and grooves
twisting to the right. There is some surface damage to the bullet but not sufficient to obscure the
distinguishing marks made by the weapon, which
are reasonably distinct and could be evidence
should the weapon be found. Bullets of this type
are only produced for S&W 38/200 so it is highly
likely that the weapon is of that type.
"(Signed) Lee Scanlon, Detective.

"Notarized by me
"Mary Ragland,
"Notary Public in the District of Columbia."

"It seems Jóhann was right regarding the type of gun," Hrefna added.

"Doesn't surprise me," Halldór replied. "He wouldn't have said anything about it unless he was certain. He doesn't speculate."

Hrefna turned to the next sheet, a report by DC Andrés, typed on an imperfect typewriter.

"On August 7, 1945, laborer H.E. came to see
the undersigned, wanting to report an incident
that might be a clue to the murder of engineer
Jacob Kieler. H.E. said he had been employed by
the army digging a trench for a drainage pipe
in the military barracks area. In his group was
a laborer S.J. who, according to H.E., is a well-
known communist who frequently tries to agitate
among his co-workers to stage protests of various
kinds.

"There was urgency to completing the drain-
age trench, as officers in the military were about
to move into the new barracks. S.J. successfully
incited his fellow workers to stage a sit-down
strike, demanding better terms as the job was
unusually dirty. Engineer Jacob Kieler, who was in
charge of the project, arrived at the site and politely
asked S.J. to a negotiation meeting, where after
they left the site in J.K.'s vehicle. J.K.'s assistant

engineer subsequently arrived on site with a mes-
sage for the workers that they would all be dis-
missed and blacklisted by their employers if they
failed to complete the work on time. Solidarity
among the workers proved weak when S.J. was no
longer on site, and they resumed working. When
S.J. returned on foot to the site toward the end
of the working day having, as far as he was con-
cerned, attended a negotiation meeting with engi-
neer J.K., the job was nearly finished. S.J. became
very angry and swore, in the hearing of a number
of workers, that he would kill engineer J.K.; H.E.
said he would be able to name witnesses to these
words. On numerous subsequent occasions, S.J.
had expressed his hatred of engineer J.K. and his
desire to do him harm. H.E. confirms this testi-
mony with his signature."

The next sheet, also from Andrés, was handwritten and dated
August 8, 1945. The handwriting was poor and the ink had faded,
making it difficult for Hrefna to read:

"Sigurdur Jónsson, laborer, who was arrested
earlier today at his place of work at Reykjavik
harbor, has been brought in for questioning.
When asked, Sigurdur says he cannot remember
where he was on the night of July 14 and the early
morning of July 15, but thinks he was probably
at his home, and that his wife is more likely to be
able to answer this as she is much better than he

at remembering his absences from home at night. When asked, Sigurdur acknowledges altercations between himself and engineer Jacob Kieler and admits to having shed few tears on hearing of his demise. Sigurdur claims neither to own a gun nor to know how to use one. He says he knows nothing about who committed Kieler's murder, and that he had nothing at all to do with it. After questioning, Sigurdur was placed in custody."

Following this interrogation, a warrant had been issued to search Sigurdur's home, and Andrés had written a report on the execution of the search.

"Today, August 8, 1945, I, the undersigned, and police officers N.L. and O.A. went to the home of laborer Sigurdur Jónsson at Brekkustígur 25, where we found his wife Kristín Jósefsdóttir and their three young children. Kristín presents as a simple and straightforward person. When asked, she admits that Sigurdur only arrived back home toward morning on July 15, but that this is actually a fairly frequent occurrence. We searched the home for a gun but did not find one. Two unused rounds were discovered in a box containing a number of toys under a child's bed, and Kristín says she thinks that the children must have brought them into the home. They appear to belong to a larger weapon than that which killed J.K., but they were removed for further examination."

The next sheet was dated three weeks later.

> *"The prisoner still refuses to disclose where he*
> *was on the night of July 14 and the early morning*
> *of July 15. An extension to custody is requested."*

Hrefna leafed quickly through the rest of the papers. "They seem to have lost interest in this case after that."

"I know Andrés very well; he was still here when I first joined," Halldór replied. "I'll talk to him tomorrow and find out if he's got anything to add to this."

Diary III

July 2, 1915. Pannonia *has now come through the worst of the war danger zone and the atmosphere on board is improving. I have met a young American, a Mr. Stephen Green, who dines at my table. He is a writer who lived in Paris before the war, and is now on his way home. I try to talk as much as possible to him to practice my English...*

July 8, 1915. Pannonia *arrived at Lower New York Bay toward the evening and sailed at half speed through the Verrazano channel into the Upper Bay and then up the Hudson River. There is a considerable amount of shipping traffic here in spite of the darkness of the night. It is hot and muggy... We saw the Statue of Liberty, donated by the French, which has stood here in the harbor since 1886. The statue is made of a copper-clad iron frame and is 151 feet high...The tall buildings of Manhattan Island are to the right and the wharves for the passenger liners lie ahead...*

July 9, 1915. Have now landed in New York. I had an easy time at the Immigration Office. I was able to present the telegram from Lautmann, and the people of this country do not seem to worry at all about my stay in Germany; these nations are not at war, of course...I wanted to be on my way as quickly as possible, and Mr. Green assisted me with getting to the railroad station, where we took our leave. I can get on to a train to Chicago in two hours. It is strange to be here where there are no worries, having dwelt in the war zone in Europe. Here there is no lack of anything...

July 10, 1915. We are approaching Chicago. The train has passed through New Jersey, Pennsylvania, Ohio, Indiana and, just now, Illinois...

CHAPTER 21

Egill was puzzled.

Jóhann had just presented him with a fingerprint card that had been tucked into a folder on a corner of his own desk, and said that the owner of these prints had been in Birkihlíd just before the murder, examined the stamp frames, and probably played the piano.

Egill and Halldór compared the fingerprint samples that had been taken in Birkihlíd with those on the card, and agreed there was every indication that Jóhann was right. The odd thing was that the owner of the fingerprints did not have a criminal record, and the card belonged to a completely different case, some burglary.

"How did you make the connection?" Egill asked.

"It was just an idea," Jóhann replied, not offering any further information.

Just after seven o'clock Egill and Marteinn were sent to fetch the man whose name appeared on the card, one Sigurdur Sigurdsson, born 1950, and bring him in for questioning. The address given was a house in the middle of the Old Town. It was quite straightforward, really, Egill reflected. The guy only needed to explain why he had been in the house, that was all, but it was better to bring him in to the station to do that. After all, neither Matthías Kieler nor Sveinborg the housekeeper had recognized the man's name, nor were they able to imagine what business he would have had at Birkihlíd.

"We are going to practice like crazy this winter," Marteinn confided in Egill on the way downtown. "It's been five years since we became Icelandic Champions and we're determined to get the title back." Marteinn was missing a soccer practice and he was upset about it.

When they arrived at their destination, they found an old, corrugated iron-clad building with two stories and an attic.

"I've been here before," Egill said, as they stood outside the house. "There's loads of weed here. We did a house search once and there were mysterious potted plants on all the floors."

Sigurdur's name was one of those listed on the directory by the front door, so Egill rang the bell. A few short minutes later, the door was opened by a barefoot young man with dark shoulder-length hair, wearing a brown cotton tunic and threadbare jeans.

"Good evening, we are from the detective division," Egill said, flashing his ID card. "Sigurdur Sigurdsson, does he live here?"

"Yes," the young man said suspiciously, "he lives here."

"Is he in? We need to ask him to come with us."

The young man shot them a wary look and then turned and yelled, "Siggi." There was no reply so he tried again, a little louder this time. "Siggi! There's somebody here wants to talk to you." Still no answer.

"He's probably asleep," he concluded, shrugging his shoulders. "Come in, I'll get him."

Egill and Marteinn stepped into the lobby and the young man disappeared into the apartment.

"We're getting a new trainer this spring, an English guy, he's bloody good," Marteinn said, continuing their previous conversation. "We're not allowed to talk about it yet; the contract isn't set."

Egill sniffed the air. "There's always this cloud of incense in these communes. You might just think they were trying to hide something."

"My mum's got incense like this; she's not trying to hide anything," Marteinn replied. "It just hides the smell of food, she says."

"I think I'd prefer the smell of proper Icelandic food," Egill said, wrinkling his nose.

"The guy can certainly sleep," said Marteinn, after a few more minutes slowly passed.

"This lot never have a clue whether they're awake or asleep," Egill said. "Hello?" he called into the apartment, but there was no reply.

"Hello?" Egill called again, this time stepping cautiously into the apartment, but still there was silence. Marteinn followed him into a large, dark room whose only furnishings were a few bean-bag chairs and some mattresses on the floor. There was a table-top, painted glossy black, resting on four brown beer crates. A number of half-burned candles stood on the table in a solidified pool of wax. The wine-colored walls were covered in revolutionary political posters and hand-painted peace signs.

They looked into the other rooms but there was nobody to be seen anywhere. A large window in the bathroom stood open, and when the two men peered out, they spotted a set of footprints in the snow outside.

"He's gone," Marteinn said, surprised. "I wonder if that guy was our Sigurdur?"

They knocked on the doors of the other apartments but nobody could give them any further information about Siggi.

They all said the same thing: If he wasn't in his apartment, then he wasn't at home.

They returned to the apartment and looked around for any photographs of the occupant without success. Before returning to the car, Egill took a measurement of the footprint outside the window; it was made by a clog, twenty-nine centimeters in length.

Diary III

July 11, 1915. I took a room at the Richmond Hotel late yesterday and slept like a log all night. It is an expensive hotel so I only spent the one night there…I presented myself at the office of C&NW early this morning and was well received. Mr. William O'Hara was given the task of looking after me to begin with. First he showed me the railroad station and a 4-4-2 Atlantic no. 125 locomotive that stood there. He then assisted me in settling in at a guesthouse in Bridgeport; this gives me a fixed residence that is reasonably priced, though in practice I shall be traveling a lot of the time…

July 12, 1915. A meeting with the railroad engineers this morning. Although I consider my knowledge of English to be quite good, I still missed much of what was said. I was given a few simple tasks to begin with. I am to go to St. Louis via Peoria and check the condition of some small bridges en route. O'Hara will be accompanying me...

July 16, 1915. In St. Louis for the first time. Looked at the Eads Bridge over the Mississippi River. It was opened in 1874 and is over 6,000 feet long. As we were standing there looking at the bridge a C&NW train arrived and passed across it. Today is Matthías's birthday; I shall write him a letter and send him a little something...

August 20, 1915. Completed my first design of a short switch at Burlington. We drank a toast with brandy at the office when Mr. Wolfert, the chief engineer, signed it off...

CHAPTER 22

By the time they had finished reading the police reports on the death of Jacob Senior, it was nearly nine o'clock in the evening. Halldór, who was expected at home, asked Hrefna to go to Birkihlíd to fetch the old diaries; he wanted her to go through them to see if she could find any information that might provide a link to the present day. Since the same weapon had killed both father and son, it was highly likely that the same person had committed both murders, so Hrefna was to look for entries mentioning people who were still alive today and had some connection with the family.

She decided to take a police car to Birkihlíd. Hrefna rarely drove; she was unable to afford a car herself, and the detective division cars were supposed to be left at headquarters, unless exceptional circumstances demanded otherwise, and this was one such occasion, she decided. After all, she wouldn't be able to manage the large box of diaries on the bus, and Halldór had asked her to begin reading tonight.

The front door at Birkihlíd had been sealed with wire strung between two small steel eyes screwed into the doorpost and the door, and then fastened with a lead seal. Hrefna simply cut the wire and entered the house. It was cold and rather dismal, but in spite of that she did not turn on any lights apart from the one in the office, where she quickly stacked the books she needed in a box she had brought along, and then hurried out, refixing the seal before driving home.

It was a lovely starry night, and the snow squeaked underfoot as she walked toward her house clutching the box. She was tired and the box was heavy, so she was relieved when Pétur opened the door for her. He lived on the top floor of her building and earned his rent by looking after the property for the owner: a bit of maintenance and cleaning, and then collecting the rent every month from the other tenants were his only duties. During the day he worked as a jackhammer operator. He was a burly fellow, with round cheeks and small eyes that were barely visible beneath his bushy eyebrows. There was certainly nothing wrong with his eyesight, though. Pétur was a curious—some would say nosy—soul.

"I heard on the evening news that a man had been shot," he remarked by way of a greeting.

"Yes, apparently," Hrefna replied, as she climbed the stairs followed by Pétur, carrying a bucket.

"Any idea what his name was?" he asked.

"No."

"No, of course not. They spare you girls these nasty cases, of course."

"Yes, yes," Hrefna agreed, slipping into her apartment and shutting the door without saying good-bye. Her daughter was sitting cross-legged on the floor reading. Classical music was playing on the radio. "It's a Stravinsky concert," Elsa volunteered.

"That's nice, darling," Hrefna replied, half-listening. "Did you have anything to eat?"

"Yes, I made some porridge. There's a bit left in the pan."

146

"I came home in a car, so I can drive you to school tomorrow morning," she said with a smile.

"Great!"

Hrefna reheated the porridge and dished some out in a large bowl, adding lots of cinnamon sugar and cold milk on top. This was one of her favorite meals, and she ate it heartily. After cleaning up, she turned to the diaries.

She took them from the box and laid them out on her small desk. She read well into the wee hours, and when she finally went to bed, she dreamed of nothing but trains the whole night long.

Diary IV

March 17, 1916. When I travel by rail between assignments, I usually go in the rearmost car; here it is called "caboose," a word with maritime origins, meaning originally a ship's galley. The caboose car is red in color and is where the conductor sits, also where he keeps his tools, lanterns, and flares. He can observe the whole train from a small tower that sticks up from the roof of the car. I chat with the conductor during the journey and think I have learnt more about railways from these fellows than throughout all my college years…Today I traveled with old Joe Benson. He told me that it had been one of C&NW's conductors who had the idea for the tower, which is called "cupola," back in 1863. By chance, an old railway car with a hole in the roof had been used as a caboose, and the conductor had stuck his head through the hole and seen how easy it was to monitor everything from this angle. He presented this idea to those who were building caboose cars for C&NW in Clinton. In Germany, this car is called "Güterzugpackwagen," and is located behind the locomotive. It has, however, not got a tower...

May 20, 1916. The dispute between America and Germany has subsided for the time being. The Germans have undertaken not to fire on passenger ships without warning, but they demand that the Americans persuade the British to lift the maritime embargo...

November 11, 1916. I really like living here in Chicago now. I have got to know the city very well and attend cultural events frequently. I am learning to drive an automobile...

CHAPTER 23

FRIDAY, JANUARY 19, 1973

The paper had arrived on time this morning, and Halldór was perusing the front page as he sipped his tea. Stefanía sat opposite him at the table. "It was absolutely pointless to stop at four hearts in the second round of bidding when we had a slam there," she said, referring to the previous evening's card game.

"Hmm," he replied, reading the headline on the front page of the paper: "Scientists at Kiel Marine Research Institute Support Iceland's Stance after Full Review of Dispute."

"Or to play a club when they had already bid five clubs. You were clearly not yourself," she continued, taking a sip of her tea.

"I just forgot for a moment," he said, turning the paper over. "Police Investigating Death of Reykjavik Man," read the headline above a small news story.

"You're always absentminded these days. You come home far too late and then think about anything but cards."

"Erlendur and Ása are taking the children to Austria, skiing," Halldór announced, changing the subject and then turning the page again.

"Yes, it's all right for some," Stefanía remarked glumly. "Whereas we never get to go abroad."

"Hmm. I'm going to be late," he said, folding the paper regretfully.

Outside, it was raining and a thaw had set in.

Diary IV

December 27, 1916. Christmas is over and I am ill. I feel somewhat sad and pessimistic. I sent a message to the office that I would not be in today. I am struggling to write this out of my system. I recognize this condition from my time in Germany, although then it was not as bad as this time. O'Hara invited me to visit at Christmas, but I concocted an excuse. He is a Catholic and would probably have expected me to accompany the family to mass, which I could not bring myself to do...

December 28, 1916. My landlady summoned a doctor for me even though I had asked her not to. He asked if I was prone to experience depression...

December 29, 1916. It is cold and dark, and I slept all day.

December 30, 1916. I have thought a great deal about Elizabeth today. As a rule I dismiss all thoughts about her, but at the moment I cannot help myself.

December 31, 1916. New Year's Eve. I got up and had a hearty meal. I am feeling a little better…

February 10, 1917. The Americans seem to be preparing to enter the war, and have broken off diplomatic relations with Germany. President Wilson is still hoping to be able to avoid hostilities, but the Senate has passed an appropriation for military expenditure…

April 6, 1917. The United States has declared war on Germany. Initially they will support the Allies by lending them money and supplying them with military equipment. General conscription is to be passed into law. All German ships at moorage here have been seized…

April 23, 1917. Yet again I am experiencing living with a nation on the brink of war. Nationalism is on the rise and the masses are being stirred up for fighting. Pray God this will soon pass…

CHAPTER 24

When Hrefna had moved to the Hlídar district the previous fall, Elsa had decided to continue going to school in their old area, in the west part of town, which meant she had to get up early to catch a bus. It was especially hard on cold mornings, but that was the choice she'd made.

This morning she was able to get an extra half hour's sleep, as Hrefna was taking her to school by car. They stopped first at Erlendur's home. He had asked Hrefna to pick him up so that Ása could have the car that day; there were a lot of errands to do before they left for their ski trip the following day.

Halli was busy shoveling wet snow off the front path when they pulled up in front of the house. It was hard work, and he didn't notice their arrival.

"It'll be such fun for Halli to go to Austria," Hrefna remarked.

"Yeah, I'm dead envious," Elsa replied. She skied a lot as well, and often bumped into Halli on the slopes.

"We'll go, too, when I'm rich," said Hrefna. "Is Halli a good skier?"

"Yeah, really good. He does competitions, too, but he usually falls. He gets so worked up that he ends up going off-trail. If he makes it all the way down in the first round, he usually gets the best time, but then he always goes off-trail at the first gate in the second round. They call him 'Drop-dead Halli,' because he is always dropping out," Elsa explained.

"And he's a bit gorgeous," Hrefna added.

"Yeah, it's such a pity he's so weird. It was hilarious at Kerlingafjöll, when the new girls were all out to hook him the first evening. They were so embarrassed when they realized he was retarded."

Halli spotted them and straightened up. He smiled, carefully examined the car license plate, and then walked over to greet them.

"Have you been skiing this winter?" Hrefna asked cheerfully.

"Oh yeah, several times, absolutely," Halli said.

"But the weather's been so bad."

"We went yesterday and also on Sunday."

"Did you go by bus?"

"Oh yeah, and I sat at the front."

"Did you compete last Sunday?"

"Yes, absolutely."

"You must be a senior class by now? How old are you?"

The smile suddenly disappeared from the boy's face.

"I'm not yet seventeen, no, absolutely not."

Then he said enthusiastically, "If you multiply the first three digits on your car license plate by two, because they are two different numbers, and add nineteen, because it's January the nineteenth today, you get 1973; and it is exactly 1973 now. Absolutely."

A broad grin lit up his face again.

Erlendur emerged from the house, made his way down the shoveled path, and climbed into the backseat. They waved to Halli and pulled away.

"Halli was a bit down earlier when I asked him his age," Hrefna said to Erlendur a moment later.

"Yeah, poor chap," he said quietly, shaking his head. "He was seventeen in November, but they decided his IQ wasn't high enough for the driving test. He's not likely to develop any further, so that's probably a final decision. He's taking it hard, so this is how he deals with it; he pretends he's not yet seventeen."

"Well, I'm not going to take a driving test when I'm seventeen," Elsa said.

Erlendur smiled. "No, but Halli has been car mad since he was a toddler. I'm sure that I could teach him to drive safely, but it's no use arguing about it. The trip to Austria is a way to make it up to him."

Diary IV

May 2, 1917. They are entrusting me with more and more complicated projects. The railroad company is very busy, and I am continually traveling round the state of Illinois. Mr. Wolfert has given me good references...

May 8, 1917. Traveled in one stage from St. Louis to Chicago today. Passed the whole journey in the caboose car with Joe Benson. We talked about the war. He wanted to hear about the Germans, and finds it difficult to understand that most of them are just ordinary folk like he and I. Joe complains bitterly about being too old for military service. He was a Federal soldier in the Civil War...

May 9, 1917. I have lived abroad for nearly 7 years now, and have dwelt in Denmark, Germany, and now in the United States. During this time I have had to become fluent in three new languages. I fear that my Icelandic would have suffered had I not placed such emphasis on keeping this diary; each evening I must sit down and think in my own native language for a while as I write these lines...

CHAPTER 25

E gill was sitting at his desk, staring irritably at a small black-and-white photograph of a boy with slicked-down hair.

Erlendur, on the other hand, was in a good mood. "If you let your hair grow to just below your ears, you might be able to connect a bit better with the younger generation," he advised.

Egill didn't even bother to reply. He had been up since before six a.m. to check if the fugitive had returned to his apartment in the Old Town. This time he had brought two police constables with him to watch the windows behind the house while he knocked on the door. A skinny youth with scruffy hair had answered the door in his underpants, and let Egill in to look for Sigurdur, but the search had been fruitless. The young man had no idea where Siggi might be, but promised to contact Egill if he heard anything.

Egill found it difficult to look for someone without having a photograph, so he had gone to the main office at Central Police Headquarters as soon as it opened that morning, only to discover that Sigurdur had never applied for a passport or a driving license. All they had was a photograph he had brought in when he got his ID card at the age of twelve. Egill had borrowed this picture but doubted that anyone would recognize the guy from it; he certainly didn't.

"Shall we put an announcement on the radio?" Egill asked when Halldór arrived at the office.

"That's hardly necessary," Halldór replied. "Just keep looking for him today. He must be with a friend, and if you ask around you should be able to find him."

Egill picked up his little exercise tool from the desk and squeezed it vigorously several times. He had no idea how to deal with this hippie generation, and now he was supposed to extract information from them in a nonconfrontational way. He only knew how to talk to these people when he had them on his own turf; that is to say, in custody.

"Can't the girl do this?" he suggested.

"It wasn't me that lost him yesterday," Hrefna replied, overhearing their conversation. "And besides, I have quite enough on my plate."

Egill knew that Halldór's silence meant he agreed.

What had he been doing knocking around Birkihlíd? Egill wondered, looking at Sigurdur's picture again and trying to imagine him with long hair. He could hardly be involved in the current murder, given that the ballistics investigation had linked it to the death of Kieler's father. This guy hadn't even been born when that happened. So why was he running away? He must be involved in some dope case; it would definitely be possible to squeeze something out of him.

He got up and poured himself some more coffee, and then gave a well-rehearsed lecture to those present on his opinion of hippies, gays, and other "perverts." When he had finished, Hrefna said, "Incomplete list. Try a mirror."

Egill didn't understand what she meant, and it bothered him for the rest of the day.

Diary IV

July 2, 1917. It is hot and humid. I find it very difficult to get accustomed to this weather and am not sleeping very well...Had a letter from my father. He writes that ships sailing between Britain and Iceland have been sunk and many sailors perished. Here in Chicago accounts have been coming in of casualties among the American forces in Europe. Warmongering is no longer so glamorous when the names of these young men are published in the newspapers...

August 17, 1917. Bought two powerful hunting weapons, a large rifle and a shotgun. I have been invited to go stag hunting this fall. I also bought a cheap little Colt 22 pistol that fits in a pocket. It is old but not much used. I must practice shooting with the rifle...

December 13, 1917. Am traveling in Canada with some colleagues from C&NW. We are checking out the new railroad bridge across the St. Lawrence River (Quebec Bridge) that was inaugurated ten days ago. We met up with Canadian railroad engineers from the Grand Trunk Railway and among their group was a young West-Icelander named Peter Asmundson. He speaks very good Icelandic even though he has never set foot in Iceland. His parents come from Skagafjördur...

CHAPTER 26

Kirsten Kieler and her daughter, Elísabet, came to see Hrefna promptly at ten o'clock, having been asked the previous evening to a meeting. Hrefna thanked them for coming and extended her condolences before inviting them into the interview room; she fetched them coffee and tried to make the atmosphere as comfortable as possible.

Once she was seated, Hrefna took in the mother and daughter opposite her at the table; they were both petite with delicate features. The mother wore a dark woolen overcoat and a black hat, and the daughter had long hair and was wearing a dark green sheepskin coat. They had very similar features, but as far as dress and manners, it was clear that they belonged to different generations.

"You know the circumstances of Jacob's death?" Hrefna began.

"Yes," replied Kirsten. "The detective who spoke to me yesterday was very kind."

"You were in the north?"

"Yes, I was at home, but I caught a flight yesterday evening."

"Can you think of anything that might help us to solve this case?" Hrefna asked.

"No. This is just as dreadful as when Dad died."

"Do you remember that well?"

"Yes, very well."

"Would you mind describing that day to me?" Hrefna asked.

Kirsten thought for a long moment before she began her account. "We got up early that day and Dad drove us—me, my brother Jacob, and Mom—to our summerhouse at Lake Hafravatn. I was fifteen years old and my brother twenty. Dad then returned to town to complete some business, but he was planning on coming back the following day to spend two or three days with us. We never saw him alive again."

"Had this trip been long in preparation?" Hrefna asked.

"I can't remember. We went to the summerhouse often during those years. The staff were given leave while we were there."

"Was your father usually with you?"

"Sometimes, not always. The engineering firm was always so busy in the summer."

"So it was common practice for your father to take you there and then go back to town?"

"Yes. Hjörleifur, the caretaker, usually drove us if Dad wasn't coming, but I remember that this time Dad wanted to take us."

"Did he return to town immediately?"

"No. The weather was wonderful, and he walked with my brother and me up Reykjaborgin, the mountain nearby. I remember so clearly how bright and beautiful the view was."

Kirsten wiped a few tears from her eyes.

"Who brought you the news of your father's death?"

"It was the parish pastor. Hjörleifur drove him to our summerhouse to see us."

"Is Hjörleifur still alive?"

"No, he and his wife are both gone."

"How did you react to the news?"

"Mom and I broke down completely, of course, but my brother Jacob was stronger at first and looked after us. It was later that the shock overwhelmed him, and I don't think he ever recovered after that. Dad was his role model and the head of the family, and when he was gone my brother felt he had to take on that role, but he wasn't ready for it by any means. The person who killed my father also took a large part of my brother's life."

"How did you and your brother get on?"

"Extremely well. My brother Jacob was very good to me when we were little, and we had a good relationship after I got married and moved to the north. It was only in the last few months that some problems came up."

"What kind of problems?"

"It had to do with Birkihlíd. He wouldn't hear of selling the property."

"Who wanted to sell it?"

"Matthías and I. It had become ridiculous keeping the house just for my brother Jacob. Then he wanted us to donate the house to the City of Reykjavik to be made into a museum, and he even offered it to the city without asking us. His behavior had become morbid."

"How did he react when you rejected this idea?"

"Very badly. He accused us of wanting to wipe out Dad's and Mom's memory. It was all becoming very difficult for us."

"Are we talking large sums of money?"

"Yes, the property is big and very well situated. We assumed that we would be able to sell the house for a good deal of money. Matthías is retired and needs something to live off. The money would also come in handy for me, as I would very much like to support Ella in her studies."

"Then what happened?"

"Matthías and I had to secure a lawyer, but the matter was concluded when Jacob said he would buy the house and its contents himself."

"Where did he get the money to do this?"

"I have no idea. He wanted to draw up a conveyance and we couldn't refuse. He agreed to pay the sum the realtor set for the house, and an appraiser was brought in to value the contents."

"Did you not want any items from the house?"

"Yes, of course there are many things I would have loved to have, but I didn't want to upset my brother Jacob any more than we already had."

"Had he finished paying for the house?"

"No, he paid twenty percent on signing, and planned to pay another forty percent in four installments this year. The rest was payable as a four-year bond."

"So he must have produced a considerable sum of money at the outset?"

"Yes."

"Do you know where he got this money?"

"No."

"Did he give any indication of this?"

"No, I didn't dare ask. He had become so strange. He had such incredible delusions about the rest of us in the family and our plans. I think he may have been ill by then, but I didn't dare suggest he see a doctor. I do know, though, that he has been in such financial difficulty that Matthías and I have had to pay the property tax for the house over the last two years to save it from being seized by the authorities. But we did finally reach an agreement that he should pay the house expenses while he was living there."

Hrefna realized they should make it a priority to examine Jacob Junior's finances; they might provide some clues about his fate. But for now, she decided to change the subject.

"Could there be any links between the deaths of father and son? Are there any friends of the family who were around in 1945?"

Hrefna purposely kept silent about the ballistics report, which had established that the same weapon had been used in both murders.

"There were of course very many people who visited the home while Dad was alive," Kirsten replied. "He ran his engineering firm from there and had assistants. There were also lots of other visitors all the time, but I don't know that any of these people maintained connections with my brother Jacob in later years."

"Were you aware that your father had any enemies?"

"No. I was, of course, very young. There was actually some communist that was arrested when Dad died and it was said that he had threatened Dad."

"Mother," Elísabet suddenly interrupted, "you know perfectly well that man was innocent. Also, he's been dead a long time."

"Oh, well, I didn't know that," Kirsten said.

Hrefna looked at Elísabet. "Do you know of this old case?"

"I have familiarized myself with it, to the extent that I know that it is recognized as one of the most serious abuses of authority in this century. The man was kept in prison for months on end without justification, a gross infringement of the principle of *in dubio pro reo*, since he was never charged with any offense. The case is considered to have been instrumental in shifting the burden of proof to the prosecution; thankfully, it's no longer acceptable to stick people in jail for months in the hope that they'll eventually confess to all charges."

Hrefna was taken aback by young Elísabet's statement. She was far more knowledgeable about the case and the law than she had expected.

"Have you kept in touch with your uncle?" Hrefna asked.

"No. When I came south to go to university, the plan was for me to live in Birkihlíð, but I moved out after a couple of days."

"Why?"

"I was supposed to sleep in my grandmother's room, and I wasn't allowed to change anything in there. I was scarcely allowed to change the bed linen, and I couldn't empty the wardrobe at all. He expected me to keep my clothes in my suitcase. I couldn't smoke in there and nobody was allowed to visit. It was like living in the National Museum."

"It would, of course, have been ideal if Ella could have made a little apartment in the basement," Kirsten added. "There was plenty of space, but my brother didn't understand at all."

Elísabet continued, "On top of that he expected me to help Sveinborg clean the house, but never lifted a finger himself."

"Did you never go back to Birkihlíð after that?" Hrefna asked.

"I would occasionally drop in for a cup of coffee with Sveinborg when Jacob was at work. She has always been a kind of auntie to me, and I like seeing her. I think she enjoyed the company as well," Elísabet replied.

Diary V

January 30, 1918. Went to a concert. One of the pieces the orchestra played was the New World

Symphony, which I had not heard since that concert long ago with Elizabeth. I had a bit of a lump in my throat...

June 5, 1918. I am mesmerized by the locomotives. They are almost human; the pipes are the arteries, the boiler the lung. A rigid body that breathes, clears its throat, and sighs. She groans with effort when she labors, and she sings as she runs at full speed. Her heartbeat ticks as the cars run over the rail joints: clickety-clack, clickety-clack, clickety-clack...

October 6, 1918. The new German Chancellor, Prince Max von Baden, has sent a request to the President of the United States to conclude a peace treaty. An end to the war seems to be in sight.

November 12, 1918. The newspapers report that a cease-fire was signed yesterday. The war has ended; God grant that there never be war again...

November 25, 1918. Matthías writes to me that Iceland is to be a free and independent state. The Act of Union was agreed in a referendum with a majority of votes. He also writes that the British consul came to see my father and asked for my address. I wonder why...

CHAPTER 27

It was midday, and Jóhann and Hrefna were on their way to Birkihlíd to conduct a thorough search of the house for any clues that might possibly help the investigation. In particular, Halldór had asked them to look for the gun, which he suspected had never left the house.

The sun had broken through, and it was getting warmer. Hrefna drove, while Jóhann leaned comfortably back in his seat; both were silent, lost in thought. Jóhann was reflecting on Birkihlíd itself; it was an unusual house and he suspected that this case would have an unusual conclusion. In addition, he was not totally satisfied with the results of his investigation the day before. He had the feeling he had overlooked something.

He could smell the faint fragrance of Hrefna's perfume. He felt good being close to her, and was sorry they reached their destination so quickly.

They broke the seal on the front door and let themselves in with a key. Something obstructed the door as Jóhann tried to push it open—it was a copy of *Morgunbladid*, lying on the floor in the lobby. He picked it up and scanned the front page. The main story was on the Kiel Marine Research Institute review, and a smaller story on the Kieler murder.

"This is today's paper," he said.

"Yes, of course," Hrefna replied. "What else would it be?"

"If today's paper is lying here, then where is yesterday's?"

Hrefna looked around. "There's usually somewhere in a home where newspapers are kept," she said.

They entered the inner lobby and Jóhann spotted a stack of them on the shelf under the telephone. "I should have checked here yesterday," he said, picking up the paper on the top of the pile. It was dated Thursday, January 18.

"This explains the footsteps we spent all that time examining yesterday," he remarked. "They belong to the person who delivered the paper, of course. He must have arrived at the house early in the morning, while it was still snowing."

"But how did it get onto the shelf?" Hrefna asked.

"The old housekeeper must have put it away before we arrived. She wouldn't have left it on the floor for everyone to trample on."

"That's probably right," Hrefna agreed. "I'll give her a ring and have her confirm it."

While Hrefna went to make the call, Jóhann entered the parlor and went around opening the drapes to let the light in; there were potted plants on the windowsill and their flowers already seemed to be fading.

"Sveinborg remembers having picked the newspaper off the floor when the policemen arrived," Hrefna announced, entering the parlor. "You were right. She didn't want them to trample over it."

"Right. That means we have no footprints to work with," Jóhann said, disappointedly. "They didn't fit with the time of death, anyway. The pathologist said he had died between one and two, but it didn't start snowing properly until after that."

They divided the workload; Hrefna went upstairs to look through Jacob Junior's personal papers, and Jóhann checked things downstairs, starting in the office.

He sat down at the desk and examined it carefully. It had four drawers on the left side and, on the right, a locked cabinet. In the top drawer he found a *Directory of Engineers*, dated 1966; he looked up Jacob Kieler's name:

Jacob Kieler, b. March 4th 1890 in Hafnarfjördur, d. July 15th 1945. Parents Alfred Kieler, merchant, son of Jacob Kieler, store manager, and his wife Kirsten, born Pedersen.

Graduated from MR High School 1910, degree in propaedeutic (cand. phil.) from Copenhagen University 1911, BA in engineering from Polyteknisk Læreanstalt in Copenhagen 1913, MSc in railway engineering from Technische Hochschule in Berlin 1915. Assistant engineer at the Chicago & North Western Railway Company in the United States 1915–1918. Engineer at the James Leslie engineering firm in Leicester, England 1919–1920. Operated his own engineering firm in Reykjavik 1920–1945.

Married June 15th 1919 to Elizabeth b. August 26th 1894, daughter of Joseph Chatfield manufacturer of Leicester and his wife Marjorie, née Stewart. Children 1) Jacob b. Oct. 12th 1925, historian 2) Kirsten b. Nov. 21st 1930, married to Árni Jónsson, headmaster.

The next drawer contained old writing utensils, an ink-pot, and some penholders; the third drawer held writing paper with the printed letterhead "Jacob Kieler MSc"; and in the bottom drawer were envelopes containing old photographic films and various pictures. The locked cabinet was no doubt the safe, Jóhann guessed.

Grasping the desktop from beneath, Jóhann tried to lift the desk, but he could hardly move it. The cabinet must be made of really thick steel, he reckoned. Before they could open it, they would need a court order, which Halldór was working on, though that might take all day. They would also need to get a locksmith here if they could not find the key.

He decided to turn his attention to the books on the shelves next. He checked them all, taking each one out one by one and leafing through them before putting them back. It was here he finally found dust. The books had clearly not been touched for ages. They were all old, and most had good quality bindings; the number of English titles was striking. He found the photograph albums and looked through them with interest. In these pictures, one could trace the history of the family and of the house they had lived in; pictures of parties and other holiday celebrations, but also scenes from daily life: girls working in the kitchen and doing the laundry in the basement, a laborer shoveling coal into the coal store, and a man cutting the grass in front of the house with a scythe.

There was a gap on the shelf next to the picture albums where the diaries had been; Jóhann knew that Hrefna had been given the task of going through them, and wished he could have had a chance to look at them as well.

The gun cabinet on the other side of the room was locked, but you could see the contents through the glass. Jóhann recognized the only revolver in the cabinet, which was a .22-caliber Colt, manufactured before the turn of the century, and small enough to keep in a pocket. He knew it was too small to have been used for the murder.

Opposite the gun cabinet was a model of a railroad station on a low table. It was not a toy, but a near-perfect replica of the buildings and equipment one would need to run a railway. Tiny letters on the railway carriages read "Iceland Railroad Company Ltd."

He went back into the parlor and checked under the sofa cushions; even here there was no dust. He looked into the fireplace and peered up the flue. A faint burned odor could be detected, and as he rummaged around with the poker, he could see a thick layer of soot on the slabs of the hearth and that the ventilator grill was in the open position. The fireplace had clearly been used frequently.

Then he carried the dining chair that stood forlornly in the middle of the parlor floor back to the dining room. The rooms looked far better with the chair back in its place at the big dining table. Jóhann examined the sideboard carefully, looking inside, under, and behind it, where he found a Christmas card from 1965 that seemed to have fallen down there and been forgotten. The greeting was to Jacob Junior and his mother, from Ingimar and family.

The kitchen was fascinating. Ancient, battered utensils hung on the walls; they had probably not been used for decades, but it was interesting to see what housewives from the first half of the century had to put up with.

There was nothing of note in the inner lobby apart from the telephone table and, beneath it, the newspaper rack, whose contents they already knew about.

In the outer lobby there was a door leading to a small guest bathroom, and another into the engineering studio. In the bathroom, the fixtures were of the same generation as elsewhere in the house, and everything was clean and shining; the toilet had a varnished wooden seat, and from the cistern high up on the wall dangled a chain with a porcelain handle. Jóhann took off his shoes before stepping up onto the toilet lid in order to peep into the cistern, but there was nothing unusual there.

Jóhann found the engineering studio most interesting of all. He could sense that a scientist had worked here. The drawings, the equipment, and the instruments were fantastic collector's items. He examined the drawing of the railroad station that hung on the wall, and recognized immediately the same structures shown in the model in the office. He went through cabinets and drawers, and spent a long time looking at drawings and other materials. He found a file containing press cuttings about the railway, including a magazine article by Jacob Senior. Jóhann sat down and read:

The Railway, by Jacob Kieler, engineer, written in June 1920.

There is increasing interest in harnessing mechanical power to the maximum for the facilitation of labor of all kinds, not least as regards the transportation of goods, as is evidenced by the ever-growing importation of automobiles. It is, therefore, not unreasonable to assume that greater support now exists for the mechanical transport method considered by most people to be the safest and most productive, that is to say the railway. It is clear to all thinking people that the automobile will never achieve a level of efficiency to make it possible to rely solely on that particular technology. With the arrival of the railway, it will naturally follow that the commercial transportation of goods and people by automobile will be prohibited on those routes served by the railroad.

The proposed railroad is intended to link Reykjavik eastward to the lowlands of southern Iceland. Surveys show that arable land in the lowlands in the south extends to 2,372 square kilometers, equivalent to more than a fifth of all arable land in Norway. The value of a railroad connecting this region to the world at large is, therefore, incontrovertible. It has been calculated that the price of milk will be reduced by a quarter on arrival of the railroad.

Over the past year, a survey has been carried out of all traffic along the Thingvellir Road and across Hellisheidi. These roads are far from being of quality, yet it transpires that the traffic is incredibly heavy, with 28,000 people crossing Hellisheidi, along with 5,000 tons of goods and livestock.

There has been much discussion on the gauge of the railway. This must be coordinated over the whole network so that the same type of rolling stock may be used throughout, and, rather than having to transfer freight between wagons, it will merely be necessary to attach previously loaded wagons to a train. In this discussion it is very important to strike a balance between excess and parsimony, as not only must the main tracks have sufficient capacity to meet

all potential transport needs for the unforesee-
able future, but one must also give due consider-
ation to the construction costs of both main and
prospective branch tracks.

Electricity would be the most practical motive
power for the rolling stock. The main advantages
are these: Electric cars run more evenly and are
more stable than steam locomotives; they therefore
create less stress to the infrastructure and are less
likely to derail even at high speed; they are ready
to go at a moment's notice while steam locomotives
take a long time to fire up; and they have both
acceleration and deceleration rates that are twice
those of steam locomotives, making for a quicker
journey when railroad stations are close together.

In order to provide enough electricity for the
railroad and other developments it will be neces-
sary to embark as soon as possible on harnessing
the river Sog, something that has already been
proposed. With a moderate increase in costs, it
will be possible to provide villages and whole
regions along the path of the railroad with as
much electricity as production permits.

It is of great detriment when planning major
projects not to allow for natural growth. We Iceland-
ers have often fallen into this trap, and it has done
us much harm; it cannot be overstated that when
embarking on expensive developments, one of the
main issues is not to do a shoddy job for the sake of
short-term economy, but rather to go for perfection
from the start in order to secure the long term.

Behind the article in the file was a folded map, showing railroad routes under consideration in thick pen markings. The map was shabby, its corners worn.

Jóhann leafed through several pages of expense calculations and plans before coming across a newspaper article that someone had marked throughout in red pencil.

Comments on the Railroad Affair by A Southerner.

In my opinion it is totally unacceptable that the citizens of Reykjavik and "those below the heath" should be the only ones to take part in the discussion on the transport affairs of us southerners, and for this reason I contribute these few words to the debate. It looks as if, for whatever reason, the fiercest railroad preachers here to the east have more often than not had some vested interest not unconnected with the proposed railway. And they keep banging that particular drum to this day, that a railroad must be built, without offering any reasoning in support of their case.

I am not in possession of information enabling me to discuss the railroad affair in detail. I am not in possession of engineers' estimates of the cost of laying railroad tracks here to the east, although I seem to remember a sum being mentioned of approximately six million krónur, according to the latest "reduced" and "amended" estimates. So it would not be far off the mark to assume that the cost would in all probability reach not less than nine to ten million krónur, bearing in mind those engineers' estimates for some enterprises here in the east that we remember with pain and heavy hearts. We have probably had greater and more costly experience of engineers' estimates than other regions of Iceland and, if truth be told, we have concluded that it would be foolish indeed to assume anything other than that all such estimates are more or less wrong, and always far too low. Low estimates are more dangerous than high ones, as they frequently lure people into enterprises they would not dream of undertaking if they knew precisely from the outset what the cost would be.

And then the railroad is supposed to be our only salvation. Apparently there are those who have convinced themselves that all our problems will vanish when it arrives. And yet they would have a job on their hands showing that the railroad can meet any of our region's needs that cannot be met with other and much cheaper means. The railroad would not pay for itself, not even given the desperate and heavy-handed measure of granting it a monopoly of commercial transportation.

But the nation, all Icelanders, would have to carry the can forever, for the benefit of no one except possibly the very few.

I readily admit that we who are against this business have kept quiet for too long, but our silence stems from a natural apathy coupled with our tendency to trust in the common sense and conscience of our nation's guardians to ensure that matters such as this would never proceed.

Jóhann continued to leaf through the file, finding more articles both for and against the railroad. The discussion seemed to
have gone on for years, and many weighed in on the argument.
Among the papers were also parliamentary documents showing
that this had been frequently debated in the Althing. In time,
the affair seemed to have died a natural death, despite engineer
Jacob's attempts to engage the interest of persons of authority
through correspondence. In the end, he had formed the Iceland
Railroad Company Ltd. and taken matters into his own hands.

Diary V

*December 24, 1918. I have just received the most
tragic news that Lieutenant Peter Faidley, Elizabeth's
fiancé, was killed at Verdun in November 1916. I
had a letter this morning from Miss Annie Barker,
who says that she asked her father to exercise his
influence in the Foreign Office to find my address.
Now I know what the consul in Reykjavik wanted
with me. Annie says that Elizabeth is very unhappy.
I have been thinking this over all day and there
is no doubt in my mind; I must go to England
immediately...*

*December 25, 1918. It is a cause of great regret to me
that I had to interrupt Mr. Wolfert in his Christmas
celebrations, but I could allow no delay in resigning
my post here. He accepted my resignation, but urged*

me strongly to come back to work for C&NW, saying as we parted that there would always be a place for me in his office...

December 26, 1918. O'Hara was kind enough to come in to the office and take over my assignments. I had finished briefing him on all matters by noon, and set off immediately for New York...

December 27, 1918. I bought a ticket on the first sailing to England. It is the Mauretania, *leaving tomorrow morning. The ship is engaged in transporting American soldiers home from Europe, but they take civilian passengers on the return trip...*

December 28, 1918. When Mauretania *set off from harbor this morning, I realized that I was exhausted. I have not slept at all since I got the letter from Annie, but now I can relax. I am on my way to Southampton, and can rest in the knowledge that the ship will carry me safely and at full speed across the ocean...*

December 29, 1918. Slept for the best part of the day...

December 30, 1918. Mauretania *is 31,938 tons, 232 meters in length, and achieves a maximum speed of 25 knots, one of the fastest ships now sailing across the Atlantic Ocean. Launched on September 20, 1906, it is the sister ship of* Lusitania, *which perished in the war...*

December 31, 1918. A new year is beginning. The passengers were not able to agree on which time zone to use for midnight, so we raised glasses to the New Year every hour all evening. My feeling is that this year will bring good fortune...

CHAPTER 28

Hrefna climbed the stairs, heading straight for Jacob Junior's office, according to the plan of the house they obtained for their investigations. She sat down at the desk and considered the neat rows of ring binders on the shelves, their contents labeled in block capitals:

FINANCE, ACCOUNTS
ACCOUNTS AND SUPPORTING DOCUMENTS 1972
ACCOUNTS AND SUPPORTING DOCUMENTS 1973
OTHER DATA

She pulled the records down and began leafing through the pages of the Finance, Accounts binder. Jacob Junior had kept very accurate books of the domestic finances, all double entry in separate debit and credit columns, and all written in pen with blue ink.

Expenses were divided into a number of categories: domestic running costs, house maintenance, food, clothing, entertainment, and so on. Income was split into two columns: salary and other income. Each page covered one month, and at the end of the month the columns were totaled and the balances carried forward to the next. Hrefna noted that Sveinborg's name was a separate item, and that each month a sum was entered for her wages under "domestic running costs"; there were no entries, however, to indicate that she had been paid.

The debt was quite large by now, and it seemed that Sveinborg had not received any wages for nearly three years. Jacob's salary from the bank was paltry; Hrefna would not have felt able to run her own home on that amount, and indeed it seemed to her that the expense items in Jacob Junior's accounts were considerably higher than his salary. The difference was explained by the "creditors" category, which showed that a considerable debt had been accumulated. Who these creditors were was not specified.

She closed the accounts binder and opened the one labeled "Other Data," which seemed to contain mainly letters and copies of letters. On top was a copy, made with blue carbon paper, of a typewritten letter to the mayor.

> *To: The Mayor, City of Reykjavik*
> *Reykjavik, November 10, 1971*

> *Sir,*

> *With reference to our conversation in your office on last Tuesday, I am very keen for the City of Reykjavik to acquire the property Birkihlíd complete with all its contents. The objective would be to establish a museum of the life of a family of Reykjavik townsfolk during the first half of the century. I should like to invite you to send your repre-*

sentative to meet me and examine the house and to discuss the implementation of this arrangement.

Respectfully yours, Jacob Kieler Jr.

There followed another letter to the mayor:

Reykjavik, March 12, 1972

Sir,

Thank you for sending your representative from the city curator's office to meet me and examine the property Birkihlíd and its contents, and to evaluate its conservation status. As he is able to testify, the house is already in a state fit for showing.

I appreciate fully that it is not easy to finance such an investment, but we owners will most certainly be agreeable in any negotiations. I am working toward an understanding that we offer you the house without payment of consideration, in return for the city assuming any unpaid current debts.

I am, subsequently, prepared to work in the museum as consultant in return for a small fee.

The present owners' conditions for handing over the house would be as follows:
1. The City of Reykjavik will establish a museum to commemorate engineer Jacob Kieler, and operate it for a minimum of 99 years.

2. *The museum shall be named "Engineer Jacob Kieler Museum."*
3. *The museum shall be open to the public for a minimum of four hours each day.*
4. *Entrance fees shall be accumulated to finance the writing and publishing of a biography of engineer Jacob Kieler.*

I hope that this matter will be dealt with swiftly and satisfactorily by the city administration.

Respectfully yours, Jacob Kieler Jr.

And another one, over seven months later:

Reykjavik October 25, 1972

Sir,

I regret to say that I am not able to keep to my undertaking that the present owners of the Birkihlíd property will transfer to the City of Reykjavik the house and its contents without payment of consideration. I had overestimated my relatives' readiness to preserve the memory of my parents. I am, however, requesting that the City of Reykjavik purchase the house with the objective of establishing a museum as discussed in my previous letters and in discussions with yourself and your officials. I feel certain that agreement as to an acceptable price can be reached.

Respectfully yours, Jacob Kieler Jr.

Behind these copies was a letter bearing the blue letterhead of the mayor of Reykjavik himself:

Reykjavik, January 8, 1973

Dear Jacob Kieler,

Your proposition as regards the property Birkihlíd and its future has now been discussed by Reykjavik city council and the city curator's office. The conclusion reached was that there are no grounds for the City of Reykjavik either to establish a museum to commemorate engineer Jacob Kieler, nor to undertake any commitment as regards its operation.

In spite of coming to this conclusion, we wish you well in your attempts to establish the museum. Should your plans not materialize, the Árbæjarsafn Museum would be happy to accept articles from the estate for conservation.

Respectfully yours, Mayor of Reykjavik (signed)

Hrefna continued to leaf through the papers, coming across two deeds of conveyance dated December 3, 1972, referring to Jacob Junior's purchase of Matthías's half share of Birkihlíd, and his purchase of Kirsten's quarter share of the property and her half share of the contents.

Hrefna pondered over what she had found. While Jacob Junior was busy buying his relatives' shares in the house and its contents, he had still been trying to interest the city in the purchase of the house as a museum. The conveyances seemed to have been an attempt to gain time, but then the mayor's letter had shattered his hopes. And according to the accounts, Jacob Junior lacked the means to meet the financial obligations that the conveyances imposed on him, let alone pay any of his other debts. He was clearly bankrupt. These last days of his life must have been difficult. His dream of a museum in Birkihlíd had come to nothing and he himself was insolvent.

Further on in the binder Hrefna found a magazine clipping with the headline "Icelanders Offer Kingship to German Citizen."

Evidence has been uncovered to substantiate the rumor that in 1938 certain worthy Icelanders invited a German nobleman, Rudiger von Kuppel, to become King of Iceland. The authorities here, however, have wanted to suppress the affair, officially claiming no knowledge of it. Von Kuppel came here himself in 1967, having previously written to announce his arrival, but was received as if he was not entirely sane, and departed a hurt and disappointed man. On arriving home he wrote a paper about his experience, which ended up in an archive in Cologne, along with other papers belonging to the von Kuppel family, when he died last year.

The paper revealed that in the summer of 1938 a number of Icelandic patriots had arrived

*in Berlin looking for a suitable candidate to be
king of a new, independent monarchy. The king
had to be in the prime of life, have a son, and
be of a former ruling family. Von Kuppel was,
of course, extremely surprised when he was
approached, but having given the matter some
consideration was able to confirm to the Icelandic delegation that he would accept their offer.
These plans, however, came to naught, thanks
to developments in Germany with which we are
all familiar.*

*Von Kuppel says in his paper that the Icelan-
dic delegation numbered five, but that he could
name only two of them. It is probable that they
only introduced themselves orally when they met,
and that von Kuppel was not able to memorize
the Icelandic names. There were, however, two
people in the group whose names von Kuppel
found it easy to remember as they were of German origin. They were the brothers Jacob and
Matthías Kieler.*

*During this period engineer Jacob Kieler was
making his final attempts to turn his railroad
company into reality, seeking help in Germany
for this purpose. One may suppose, therefore, that
turning Iceland into a monarchy was but a small
matter for him in his quest to gain backing for the
railroad business. The most likely explanation, in
fact, is that he became a guide to the royalists on
their trip to Berlin because he knew the city well,
having studied there, and then used the opportu-*

nity to gain support for his business at the same time. Matthías Kieler actually lived in Berlin during these years, and was thus very likely to have been of assistance to the delegation.

The present writer has experienced some difficulty in finding further information on this story. Engineer Jacob Kieler was shot and killed in 1945, while Matthías, who now resides in Austria, has not responded to written enquiries on the matter. It is tempting to speculate that Jacob Kieler's fate was somehow linked to the royalist mission, and it is a known fact that Matthías Kieler experienced a crisis in Germany during the war that has not been explained. It must have been difficult for the engineer to carry this secret with him when he became chief contracting agent to the British and, later, the American occupying force, here in Iceland during the war. The fact that their royal candidate was a professed Nazi with personal connections to the leaders of the Third Reich would have caused Jacob Kieler considerable concern.

The article bore the signature of Yngvi Jónsson, historian. The document right behind it in the ring binder was a handwritten draft of a summons issued against Yngvi Jónsson for libel. Hrefna removed these papers from the binder and tucked them into her bag. She put everything else back in its place and went downstairs, where she found Jóhann in the engineering office, buried deep in old papers.

"Have you discovered anything?" she asked.

"No," he replied, shamefaced. "I'm mainly just nosing around. Jacob Senior seems to have been incredibly interested in railways."

"Yes, that's what his diaries show," Hrefna said, looking around the room. "So this is where he worked."

"Yes, it's as if he walked out of here yesterday."

Hrefna perused the filing cabinets, opening them and examining the contents.

"He must have been very orderly," she said. "I wish I was like this."

She turned to a long, wooden box standing by the outside wall.

"Have you looked into this box?" she asked.

"No, I hadn't got that far."

Hrefna opened it and found two tripods and a steel measuring tape. A compartment in the lid of the box contained a booklet in Danish, with the title *Jäderin's Basisapparat.*

"What's all this for?" she asked.

Jóhann took the booklet and leafed through it. "It's equipment for measuring distances," he said.

"Surely the measuring tape can do that on its own?"

"No. To get an accurate reading, the tape needs to be pulled taut with the correct force. You place the tripods over the points whose distance you want to find, stretch the tape across the tripods, and hang a heavy weight from it to create the correct tension. Then you apply the angle of slope of the tape to the distance measured to get the correct result."

"Well, well. Very interesting," Hrefna replied, about to close the box.

"Just a minute," Jóhann said. "It looks as if everything's in the box apart from the weight. Here's a compartment where it obviously should be, but it's not there. It's unlike the Kieler menfolk not to have everything in place."

"Put it in your report, then," Hrefna suggested skeptically.

Diary V

January 3, 1919. Sent a telegram to Miss Annie Barker that I have arrived in England. I presume that she will arrange for me to meet Elizabeth...

January 4, 1919. Received an invitation at the hotel to come for supper to Mr. and Mrs. Barker's home tomorrow evening...

January 5, 1919. I arrived at the Barkers' home a short while before Elizabeth. When she came in and saw me, we stood and gazed at one another, not able to utter a word. Finally we shook hands. She was pale but very beautiful. She has matured and now looks like a rose that has just come into bloom. Elizabeth is complimentary about my knowledge of English; she says I speak just like an American...This time I shall not hesitate. Tomorrow I am going to ask for Elizabeth's hand in marriage. I am not going to make the same mistake twice in my life...

January 6, 1919. I dressed in my best clothes and took a carriage to the home of the Chatfield family.

I asked to see Elizabeth and immediately put the question to her whether she would permit me to ask her father for her hand in marriage. She said yes. Mr. Chatfield has agreed to see me tomorrow...

January 7, 1919. I met Mr. Chatfield at his club. He made me tell him my life's history and describe my family. Then he asked me about my future plans. I told him that it had always been my determination to go to Iceland and build railroads there. I showed him my letters of recommendation...

January 8, 1919. I was summoned to the Chatfield residence very early this morning. Mr. and Mrs. Chatfield were having breakfast. Mr. Chatfield said that he and his wife were prepared to agree to our marriage if my affairs proved to be in order. The engagement is to last for six months. Then I was allowed to see Elizabeth...

CHAPTER 29

After lunch Halldór went to see Andrés, the retired DC. The old man was astonished to learn that there had been a repeat of the Birkihlíd incident, and, what was more, with the same weapon. He tapped out some snuff from his snuffbox, but then paced up and down the parlor floor with it untouched on the back of his hand.

"Well I never, you don't say, well I never," he kept repeating. Finally he sat down, sniffed the tobacco up one nostril, and began to look through the papers Halldór had brought along.

"Of course I remember this case very well," he said. "We never managed to solve it, as you know, but it was fully investigated. There was even an agent from an English insurance company who came over to check the evidence."

"Really?"

"Yes, apparently the engineer was insured for a large sum of money, and they wanted to be certain he hadn't shot himself."

"Was that ever a possibility?"

"No, the gun would have been found nearby, of course. The English investigator made the caretaker swear he hadn't removed the weapon from the house after finding Jacob dead."

"Did you know engineer Jacob while he was alive?" Halldór asked.

"I knew him quite well. He helped us a lot with things involving the military."

"What do you think really happened there?"

"I don't know. There were all sorts of speculations; some thought it was a communist conspiracy, and then there were those who claimed the Allies had murdered him because he had been spying for the Germans."

"Really?"

"Yes, apparently he had studied in Germany and also been there just before the war. He seems to have been trying to interest them in going into business with him."

"Do you think he could possibly have been a spy?"

"No, not the man I knew."

"Could it have been a felony murder, then?"

"Yes, maybe. I always believed that the killer was just some drifter who got hold of this gun and had it with him when he broke into Birkihlíd. He must have thought the house was unoccupied."

"What about the guy who was arrested, this Sigurdur?"

"That was just nonsense. He definitely had nothing to do with it. It's just that he was so bloody stubborn, he wouldn't talk. But there were those within the police force who believed he was guilty."

"Do you know what happened to him?"

"Yes. He was killed in a work accident at the harbor. I went there and did the report."

"When was this?"

"Probably 1950."

"What happened?"

"They were unloading a freighter when a sling broke. There were two of them in the hold who had a whole stack of timber collapse over them. The other guy got a broken leg, but there was nothing that could be done to help Sigurdur. It was one of the ugliest accidents I've ever seen."

"He had a large family, didn't he?"

"Yes, he left five kids and a pregnant wife. I got the parish pastor to go with me to tell her of the accident."

"What became of the family?"

"They stayed where they were, a squalid place in the west end of town. I seem to remember us having some dealings with the older boys, but nothing serious. The address is probably still the same as the one in my report."

"Do you know of anyone who knew Jacob Senior who might be able to help us now?"

"The assistant engineer, Thórdur, is the most likely; I think he took over the running of the business, and has done well for himself. The caretaker who found Jacob's body passed away many years ago."

"Anything else you can think of about the case?"

"No, but I'll try and run back over it. Actually, there was a guy here the other day asking questions about it. Called himself a historian, but he was nothing but a hippie. I pretended not to remember anything, just made fun of him," Andrés laughed.

"Can you remember his name?"

"Yngvi, I think it was," Andrés replied. Halldór wrote the name down.

"Did he tell you why he wanted to know about this?"

"No, and I didn't ask. It was none of his business."

Halldór riffled through the old reports and photographs. "You didn't have much to go on in this case," he said.

"No, it was terribly inadequate. A broken windowpane and a dead man, that was all."

"At least you had the bullet."

"Yes, it was sent abroad for examination, but we never found a gun for comparison."

"Weren't there some Smith and Wessons around?"

"Well, we suspected so. Some of the British officers carried guns like that, and they lost a few, but it was impossible to lay hands on suitable ammunition after the British army left."

"So you never found a gun like it at all?"

"Yes, a couple, but they had no ammunition, proving they were not involved. One was broken, and the other belonged to a member of parliament who shall remain nameless." Andrés helped himself to some more snuff. "I really hope it can be sorted now," he added. "This case has often kept me awake at night."

Diary V

January 9, 1919. Wrote to my parents with the news of my engagement. They will probably be very surprised, as they still don't know that I am now in England...

January 12, 1919. I rented a room in a decent house on Halford Street. It is within easy walking distance of the Chatfield family home...

January 15, 1919. With the help of Mr. Chatfield, I am now employed by Mr. James Leslie's engineering firm here in the city. Mr. Leslie specializes in civil engineering, so I shall not be involved in railway engineering in the immediate future. This will, however, be good experience, since it is by no means certain that I shall always be able to find work building railroads in Iceland, and it will then be good to be able to work on other projects...

January 17, 1919. Elizabeth and I take long walks round the city, when the weather allows. This morning she showed me Jewry Wall, which was built by the Romans. We have also looked at St. Martin's Cathedral, where we are planning to get married this coming summer...

March 5, 1919. Had a long talk with Mr. Chatfield about my and Elizabeth's financial arrangements. He will provide a dowry in the form of a trust fund that will be available to us subject to specific conditions. In return he wants me to take out a life insurance policy for myself...

March 6, 1919. Mr. Leslie has been instructing me on how to design drainage systems. He is a clever engineer and a good teacher, but what a tedious subject this is...

March 23, 1919. Went to meet the agent at the life insurance company. He said that the medical had gone well, and that I have a clean bill of health. He read to me the whole of the life insurance policy document, and gravely reminded me that the policy would be invalid if I were to take my own life. I promised to remember this. There is a lot of money at stake...

April 4, 1919. Had a letter from my parents. They will be attending the wedding this summer...

CHAPTER 30

It was nearing six o'clock when the investigative team convened at the Borgartún headquarters.

"This country would be in far better shape if we had a king. Then there'd be someone to look up to," Egill said, in regards to the magazine article Hrefna had found about the German royal candidate and was passing around.

Nobody else seemed to agree with his comment, and Halldór moved on to the more pressing point. "We must check Matthías's reaction to these allegations; they might be relevant to the case." Then he peered beseechingly at Hrefna and asked, "Would you be prepared to go and talk to him right away?"

Hrefna agreed, despite the late hour. She was keen to get to know Matthías Kieler firsthand anyway.

"We also need to speak to this historian tomorrow," he continued. "He has shown a lot of interest in all this." Hrefna understood that she was to take this on as well.

Jóhann had found the teenage girl who delivered *Morgunbladid* to Birkihlíd; she had not noticed anything unusual when she delivered the paper there on Thursday morning. Her winter boots had fit perfectly into the plastic cast Jóhann had made of the footprints in the snow.

Egill and Marteinn had not yet found the left-handed guitar-ist, but they planned on continuing the search that evening.

Diary V

*June 15, 1919. Today is our wedding day. The
ceremony at St. Martin's was very well conducted.
Afterwards our photograph was taken before
the church doors. There was a large reception at
the Chatfield family home...My father made an
admirable best man, and my mother had tears in her
eyes. Elizabeth and I are on our way to London for
our honeymoon...*

*July 1, 1919. Elizabeth and I moved into a small
apartment on Elmfield Avenue. We shall be living
here for the coming year, but have decided to move
to Iceland next summer...*

*July 23, 1919. Mr. Chatfield wants to lend Elizabeth
and me his new automobile in order for us to travel
during our summer holiday...*

*August 2, 1919. Drove through Dorset in the late
afternoon and arrived at the hotel at five o'clock. We
rested until supper time...*

August 4, 1919. This morning Elizabeth and I climbed Bulbarrow Hill. The view from there is wonderful. There are countless variations of green as far as the eye can see, small meadows broken up between windbreaks...

CHAPTER 31

Hrefna took a taxi to Matthías Kieler's home that evening, wondering on the way what she should say to him. There was just no casual way to broach the subject. *So, do you feel we should have a king?* Then again, maybe it looked different to the generation that took part in the establishment of the republic. It was possible that people had been of two minds then; she had never thought about it before.

Hrefna found Matthías's apartment on the second floor of a tidy house in Thingholt. She knocked gently on the front door, which was promptly opened by a short, slightly plump man in his sixties, dressed in a dark gray vest and trousers, with a crisply ironed white shirt and a black bow tie. He wore a short, green apron.

"Yes?" he said quietly.

"Matthías Kieler lives here, doesn't he?" Hrefna asked.

"Yes, he lives here."

"My name is Hrefna; I'm from the police. I need to trouble him with a few questions regarding his nephew Jacob's death."

"Please, come in."

Hrefna studied the man as she passed him. So this was the manservant Klemenz. He had large, slightly protruding, dark brown eyes, round cheeks, and a handsome mouth. Prodigious crow's-feet around his eyes gave his face an amused expression, and his hair was jet-black and combed straight back, held firmly in place by some sort of hair product. Hrefna detected a faint but agreeable scent on him, and he smiled kindly when she looked him in the eye. A cute old guy, she decided.

The sound of a string instrument came wafting through the apartment. "Mr. Kieler is practicing," Klemenz explained. "Perhaps you would care to take a seat and wait while he finishes the piece?"

"Yes, please," she said.

The manservant showed her into the room where Matthías sat by the window, playing the cello. Hrefna sat down, and Klemenz disappeared into the next room. She withdrew the magazine article about the business with the king from her bag, intending to read it again while she waited, but she couldn't concentrate, and just listened to the music instead. It was a lovely piece, beautifully played. Matthías guided the bow expertly across the strings, his eyes closed in deep concentration; he showed no awareness of her presence. Hrefna leaned back in the chair, realizing how tired she was.

She had never heard this piece before, nor had she ever heard a solo cello. She had actually never been particularly interested in classical music, but this piece took hold of her. She nearly forgot the purpose of her visit, allowing the music to wash over her. She felt more relaxed than she had in a long time.

The atmosphere in the room was extremely pleasant. It was airy and clean. Candles had been lit, and the light was just right.

As the final note died away, Hrefna wanted to applaud but sensed that it was not appropriate given the circumstances.

Klemenz reentered and waited for Matthías to look up.

"There is a young woman here from the detective division who would like to speak with you, sir," he said.

Matthías gave Hrefna a friendly smile.

"That was 'Berceuse de Jocelyn,' by Godard. Perhaps you are familiar with it?" he said.

"No, I've never heard it before. It's very beautiful."

"Yes, you think so? That pleases me. I myself made this arrangement for solo cello—it is quite a bit longer than the original. I want to play it at my nephew's funeral."

"He is the reason I am here."

"I suspected as much."

"Have you seen this, sir?" Hrefna asked, handing Matthías the newspaper clip; he held it at a slight distance as he read a few lines. Farsighted, Hrefna thought.

"Yes, I have seen this," he said, handing the paper back to her.

"Are these claims true?" Hrefna asked.

"No, they are not. This piece is pure fantasy from beginning to end."

"Do you know the author?"

"By reputation. This self-styled 'historian' has been relentless over a period of many years as far as my family is concerned. All respectable academics regard this charlatan as a disgrace."

"What about the paper the royal candidate wrote? Does it exist in Germany?"

"Yes, I understand that it actually does, but this man was a mentally confused eccentric, subject to ridicule by everybody. He must have found the names of me and my brother in some documents dating back from when my brother had some business dealings in Berlin, and then incorporated them in these fantasies of his. He says somewhere else in his paper that the Third Reich's propaganda minister had offered to accompany him to Iceland

and enter his service here. None of it made an ounce of sense, and it is unfathomable that the poor man's relations didn't destroy those documents after he died."

"What was this business your brother was engaged in?"

"He was raising finance for his railroad company. He was all set to commence construction of a railroad in Iceland but lacked funds, and we went to see certain wealthy industrialists in Berlin who were prepared to invest in the enterprise."

"What sort of reception did the two of you get?"

"Extremely satisfactory, as my brother Jacob had done the most thorough homework for his mission. I was only there to assist him in a secretarial capacity. But all these plans came to nothing, of course, when the war started."

"This draft of a summons that was with the article, was it ever submitted in court?"

"No, my nephew and I decided to leave it. Jacob Junior was, however, keen to write a response to the piece for the magazine. He was a scrupulous historian himself and was respected for his research."

"Was that response ever published?"

"No, I think not. I once saw a draft he had written. It was measured and professional, and would have eliminated these speculations immediately, but I think he felt that the matter would die a natural death anyway."

"Have you any idea what this man's motive was for writing the article?"

"Envy, perhaps. I have come across such things in the past. My father was very wealthy by Icelandic standards, so my family was rather in the limelight. There were all sorts of stories going around about us, then as now. Most are fabrications, and the rest half-truths. It has actually not affected me much, as I have lived abroad. There is a Chinese saying that you can measure the height of a tower from the shadow it casts, and the value of great men from the slander they encounter." Matthías smiled.

Klemenz entered the parlor. "Excuse me, sir, your supper is ready. Perhaps you would care to invite your visitor to join you?"

"Yes, that's a good idea," Matthías replied and turned to Hrefna. "May I offer you supper, my dear?"

Hrefna was of two minds about the offer; her business here was not finished, yet she was actually quite hungry. Her stomach won out in the end. "Yes, please," she replied.

"Excellent," Matthías said and turned to Klemenz. "What is on offer this evening?"

"The first course is quiche lorraine and the main course is filet mignon chateaubriand."

"How does that sound?" Matthías turned to Hrefna.

"That sounds good."

"Do you know the story of Chateaubriand?"

"No."

"He was a nineteenth-century French writer and politician. It was, in fact, his chef, Montmireil, who first cut filet mignon in this manner, but the honor was attributed to his master."

"How fascinating."

Matthías turned to Klemenz. "We shall have white wine with the first course, a Sauternes Bordeaux." He looked back at Hrefna. "It is slightly sweet. Are you familiar with it?"

"No," she replied, and was about to add that since she was working, she would just have water, but sensed it would be in bad taste. A little wouldn't hurt, she decided.

"We shall stick with the Bordeaux region and have a Margaux red wine with the main course," he told Klemenz.

"Excellent, sir. Would it suit you to take a seat right away?"

"Yes, please."

Matthías went over to the record player and took an LP record from a shelf.

"I should like to listen to the Elgar Cello Concerto while we dine. Jacqueline du Pré is the soloist with the London Symphony Orchestra, conducted by Sir John Barbirolli."

He took the vinyl disk gently from its sleeve and blew some grains of dust from it before placing it on the turntable. Setting the music to play at low volume, he led Hrefna into the dining room next to the parlor. The table had been set for two, one at each end.

"This is not the sort of tableware I would have chosen, but it comes with the apartment," Matthías said apologetically, as he invited Hrefna to take a seat.

Hrefna didn't see anything wrong with the setting in front of her. Klemenz brought in a silver bucket with an open wine bottle on ice, and put it in the center of the table. He took the bottle and wiped it before half-filling Hrefna's glass, and then did the same for Matthías, before returning the bottle to the bucket and disappearing into the kitchen.

Matthías took his glass and carefully examined the wine.

"You may rest assured that the wine is satisfactory. Klemenz tastes it himself before serving it. He has a better palate than I myself do. Prosit!" He raised his glass.

"Cheers," Hrefna said, raising her glass and sipping the wine. She was not very familiar with white wine, apart from the cheapest sort in the state wine store, but this tasted very good.

Klemenz returned, bearing two plates on his left arm, and placed a quiche in front of Hrefna.

"This is my favorite dish," Matthías said. "Klemenz makes a particularly fine quiche."

They ate in silence. The music wafted in from the parlor and it somehow seemed inappropriate to talk over it. Although Hrefna had a glass of water next to her wine, she had emptied the wine glass before she realized it, and Klemenz had poured her some more.

"May I offer you some more quiche?" he asked when she had emptied her plate.

"No, thank you, but it was very good."

"Thank you. The main course will be ready shortly."

He brought larger wine glasses, placing them next to the ones that were already there, and filled them with red wine from a carafe before disappearing again.

"Cheers once more," Matthías said, raising his glass.

"Here's to the chef," Hrefna replied.

"Yes, to the chef. He will now be frying the filet mignon, which he only does when he is ready to serve. If I know him correctly, he will have spent all last week harassing the city's butchers to find the right ingredients for this course."

"You are lucky to have such service."

"Yes, Klemenz has been singularly faithful to me. He could be a head chef in any restaurant anywhere, but he prefers to cook just for me as he knows that I appreciate fine things. That means he can spend days on end preparing just a single meal."

Matthías got up, and returned to the parlor, then reemerged a moment later at the table.

"Now you will hear a cello concerto by Haydn. The soloist is still du Pré," he said, after he had taken his seat again.

The filet steak that Klemenz served her could have been eaten with a spoon, it was so tender. She'd never tasted meat like this before. The only beef she had ever come across was the extremely chewy cut used in Icelandic goulash.

The accompaniment and the sauce were also quite different from what she was used to; this was a true gourmet meal.

Klemenz topped up the red-wine glasses and asked whether he could offer them a second helping of the main course. Matthías declined, and Hrefna followed his lead; she would, actually, have been able to eat far more of this delicacy, but sensed it would not be polite. And besides, she was not exactly hungry anymore.

After the meal Klemenz served them coffee in the parlor.

"I was examining Jacob Junior's accounts today," Hrefna began. "It seemed to me that he was up to his neck in debt."

"Is that so? Well, it does not surprise me."

"Do you know where he got these loans from? You can't see it in his papers."

"No, but the lender will surely reveal himself when the estate is settled. I assume that Jacob Junior's purchase of the house will be canceled now that he has passed away, so the settlement needs to be hastened."

"What will happen to the house?"

"It will be sold, as originally intended."

"The history of the Kieler family in Birkihlíd will finally come to an end," she remarked, thoughtfully.

"Yes," Matthías replied, a brief smile crossing his lips. "One chapter in the history of this house has come to an end, but it will remain and acquire a new role; and the history of the Kieler family has also come to an end, in the sense that the name will die out here in Iceland. But all this is nothing but vanity."

"What will you do?"

"I shall go back home to Austria and hope to end my days peacefully there. I have accumulated a reasonable retirement fund, and my share from the proceeds of the house will augment that. I am assuming that Klemenz will continue to work for me, so I am not worried."

Hrefna could think of no more questions for her host, so she began to gather her things.

"I am going to play through my 'Berceuse' arrangement again," he commented. "You may listen if you would like to."

"Yes, I would like that," Hrefna said gratefully. She knew she would remember this evening for years to come.

Diary VI

May 3, 1920. The Gullfoss *set sail from Leith harbor this morning. We settled ourselves into an excellent two-berth cabin on the starboard side. This ship is very similar to the* Godafoss, *in which I sailed to Leith a few years ago. You could say that I am now completing a journey begun then. Both my wife and I are a little bit anxious. I have lived abroad for nearly ten years and Elizabeth feels she is heading for the great unknown...*

May 4, 1920. The ship makes around 12 knots, and the captain estimates that we shall be docking in Reykjavik on the morning of May 8. The weather is reasonable and I am enjoying spending time with the other passengers. Elizabeth is a little bit seasick...

May 5, 1920. Elizabeth is feeling better and was able to eat. We piled on some warm clothes and are sitting on the upper deck, where there are nice wooden benches. I am teaching Elizabeth Icelandic. She is now able to say hello and good-bye properly...

May 7, 1920. Got up at 10 o'clock a.m. The Westman Islands are rising over the horizon. The glaciers are not very visible, as their tops are draped in fog...

May 8, 1920. Homecoming. My father and Matthías met us on the pier. Little Matthías has turned into a handsome young man. My father has aged. Everything seems so small to me, in spite of all the construction projects that have taken place since I left the country. My father had borrowed an automobile to take us and all our luggage home to Birkihlíd. It annoys me how people here keep staring at Elizabeth and me. They have no manners...

CHAPTER 32

Halldór was reading an article in *Morgunbladid* about police reinforcement when the phone rang. It was only seven thirty, and it was rare for anyone to call at such an early hour. Halldór looked at Stefanía. "Are you going to answer, dear?"

"It's bound to be for you. Nobody I know would ring so early in the morning, and on a Saturday at that. It's not polite," Stefanía grumbled, going over to the phone.

"Hello," she said sharply into the receiver. Halldór noticed the scowl quickly disappear from her face.

"Oh no, no need to apologize. Of course we are up," she said cheerily.

"Yes, yes, he is here. Hold on a moment, please." She covered the mouthpiece and whispered to her husband, "It's Jón Björnsson, the bank manager. He wants to talk to you."

Jón Björnsson was a former government minister and now a bank manager—a résumé his wife would appreciate, Halldór thought to himself.

"Come on then. Don't keep him waiting," she said as he put the paper aside.

"Please excuse the intrusion," the bank manager said when Halldór answered. "I was told that you were in charge of the investigation into the death of Jacob Kieler, one of our staff members."

"Yes?"

"Well, some rather unpleasant things have come to light here at the bank. Our accountants have been going over this all night."

"Oh?"

"It seems that Jacob has been embezzling a considerable sum of money from the bank."

"How so?"

"By using a series of checking accounts. He has taken advantage of the fact that withdrawals take up to twenty-four hours longer to process than deposits. This should of course have come out when we did spot-checks, but he has been able to use his position in the bank to conceal it."

"Is it a large sum of money?"

"We haven't got the final figure yet, but he seems to have accumulated several million krónur."

"I am astonished," Halldór gasped.

"Yes, but that is not the whole story."

"Oh?"

"The late Mr. Kieler was treasurer of a society that a few worthy gentlemen here in the city belong to—Gethsemane, a Christian brotherhood. Do you know it?"

"Yes, I have heard of it."

"When the brotherhood's board checked their accounts here at the bank yesterday, they discovered they were mostly empty."

"Good grief! Was it a large sum of money?"

"Yes, quite a bit. The brotherhood has been liquidizing its assets recently, sold an apartment and other things, because they are about to extend their clubhouse. They'll need to examine their accounts further to get the final figure."

"Has this been going on for long?"

"He seems to have used money from the brotherhood to disguise the checking fraud when he needed to, but then all the money disappeared from the accounts over a period of a few weeks."

"I see," Halldór said. He now understood where Jacob had gotten the money to pay the deposit on Birkihlíd when the contracts were exchanged.

"Can you come to a meeting with us later this morning? Say around ten?" the bank manager asked, adding, "And we would appreciate for this to be kept confidential."

Halldór agreed to come to the bank, and then hung up the phone.

"What did the minister want?" Stefanía asked.

"He is no longer a minister, only a bank manager."

"Yes, but what did he want?"

"Nothing special. Just a police matter."

Stefanía shrugged a little disappointedly and turned back to her tea and magazine. Much to his relief, it looked as though she had accepted this explanation. He sat back down again at the kitchen table and picked up the paper, thinking how good it would be to have Erlendur here to help with the bankers instead of on his way to Austria. Erlendur was a business-school graduate and nearly the only one in the investigation team who knew the difference between a debit and a credit.

Diary VI

May 9, 1920. It is strange to have finally come home. Everything seems so unfamiliar and at the same time so familiar. I know the smell and the cold breeze that

*kisses me. This spring has not been good, I am told.
There is still a layer of ice on the lake...*

*May 10, 1920. I went to see the Government Chief
Engineer. He thanked me for the letter I sent him
last fall. He showed me the papers they have on the
railway: measurements, calculations, etc. There will
definitely be projects for me soon, when the finances
are there...*

*May 11, 1920. I find myself turning round when I
hear people speak Icelandic out on the streets. It is
such a long time since I have been among people
who speak the language. The best thing is hearing the
children talking...*

*May 12, 1920. There is a report in Ísafold about my
return home. It details my studies and employment
abroad, and my marriage. The editor opines that it is
very fortunate for the country that I have chosen to
return home to work here...*

*June 3, 1920. I have decided to pen various articles in
the papers, particularly on employment and education
issues and, of course, the railroad question...*

*June 22, 1920. I went to see the Government
Chief Engineer again. He gave me some surveying*

*assignments in connection with the proposed
railroad track as per our conversation at our meeting
this spring. I calibrated my optical square and
leveling instrument in the evening. Matthías helped
me...*

*June 23, 1920. I called Kristján to meet with me.
We agreed he would assist me on the surveying trip
and provide horses. I shall supply a tent and food...
My wife and I went for a midnight walk to take
advantage of the light. Elizabeth is fascinated by
these light nights. I hope the dark nights of winter
will not discomfort her...*

*June 24, 1920. Reasonable weather. We set off
east at eleven o'clock with seven horses. Matthías
is coming too...We took the South Road through
Svínahraun lava field, but where it turns east
toward the Hveradalir valleys, there is a faint track
forking off to the south west. It leads to the pass
between Stakihnjúkur and Lambafell mountains,
and goes by the name of Threngsli. I measured the
gradient, and conclude that the highest point is no
more than 252 meters above sea level, similar to
that of Kolvidarhóll. This seems the ideal route for
the railroad. After the pass, the track turns directly
south and goes through passable moorland beneath*

the western side of the Meitill Mountains, while
there is continuous lava field on the other side of the
road. We set up camp on the south side of the hollow
between Greater and Lesser Meitill. From here there
is a wonderful view toward the Bláfjöll Mountains,
standing picturesque and majestic against the
western sky...

CHAPTER 33

Egill was up early. The day before he had dragged Marteinn around town looking for a young man who didn't seem to exist, even though they both felt sure they had spoken to him in the lobby of the house the previous evening.

They had a name, and had even found an ID number in the books of the sound studio where the young man had been working when he supplied the police with his fingerprints.

They had the address in the Old Town that the employer had provided on the fingerprint card, where they found and then lost the guy once already. They also had an official home address the Public Records Office had registered against the ID number, Brekkustígur 25, but that house, they discovered, didn't exist anymore.

They had trudged between sound studios, record shops, musical-instrument shops, clubs, cafés, music colleges, and a number of other haunts where they imagined they might find people who knew a left-handed guitarist with dark shoulder-length hair named Sigurdur Sigurdsson. Egill had relied on Marteinn to do most of the talking, while he just stood by with a look on his face meant to show these hippies that they meant business. It didn't seem to matter. Nobody knew anything about the guy.

Halldór had not yet arrived at the office, and Egill was not looking forward to reporting the details of their fruitless search, even though they had kept at it well into the night. While he waited, he decided to see if the others had had better luck.

All the information that the team had gathered on the case so far was kept in three-ring binders in a fixed place, so that everyone could keep up-to-date on the progress of the investigation.

Egill paged to the report Halldór had written after his interviews with Matthías, then he scanned the reports Hrefna had written after her interviews with Sveinborg and her search through Jacob Junior's papers, and finally he read the report Erlendur had written after his interview with Reverend Ingimar.

The data on the investigation into Jacob Senior's death caught his attention. The search warrant that had been issued for the home of Sigurdur Jónsson way back in 1945 listed the same address as that of Sigurdur Sigurdsson's registered address, Brekkustígur 25. And Halldór's notes showed that Sigurdur Jónsson's widow had lived in the house following her husband's death.

Sigurdur Jónsson and Sigurdur Sigurdsson. They could be related—the younger Sigurdur's patronymic showed he was the son of a Sigurdur, and according to the Records Office, his birth date was August 8, 1950, the same year that Sigurdur Jónsson died. Could it be that Sigurdur Sigurdsson the guitarist was the son of Sigurdur Jónsson the laborer? Born after his father's death and named for him?

If so, it was certainly more than coincidence that Sigurdur Senior was arrested for the murder of Jacob Senior and then Sigurdur Junior's fingerprints were found in the place where Jacob Junior was murdered twenty-seven years later.

Egill was convinced he was on to something. He decided to check the history of the disappearing house and its inhabitants.

This was proper police work, he thought, and if all went according to plan, the next hippie he spoke to would be in handcuffs.

The abandoned lot where Brekkustígur 25 had once stood was as far west as you could get and still be in Reykjavik. Egill walked around the site, outlining the former rooms as he paced; it had been no mansion, that's for sure. He heard scraping sounds, and saw an elderly man chipping ice off the front steps of an old house nearby. Egill went over and greeted him.

"Morning," the man replied.

"Have you lived here long?" Egill asked.

"I moved here in '49."

"Do you remember a man who lived next door and who died in an accident at the harbor? In 1950? Name of Sigurdur."

"Yes, I remember him. We called him Siggi Pistol."

"Oh, why was that?"

"They said he killed a man."

"Do you know what happened to his family, the wife and the kids?"

"Why are you asking?" he asked suspiciously.

"I'm from the detective division," Egill explained, pulling his ID out of his leather wallet and showing it to the old man. "We're investigating a case they are connected with."

"I see. Are the boys in trouble again?"

"Could be."

"Well. They were good lads, but it must have been hard being brought up so poor."

"Do you know where they are living now?"

"No. Kristín, the widow, she became an invalid, and I think she's in one of those institutions now. As far as I remember, the kids moved out of Reykjavik and the boys went to sea. Except perhaps the youngest one."

"What is his name?"

"Sigurdur, what else? He wasn't born until after the accident, and was named for his father. Nicknamed Diddi."

"Do you know anything about him?'

"He's some sort of musician. I think he may have been in a band."

"What happened to this house?"

"The authorities had it demolished. It had become so run-down and rat infested; it leaked and stank of mildew. It just wasn't fit to live in."

Diary VI

July 22, 1920. I bought a bicycle for 140 krónur. Read Black Feathers *by Davíd Stefánsson. One of the poems is called "By Train." It's a long narrative poem in eleven verses. The poet describes a journey by railroad that is, at the same time, life itself. The train speeds along non-stop, and the engineer is "that kingly soul, than whom none higher, who stokes the all-empow'ring fire."*

August 3, 1920. Plotted the Threngsli gradient survey onto graph paper. Weighed myself, I am 73 kilos...

September 20, 1920. Sheep-farmers here have now brought their flocks down from the summer pastures. They do not, however, bother to keep them penned,

*and the animals target the townsfolk's gardens with
great enthusiasm. I got up twice last night and
chased them out of our garden...*

*November 1, 1920. Met with the minister this
morning. He is very pleased with the work I did in the
summer, and feels certain I shall be appointed Chief of
Railroads as soon as the office is established...*

*November 17, 1920. Attended a meeting at the
Association of Chartered Engineers on the subject
of waterfalls. There were some excellent, forward-
looking speeches on harnessing their power. I
stood up during the debate to say that I personally
was of the opinion that the first public power
company and the railroad business should progress
simultaneously. There is no need to elaborate on
the necessity of building railroads in this country;
everybody realizes this and it has practically become
a vital necessity for Reykjavik and the lowlands in
the south...*

*November 18, 1920. Elizabeth and I went to a show
given by the Students' Union. There were readings
with dancing afterwards. At the end, we all sang the
national anthem and "Mothers of our Homeland."*

It was a most successful entertainment. Elizabeth can now understand a good deal of Icelandic, but she does not care to speak the language. I find this difficult to understand, as she was very enthusiastic in the beginning.

CHAPTER 34

Halldór had to knock for some time before a janitor finally opened the door to the bank. He was shown into Jón Björnsson's office, where he had been once before to arrange a car loan; he remembered the paintings on the walls.

Although it was Saturday and the bank was closed, four men had already assembled in the manager's office. Halldór knew Reverend Ingimar and Jón Björnsson by sight; the third man, wearing thick-lensed glasses, introduced himself as Vilhjálmur Jakobsson, the vice president of the Gethsemane brotherhood; and the fourth man was the bank's auditor.

Jón paced the floor, repeating, "This simply must not get out. This simply must not get out."

Halldór could not promise anything on that score. The auditor handed him the final figures relating to the embezzlement.

"Well, that's certainly a lot of money," Halldór said, glancing at the paper.

Reverend Ingimar groaned and asked, "What in heaven's name did Jacob do with it all?"

Halldór told them about Jacob's purchase of the Birkihlíd property. "He kept thorough accounts, so I assume all this can be traced there," he added.

"So it will be possible, then, to retrieve some of these funds, will it?" Vilhjálmur asked.

"The deceased's estate will be handled by the executor, and you will have to make your claims to the estate," Halldór replied. "There should be some money when the property is sold."

Vilhjálmur was not happy with this reply, and turned to Jón. "Surely the bank is responsible for embezzlement by one of its employees?"

Before the manager could answer, the bank auditor replied, "You gave Jacob a mandate to operate your account; his withdrawals are nothing to do with the bank."

"This simply must not get out," Björnsson repeated.

"The bank has also suffered a considerable loss," the auditor remarked a little defensively.

"Who on earth can you trust when upstanding citizens like Jacob let you down so dreadfully," Reverend Ingimar said forlornly.

Halldór could see that the reverend had not recovered from the shock of this deception by his old friend. "We think he may have been ill," he offered.

"He surely must have been," Ingimar replied.

"Yes, of course, the man must have been insane," Jon exclaimed with some relief, and before repeating, "It simply must not get out."

Diary VII

January 1, 1921. New Year's Day. The weather is mild. There was a brass band playing outside the government office.

June 25, 1921. I booked a passage for Elizabeth and myself on the Sterling *north to Skagafjördur next week. We plan to walk south along the Kjalvegur route. The three royal ships arrived tonight and sailed into the sound...*

June 26, 1921. King Christian X and his queen disembarked at 10 o'clock this morning. The Prime Minister welcomed the king, and an anthem was sung. Then the royal couple headed up the town quay and through the ceremonial arch between the Eimskip Company building and Thorsteinsson's house, where the mayor and city council welcomed the royal couple. They then proceeded to the high school, with white-clad children lining their route scattering flowers in their path...

July 3, 1921. The Western Fjords. The Sterling *is slow-moving because of the poor quality of its coal, and stops at every port. There is a gale blowing from the south, but there is no snow and the sun is shining...*

July 4, 1921. We went ashore in Saudárkrókur and stayed at Hótel Tindastóll. Kristján has arrived as planned. He will be our guide on the trip...

July 5, 1921. The townsfolk watched with interest as we set off on foot from Saudárkrókur. Our backpacks that we brought from England attracted a good deal of attention; people here are in the habit of carrying luggage in sacks or heavy trunks. I also think people are amazed that we choose to go on a trip like this without horses. In these parts it is mainly vagrants and paupers that travel in this manner. The new walking boots are proving excellent...

July 6, 1921. Set off at the crack of dawn from Mælifell. We traveled up Mælifellsdalur valley and across Haukagilsheidi. It is foggy and drizzling, and not at all easy to find one's way until the track marked with cairns is reached. Kristján does not hesitate at all and takes big strides. Elizabeth and I try to keep up. We found the refuge hut at Adalmannsvatn and are planning to stay the night here. We caught a few trout and ate them for supper...

July 7, 1921. The weather has improved. It is light, and visibility is good, but there is a gale blowing from the north. It helps that the wind is behind us. The track is now well defined and marked with cairns. We have to wade across a number of rivers; Strangakvísl and Blanda Rivers are the trickiest ones. It is evening by the time we reach the refuge hut at Hveravellir...

July 8, 1921. We inspected the geothermal area. It has about 20 mud pots with boiling blue-green mud, giving off thudding and rasping noises. We have opted for the route to the west of Kjalhraun lava field, making for Hrútfell. Langjökull Glacier is to the west of us, and to the east stand the Kerlingafjöll Mountains, silhouetted against the sky. Kristján says that from there you enjoy the most panoramic and majestic views in Iceland. Glacier tongues stretch into Lake Hvítárvatn and icebergs float on the lake. We are making for the ferry where the Hvítá River flows from the lake...

July 10, 1921. Our journey is nearly over. Elizabeth is weary but does not complain. I am relieved that our loads are getting lighter as we use up our food. Kristján is indefatigable, and yet he has the most to carry... We wade across Grjótá and Sandá Rivers and reach the Gullfoss waterfall around the middle of the day. We are staying at Brautarholt tonight, and will be viewing Geysir tomorrow...

CHAPTER 35

When Halldór returned from the bank at eleven o'clock, the investigative team convened—apart from Egill, who had showed up earlier at the office that morning and then disappeared again.

Halldór, Jóhann, Hrefna, and Marteinn took turns describing what they had found out. Halldór began by explaining the ins and outs of Jacob Junior's embezzlement scheme. The import of this revelation was immediately clear to the team: Jacob had no doubt used the money to finance the running of the house for some time, and then to pay the deposit when contracts for its sale were exchanged, hence the so-called loans that he had recorded in his books. Initially, he had probably intended this to be a one-off loan, but, as so often happens with people who misappropriate funds they are entrusted with, things got out of hand. Remarkably, unlike most crooks in this sort of situation, Jacob had kept detailed accounts of his financial misdealings.

The victim's obsession with preserving his home was becoming more and more clear to Hrefna as well; it must have governed all his actions, and was probably either the consequence of some kind of mental derangement or what caused it. It did not, however, explain why he was murdered. They still had no motive; they needed to identify not only motive, but intention and opportunity, none of which had come to light yet.

Jóhann then presented a timeline he had prepared, showing all they knew of Jacob Junior's movements on Wednesday, January 17:

> *08:56 Clocks in for work at the bank. A few fellow employees remember seeing him at his desk that morning.*
>
> *12:05 Clocks out for lunch.*
>
> *12:15 Arrived at Birkihlíd, according to Sveinborg. Ate the rest of the previous day's meatballs and a prune compote. Took a ten-minute nap and went back to the bank at 12:50.*
>
> *12:59 Clocks in for work after lunch. As far as is known, spends the rest of the day at his desk. Had afternoon coffee in the bank canteen at 15:30. Sat at the same table as one of the bank's cashiers, as was his habit. They discussed the fishing limits dispute. Jacob was reportedly somewhat distressed by this conflict, being English on his mother's side.*
>
> *18:03 Clocks out from the bank.*
>
> *18:10 to 18:20 Arrives at Birkihlíd, according to Sveinborg. She is not completely certain of the time.*
>
> *19:00 Has supper, poached haddock fillet. Sveinborg recalls that the radio news program started just as they sat down at the supper table.*

> *After 21:00 Sveinborg leaves Birkihlíd, at*
> *which time Jacob is in his home office. What he*
> *was doing is not known. After that there is no*
> *information about what happened in the house.*

In Egill's absence, it fell to Marteinn to describe their fruitless search all over town the previous day for Sigurdur the guitarist. And finally, the meeting was adjourned after Halldór delegated the tasks for the rest of the day.

Diary VII

May 13, 1922. It seems that driving conditions are now safe for cars going east across Hellisheidi. The snowdrift in Smidjulautin was cleared yesterday. Now I can start to prepare for the survey...

June 26, 1922. Had a meeting with the supporters of the railroad in the Ölfus district. Many people spoke, and I answered questions. A farmer from the region performed a long poem about the undertaking. I only remember this bit:

...swift runs the train over southerly lands,
eager its song is, and clear.
In the first carriage he eminent stands,
Jacob the engineer...

As I listened I jotted these lines on a piece of paper:

Here my heart is warmed by you,
my hopes, dear friends, you nurture.
Tracks I lay this terrain through,
and trains will be the future.

I got up and recited this at the end of the meeting and was well received. Perhaps they were being polite...

August 13, 1922. Went with Matthías to Skerjafjördur to practice target shooting with my rifle...

September 4, 1922. The minister has entrusted me with calculating the cost of the railroad. Its total length will be 65.52 km, the gauge 1.067 m, the rails 18 kg/m...

September 12, 1922. I am assuming that the track bed will need 316 thousand cubic meters of material at a cost of 2,085,000 kr. With good management, this should be ample...

September 15, 1922. For the rails, I am going to use the unit price as delivered to a railroad station in Norway, i.e. inclusive of inland freight charges. I am assuming that a special ship will be chartered to transport the material to Reykjavik. It would amount to 3,300 tons of rails and 2,400 cubic meters of cross ties...

September 17, 1922. The cross ties (1.60 x 0.22 x 0.11 m) will be made of impregnated pinewood mounted with 12-cm-wide baseplates. The price, 6.00 kr. per item, is a little high, but is based on the present high price of timber and the cost of creosote being 150 kr./ton.

CHAPTER 36

Around noon Hrefna went to see the historian who had written about the royalist affair. He lived in an old timber house on Vesturgata. She recognized the house by the sign in a ground-floor window that read "Yngvi Jónsson, historian," and beneath the sign, a square piece of paper had been taped up with the words "Genealogical Services" written in thick lettering.

A fat boy wearing a black-and-white KR football shirt adorned with red ketchup stains opened the door when she knocked.

"Is Yngvi Jónsson in?" she asked politely.

"Yeah, hang on," the boy replied. He disappeared into the house and Hrefna heard him yell, "Dad! There's some woman wants to talk to you."

She couldn't hear a reply, but there must have been one, as the boy returned to the door and asked her in.

Hrefna followed him along a narrow corridor and past a kitchen, where a woman of an uncertain age sat at a table smoking. Her graying black hair was gathered into two plaits, and she wore a colorful batik tunic. She gave a friendly smile when Hrefna greeted her.

"He's downstairs," the boy said, pointing down a steep timber staircase.

Hrefna carefully descended the battered stairs to a large, low-ceilinged basement room; every piece of furniture was covered with stacks of papers and books, and atop one of the stacks lay a fat tabby cat. Yngvi Jónsson, historian, was also fat, very fat. Sitting on an old castored desk chair, he swiveled round toward Hrefna and gave her a cheery greeting. He wore a shabby pair of jeans and a red-checked flannel shirt; his friendly face was completely round and pink, with several double chins, and his colorless hair and beard were unruly. He seemed to be in his fifties, but was clearly younger than that in spirit. He got up with some difficulty, removed a stack of dusty papers from an easy chair, and offered Hrefna a seat.

"And what can I do for you, my dear?" he asked with a smile, taking the cat into his arms before sitting down again.

"I am from the detective division," Hrefna said. "We are investigating the death of Jacob Kieler."

Yngvi heaved with laughter. "I didn't shoot him," he gasped.

"Was I supposed to think that?"

Yngvi laughed again, and his stomach and double chins shook.

"No, not seriously," he said.

"Have you any idea who might have done it?"

Yngvi became serious for a moment. "No. I hadn't thought about it. To be honest, I haven't considered those Kieler chaps at all of late. You probably saw the article I wrote about the German king?"

"Yes."

"When I come across material like that, I sometimes write newspaper articles about it and sell them for a bit of money, but I didn't take it too far. It would be an interesting project for a keen writer to look into that family's history. There's plenty of material there."

"Really?"

Yngvi stroked the cat thoughtfully and then continued. "Yes, there's some stuff there. First of all, there's the myth about old Jacob the store manager, the Danish shop assistant who moved here to Iceland and became a wealthy merchant. Then there was that engineer's railroad nonsense and the royalist business, Matthías's misfortunes in Germany during the war years, the engineer's murder, and now, the boy's murder."

"He was hardly a boy."

"Oh, well. He was my contemporary and you tend to talk about your contemporaries as boys."

"All right. Let's take things in order," Hrefna suggested. "What myth are you talking about?"

"I once reported a story about events that were supposed to have happened in the last century, involving a Danish store manager who was particularly loyal to his boss and made everyone suffer for it, both staff and customers. Later it was said that this Dane had been Jacob Kieler the first—the shop assistant that became a real big shot. Do you want to hear the story?"

"Yes, if it's relevant."

Yngvi put the cat down, got up, and began pacing the floor. "Well, the Danish store had a cutter that used to sail from Hafnarfjördur under a skipper named Jón," he began. "He and Jacob did not always see eye to eye about when to go to sea, though Jón usually prevailed. One morning Jón and his coxswain were on the beach looking at the weather, when Jacob the Dane appeared; Jón advised against putting out to sea but, deviating from his custom, let himself be pressured by the store manager. Jacob watched the men row out to the cutter, as did a group of other people, among whom was an old man named Ari, who had lost two sons and a grandson to the sea and was now alone in the world. He was flensing a seal that had been knocked out and washed ashore by the heavy surf two days previously. 'May god be with them tonight,' the old man supposedly said, at which Jacob is reported to have asked, '*Tror du også det bliver blæsevejr?*' (Do you also believe it will blow a gale?)"

Yngvi's pronunciation of the Danish was very convincing, and he was putting on quite a show, acting out the story as he told it. "Then the old man said, 'I do not predict the weather, but I can see a thing or two.' To which the Dane asked, '*Og hvad ser du nu?*' (What do you see now?) Old Ari replied, 'No one on board that ship is fated to die, so she will return safe to harbor, but I do see that neither you nor your male descendants will die of old age in your beds.' Jacob's response was to shove the old man to the ground and stride away. That night a storm blew from the east, and the cutter was buffeted this way and that across the sea for days on end, but thanks to his stalwart crew and fine seamanship, Jón managed to hold his course and steer the ship back into harbor when the wind abated."

"Did the prophecy come true?" Hrefna asked.

"Jacob Kieler the merchant, whom we might call Jacob number one, fell off a horse and broke his neck. He had a son, Jacob Kieler number two, who drowned in a pond on his third birthday. His other son, Alfred, the father of engineer Jacob Kieler, number three, and Matthías the musician, was killed when his car overturned and rolled down the Kambar Mountain road. You know what happened to father and son Jacob Kieler, numbers three and four."

"So Matthías is the only one left," Hrefna said.

"Yes. Perhaps he will be the one to debunk the prophecy and live to be a hundred, dying peacefully in his sleep."

"I do hope so," Hrefna remarked.

"Yes, he has had his share of suffering, poor old fellow."

"Really?"

"Well, we know he was in a German prison camp during the war. Apparently, he has never wanted to talk about that experience, but it was definitely no more of a joyride for him than it was for others who went through the same."

"Do you know anything more about this royalist business?" Hrefna asked, changing the subject.

"I always say that in Iceland we have one president and two hundred thousand kings, so we don't need another one," Yngvi laughed. "No, I haven't gone into it any further since the article. There is probably enough material there for a whole book. I am too lazy for historical research, though. I can't be bothered to hang out in archives digging through dirty old papers; I much prefer sitting in cafés chatting with people. When I'm lucky, I get some gossip I can use for newspaper articles. I'm also good at genealogy. What was your paternal grandfather's name?"

"Never mind that," Hrefna said, a note of annoyance in her tone.

"Oh, well. And yet that's one part of this Kieler case that amuses me particularly, as I am somewhat involved."

"Yes?"

"I often sit in cafés with young university students. These kids like to hear their family traced back a few generations, though they rarely know their own grandparents' patronymics. If you write it up for them, they're even prepared to pay, or at least treat you to a coffee. One day I met a young woman who turned out to be offspring of this noble Kieler family, name of Elísabet Árnadóttir, born and raised in the north, daughter of Kirsten, who is the daughter of Jacob the engineer. But you probably know that. Well, who should be sitting at the next table over but Diddi, youngest son of Siggi Pistol."

"Who's Siggi Pistol?"

"Siggi Pistol was the guy who was jailed for several months after Jacob Senior was shot."

"Why was he called Siggi Pistol?"

"It's just an awfully cruel habit people have of dishing out nicknames. They started calling him that when he was in prison. Have you ever heard the story of the guy who happened to see a rat on the shore when he was a young boy? He shouted, 'Look, a rat!' and his friends took to calling him Óli Rat, as a joke. He was a promising young man, but this unfortunate nickname became so associated with him that it completely ruined his life. What girl do you think wants to marry Óli Rat? He hanged himself before he was twenty."

"What about this Sigurdur? Do you know his history?" Hrefna asked, trying to get the historian back on track.

"I remember Siggi well. I lived in the same part of town."

"Are you sure he wasn't involved in the murder?"

Yngvi laughed again. "Siggi from Brekkustígur was bloody good-looking and a great ladies' man. He was always having affairs with other men's wives. The night the murder was committed he was in bed with a respectable skipper's wife in Bárugata. Everybody except the coppers knew this, and Siggi was too much of a gent to tell them."

"So this Diddi is Sigurdur's son?" Hrefna asked.

"Yes, he was born after Siggi died, and was named for his father. It was a dreadful accident." Yngvi fell silent, and the smile left his face.

"Carry on with the story," Hrefna begged.

Yngvi smiled again. "Yes, well, here was Ella with me, and Diddi was sitting at the next table. I couldn't resist it, of course, and introduced them. It transpired that neither of them had heard the whole story of old Siggi's incarceration, so I told them some things about it. Since then, they have been inseparable," Yngvi concluded, laughing heartily.

"What do you mean?"

"They are sweethearts. Isn't that wonderful?"

"If they are in love, then it is indeed wonderful."

"I just love being an agent of destiny in people's lives. There was for instance—"

"Is it anything to do with this case?" Hrefna interrupted.

"No, not in fact, but—"

"Then I don't want to hear it," Hrefna scolded.

"Oh, well," Yngvi replied, shrugging his shoulders.

"What can you tell me about this Diddi?"

"His name is Sigurdur and he's, of course, Sigurdsson. He plays the guitar and writes songs; he's a bit of a troubadour, you know, like Bob Dylan, 'Blowin' in the Wind' and all that. Lives in a commune in the Old Town—I can't remember the name of the street, but I can describe the house to you."

"You don't need to. I think I know who he is now."

Diary VIII

January 5, 1923. A letter has arrived from the Norwegian expert. He thinks that the price for 4 locomotives and 30 carriages is now 746,000 kr. These are top quality locomotives with the latest modifications. Machines and tools for the workshop are included...

March 5, 1923. The national budget has been announced. There is no allocation for the railroad apart from my remuneration. Roads, on the other hand, get 377 thousand krónur...

May 30, 1923. The papers publish many articles attacking the railroad. The anger is dreadful. I am of a mind to abandon the whole business and emigrate. Elizabeth tries to give me courage...

February 20, 1924. Yet another budget that ignores the railroad. Construction projects are at an absolute minimum; they allocate just enough for basic maintenance and hardly that. New road legislation is on its way...

August 26, 1924. It is Elizabeth's thirtieth birthday today. We gave a big party...

March 13, 1925. Ísafold mentions that this year sees the centenary of the railways; on September 27, 1825, the first publicly subscribed railway train ran between Stockton and Darlington in England. Is it not time for Icelanders to make use of this invention, nearly a hundred years behind other nations...

March 15, 1925. Elizabeth told me she is going to have a baby...

CHAPTER 37

When Marteinn joined the detective division, Egill had taken him under his wing. Although their age difference was more than twenty years, they had similar views on most issues and found working together easy. Marteinn was, nevertheless, not always happy with the way his partner set about dealing with other people, but he comforted himself with the knowledge that they were all either former or future jailbirds.

Marteinn had decided at the age of ten that he wanted to be a policeman, and he was not one for changing his mind. When his peers grew their hair and objected to NATO and the police because it was the in thing, he had his hair cut short and wore a suit and a tie. He enrolled in an American correspondence course on law enforcement, and as soon as he was old enough, applied to the police force. He was initially taken on in the traffic division, and sent to the police academy, where he earned top marks in the final exam. On his first day at work, he issued a whole book of tickets, setting a record. His superiors, however, were less than impressed with this young man's ambitious nature, and at the first opportunity, shifted him over to the detective division, where he came into his own—though, unlike everyone else there, he missed the uniform.

Marteinn was just coming back from lunch when Egill turned up at the office with the name of a woman who might possibly help them trace Sigurdur the guitarist. They began by phoning hospitals and clinics in the city.

"Good afternoon, this is the detective division," Marteinn said to the first operator he spoke with. "Do you have a patient named Kristín Jósefsdóttir?"

She didn't seem impressed by the detective division at all, and made him wait a long time. When she finally came back on the line, she replied rather curtly, "No one by the name of Kristín Jónsdóttir is registered here."

"Jósefsdóttir," said Marteinn patiently.

"One mo—" she said, and again put Marteinn on hold.

"No, she is not here" was the final reply a few long moments later.

They spent a considerable time getting the same answer at the other places they phoned.

"What about the nursing homes," Marteinn suggested.

This they tried, and finally got a hit: a nursing home in Hafnarfjördur had a resident named Kristín Jósefsdóttir.

There was nobody in reception, so they went into the sitting room, where they found a neatly dressed old lady seated listening to the radio. She smiled when they bade her good afternoon.

"We are looking for Kristín Jósefsdóttir," Egill said.

"Yes." The old lady nodded.

"Is that you?"

"Yes."

"We are from the detective division," Marteinn said.

"Yes."

A voice from behind them warned, "She doesn't know nothing, not even her own name."

An ancient woman leaning on a metal walker, her back so bent she was unable to look them in the eye, asked, "What do you want?"

"We're looking for Kristín Jósefsdóttir," explained Egill.

"Kristín is in the infirmary. Room 102. The bed next to the window."

Room 102 contained three beds, the two nearest of which had clearly been slept in but were currently unoccupied; in the third bed, next to the window, as the old lady had described, lay a woman who, though she seemed younger than the other residents, looked very sickly and had an oxygen tube running up into her nose.

"Let me do the talking," Egill whispered to Marteinn. He then raised his voice. "Kristín Jósefsdóttir?"

"Yes, that's me," the woman whispered.

Egill smiled sweetly. "We're looking for your son, Diddi. We owe him money and would like to pay him. Do you know where he is?"

Kristín smiled back with some difficulty. "Well, he came here yesterday. I think he was planning to go to Ólafsvík to work in a fish factory."

Egill looked at Marteinn and smiled knowingly, then moved closer to the woman and leaned over her.

"We are from the detective division. We know your husband shot engineer Jacob Kieler."

Kristín pulled the bedclothes up to her chin and looked at him apprehensively, but gave no reply. Marteinn shifted uncomfortably.

"You were the one who looked after the gun, isn't that right?" Egill continued.

"There never was any gun. Why are you saying this?"

Marteinn whispered apprehensively, "Go easy."

"Diddi told us he got the gun from you."

"That's not true. Nobody would have said that."

Kristín whimpered and shrank away from Egill when he put his hand on her shoulder.

"You'd better tell us everything. It'll be best for him."

Kristín cried out in a cracked voice, "No, there was no gun."

"What are you doing here?" a voice demanded from behind them.

Marteinn looked around and saw a tiny woman in a nursing assistant's uniform.

"How dare you behave like this! Get out!" she shrieked. The old woman with the walker was standing behind her.

Marteinn heaved a sigh of relief, glad to be interrupted.

Egill smiled apologetically. "We are from the detective division, and were just looking for some information—"

"The police? What the…! Out of here, at once!" demanded the petite nurse.

Marteinn took Egill's arm. "Let's go," he whispered.

"We'll be back," Egill warned Kristín.

A group of old people who had gathered outside the room moved anxiously out of the way when Marteinn and Egill emerged, hotly followed by the nursing assistant.

"Let's get out of here before the grannies start throwing their chamber pots at us," Egill whispered to Marteinn.

Diary IX

May 23, 1925. I have been re-examining my cost calculations for the railroad. Prices are all coming down so it is right to review the figures. I also think it would be safe to reduce the width of the track bed by 10%. Taking all this into account the railroad should cost only 5,750,000 krónur...

June 6, 1925. I met with the minister today to discuss the railroad. I showed him the new costings and he was quite impressed with them. I reminded him that it was now 20 years since the telephone first arrived in Iceland, and that we now have 190 telephone exchanges in the country and more than 3,000 telephone apparatuses. In earlier days the telephone and the railroad were mentioned in the same breath, and many considered that the railroad was a greater necessity than the telephone...

July 10, 1925. There are reports from neighboring countries that motorized railcars are becoming more and more common on their railroads. They are of many different types, and use either gasoline or diesel oil for fuel. Their main disadvantage is the rather poor uphill traction. I can also foresee the viability of electric railcars, as it is not unlikely that the Sog waterfalls will be harnessed before long...

August 18, 1925. There was a report in Ísafold about a railroad accident in France. I do not like this reportage. I hear the opponents of the railroad use this in the presentation of their case; they say that railroads are dangerous. They ought to report all the accidents caused by automobiles worldwide. I also hear that many people think that motorcars are better equipped to get about in heavy snow, because it is reported in foreign news if a train is delayed by snowfall for a few hours; nobody thinks it newsworthy if cars get stuck in snowdrifts for days on end...

August 27, 1925. Cannot see that there will be many engineering projects to be had this fall, so I am going to do some part-time teaching in English, Danish, and mathematics...

October 12, 1925. At about half past three last night, Elizabeth was delivered of our perfect, beautiful son. She had been in labor since yesterday, under the care of Dr. Eiríkur and an experienced midwife. I was allowed into their room after Elizabeth had had a short while to recover after the birth. He is a very bonny baby. I sat and watched him well into the morning as he slept in his crib...

CHAPTER 38

At four o'clock that afternoon four men gathered in Jacob Kieler's office at Birkihlíd to open the safe: Halldór and Jóhann joined Matthías Kieler and a marshal from the civil court. An empty cardboard box sat on the desk, awaiting the contents of the safe.

The only person missing was the locksmith.

Halldór glanced at his wristwatch. "He promised to come at four o'clock."

The marshal checked his watch, too. "In that case, I'll read out the warrant while we wait."

Jóhann paced the floor while the man recited the terms of the warrant, stating that the detective division had permission to open up and investigate the contents of a locked receptacle belonging to the estate of Jacob Kieler, born October 12, 1925, died January 18, 1973.

Meanwhile Jóhann couldn't help but wonder where Jacob Junior had kept the key. Why hadn't they found it during the house search? All the keys they had found had been tried, and none had fit the lock. Jacob Junior must have had a good hiding place for it, presumably somewhere close at hand, and perhaps close at heart. And that's when the idea struck him: the elaborate model of the railroad station Jacob Kieler kept right here in his office.

He tried lifting the roof off the station building, which proved detachable, but found no key there. The roofs of the other buildings also came off, but none hid a key either.

"I shall have to cancel this meeting if he doesn't turn up soon," the marshal said impatiently.

Matthías had been standing there silently, still wearing his overcoat and hat; now he sat down, sighing. "Is this Icelandic punctuality?"

Halldór smiled apologetically.

The model station had a complex system of tracks and sidings, including a turntable onto which rolling stock could be moved and turned round; Jóhann first tried making it turn, which it did easily, and then found he could lift it completely off its base, revealing, in a compartment beneath, a large key.

Jóhann walked past the three men and fit the key into the lock; it turned, and the safe door popped open. The atmosphere in the room lightened immediately as Jóhann withdrew the contents of the safe and placed them on the desk. The marshal pulled out his notebook and began recording each item as he did so.

> *Twelve packets of ammunition, various sizes.*
> *Seven hardback books, handwritten, labeled*
> *as engineer Jacob Kieler's diaries.*
> *Old documents parceled together with string.*
> *A framed photograph.*
> *A key on a string.*

Jóhann straightened up. "That's all."

The four men examined the photograph first; it was a black-and-white of a gleaming new railway train, its locomotive in the foreground, probably painted black, bearing the inscription in Gothic lettering on its side: Iceland Railroad Company Ltd.

"Have you seen this picture before, sir?" Halldór asked. All eyes were now intently on the last Kieler male.

There was a long pause before Matthías replied. "No."

"What about this key, then?" Halldór said.

"May I see it?" Jóhann asked, taking the key from the desktop. He went over to the gun cabinet and tried the lock; the key fit.

"This will need further examination," Halldór stated, scanning the ammunition on the desk. "Jóhann will do that in the forensics lab."

Matthías stood up. "With your permission, I shall take the diaries into safekeeping."

"No, that will not be possible," replied Halldór, taken aback. "They are important for our investigation of the case."

"But my brother's wishes are clear," Matthías said firmly. "He wanted to protect these books from unauthorized access."

Halldór bristled a bit and then said emphatically, "I can assure you that they will be treated in strict confidence; one of my team will read the diaries, and all that is not relevant to the present investigation will remain private."

Matthías turned to the marshal.

"Do I have to put up with this?" he asked sharply.

"Yes, the law is unequivocal."

Matthías looked at each of them in turn, and then left without saying good-bye.

Wordlessly, Halldór watched him depart, and then, turning his attention back to the contents of the safe, transferred all of it to the cardboard box. The marshal had them each countersign the record of their meeting, and they left, locking the door behind them. On the front steps of the house they met a man dressed in a parka and carrying a toolbox, "Is there a lock here that needs opening?" he asked, after removing a half-smoked cigar from his mouth.

Diary X

March 27, 1927. AT LAST, AT LAST! The
Althing has passed a government bill granting
the Hydroelectric Company a franchise to build a
railroad between Reykjavik and Thjórsá River. The
state treasury will contribute 2 million krónur on
completion of its construction, and the Hydroelectric
Company will provide the balance, 6 million krónur,
with capital from abroad. Compared with the cost
estimates for the power station at Urridafoss, this
is relatively cheap. The state will be in charge of
operating the railroad on its completion...

March 30, 1927. I met the agent of the Hydroelectric
Company. He now has all the data on the railroad,
and we shall be having further talks before long.
He has every confidence that construction of the
railroad will start this coming summer. It will require
200 laborers, and we shall probably hire experienced

men from Norway; we shall endeavor to select
respectable, temperate, and hard-working men...

April 11, 1927. Made an agreement with Kristján
for me to employ him on a permanent basis. He is a
skilled draftsman and admirably capable when we
are surveying...

June 14, 1927. I still have heard nothing from
the Hydroelectric Company. This is becoming
inconvenient, as I have turned down other projects.
I have discussed this with the Employment Minister,
as I felt sure that the government will have assumed
that the passage of the bill into law was sufficient to
ensure commencement of the works...

July 5, 1927. I am not getting any replies to my
letters to the Hydroelectric Company. I am becoming
very worried about this...

November 15, 1927. I have not been able to do
anything today, and hardly even managed to pick up
this book to write these lines. The short days of fall sit
heavily on me.

November 16, 1927. I am ill. I feel as if my head is
burning.

November 17, 1927. I am ill.

November 19, 1927. Got up around noon and went outside briefly. The weather is bright and there is sunshine, albeit a little cold.

November 20, 1927. I felt well today and was able to work. Elizabeth is happy; she has been worried about me...

CHAPTER 39

Earlier that morning Halldór had made an appointment to see Thórdur, Jacob Senior's erstwhile assistant. And despite the fact that it was Saturday, Thórdur said he'd planned on being at his office. Halldór went straight there after the safe opening at Birkihlíd, the picture of the railway train tucked firmly under his arm.

Thórdur's engineering firm was housed in a new building on Sudurlandsbraut. This was clearly a sizable operation, with a spacious reception area and, beyond it, a large room containing many drawing boards, where a number of people were hard at work. Halldór was shown into a large, well-furnished office.

Thórdur was in his sixties, with gray hair and long sideburns. He was dressed in a woolen jacket with leather patches on the elbows. The office smelled of tobacco smoke, and several pipes hung from a rack on the desk.

Thórdur shook Halldór's hand and offered him a seat.

"I am here about Jacob Kieler Junior's death," Halldór announced plainly.

"Yes, these are dreadful events," replied Thórdur. "I still haven't recovered from hearing about Jacob Junior's death. He was a fine man."

"Do you recall the death of Jacob Senior?" Halldór asked.

"Yes, of course. I understand from the news that Jacob Junior suffered a similar fate."

"Were you working for Jacob Senior when he died?"

"Yes, but we were actually on summer holiday at that time. Otherwise it would probably have been me who found him."

"Have you seen this picture before?" Halldór asked, passing Thórdur the picture of the railway train.

Thórdur took the picture and examined it carefully.

"Yes, I've seen it once before."

"When was that?"

"Jacob Senior received it in the post a few weeks before the war broke out in Europe. Nobody was supposed to know about the trains here in Iceland at that time, but Jacob was so overjoyed about it that he couldn't resist showing me his treasure. He knew, of course, that I wouldn't break his trust. I never saw the picture again, and I have never discussed this with a soul apart from Jacob, until this moment."

"Whose train is this?"

"This is Jacob's train, of course. After tireless effort, Jacob had found backers in Germany to provide a substantial part of the finance for the railroad, and an operating company, Isländische Bahn AG, was set up there to produce the rolling stock and lease it to the Iceland Railroad Company. This was the first of two trains that the company made. It was a sensitive subject because of the political situation in Europe, and the identity of the company behind the rolling stock had to be kept secret in Iceland."

"But the tracks, they didn't even exist here."

"That's right. The Iceland Railroad Company was supposed to look after that side of things, and the steel for the first stretch of track was ready on the quay in Hamburg. The cross ties were coming from Norway. That summer they were going to build the first few kilometers from the harbor, and ship the train to Iceland. Jacob was hoping some local funding for the enterprise would come forth once people saw that it was about to become reality. The war ruined all those plans, of course."

"What happened to the trains when the war started? Were they used for war operations?"

"No, hardly. You see, Jacob had made the bold decision to use a gauge of just one meter for the track here in Iceland, rather narrower than the standard gauge most commonly found in Europe. As the Icelandic railroad would never be directly linked to another system, he took the view that it didn't matter if we used a narrow gauge, and it created considerable savings on infrastructure cost."

"So our trains would have been too narrow for German tracks?"

"Yes. We had some vague news that they had remained dockside in Hamburg, but had eventually been destroyed in the Allied bombardment."

"They'd have been handsome, those locomotives."

"Yes, and technologically advanced, able to use either electricity or diesel."

Thórdur reached for a pipe on his desk and began to stuff it with tobacco.

Halldór decided to change the subject. "You were Jacob's colleague for some time, weren't you?"

"Yes, I graduated from the Technical University of Denmark in Copenhagen in 1935, and began to work for Jacob immediately. We had worked together for ten years when he passed away," Thórdur replied.

"What did you work on?"

"Mainly incidental engineering jobs: surveying, project supervision, and design. There was actually not much of that sort of thing going on during those years, but when work was scarce, Jacob used the time for research and preparation for the railroad."

"Were there others working with you?"

"Yes, there was a man called Kristján Jónsson who assisted us with surveying and technical drawing."

"Is he still alive?"

"Yes. He is a resident of the Grund Nursing Home."

"Can you describe Jacob to me?" Halldór asked, after jotting down the name of the nursing home.

"He was a short man, less than one meter seventy tall, but well proportioned and so seemed taller. He had a knack for carrying himself in such a way that people did not look down upon him. He was a likable man, extremely intelligent, and a skilled engineer."

Thórdur lit his pipe and puffed on it enthusiastically before continuing. "Dear Jacob would have appreciated the present times, when there are so many big projects going on and new technology to help us realize them," he remarked more cheerfully. "Now you can stick a bunch of punched cards into a machine and it calculates equations and curves that previously took us days to work out using slide rules and books of tables. These are great times for the engineering profession."

Thórdur's tone changed and he became serious again.

"But Jacob's problem was that he suffered from depression." He paused, and then added, "It was, actually, both excitability and depression; he was a manic-depressive."

"How did it manifest itself?"

"When he was overexcited, the railroad and other dreams took over all his thoughts, whereas during the fits of depression he would lie in bed, and we wouldn't see him downstairs in the engineering studio for days on end. In between, he was completely normal and a hard worker."

"Can you describe his manic fits a bit more?" Halldór asked.

"Endless chatter, almost limitless energy, and unrealistic ideas about himself and his abilities. When he was at his worst, he didn't sleep for days on end and got all kinds of delusions; but when he was in that kind of mood, he could be really persuasive to those who didn't know him, and I think, for instance, that he must have been on a real high when he got the Germans to invest money in Isländische Bahn. It must have taken a great deal of persuasiveness to get them to build the trains before even one meter of track had been laid here in Iceland."

"What happened to the railroad company here?"

"By the time Jacob died, it had broken even. A great deal had been spent buying material for the railroad; material that never made it to Iceland and was lost in the war. But the engineering firm had gotten good jobs and received considerable income in the intervening years, so Jacob had been able to pay up all the shares he had underwritten in the company, which was a considerable sum. This money was used to pay outstanding debts. There were, naturally, many others who were fully paid-up shareholders in the company, but it was declared insolvent, even though it owned a nearly perfect railroad design."

"So did the investors have to write off their shares?"

"Not totally. Jacob had a life insurance policy with an English company for a considerable sum of money, which went to Elizabeth. She was very keen for the railroad company to be honorably wound up, so she made an offer to all the investors to buy their shares at twenty percent of the nominal value. It was her wish that I should deal with these matters, and I went to see every shareholder about it; people were, on the whole, reasonably satisfied with the outcome."

"Was the company then dissolved?"

"Yes. When I had got hold of all the shares, a formal company meeting was held and the company was dissolved, with the assets that remained passing to Elizabeth—nothing but valueless designs and documents, of course."

"Why valueless?"

"It transpired during the prewar years that what Iceland needed was roads. A railroad would never have paid for itself at that time, but Jacob just wouldn't face that fact, however many times I tried to make him realize it. But I am convinced that the railroad would have been of great value for the nation had we built it earlier, at the start of the century."

"Did you own shares in the company?"

"Yes. We, the staff, got part of our salary paid in shares, so I was, of course, relieved to be paid this percentage. I made an agreement with the widow that I would deal with the dissolution of the business, and all that that entailed, in return for retaining the engineering firm's goodwill. She refused to sell the furniture and equipment, but there were a few projects in progress, and I was allowed to take them with me. I have done very well since then, as you can see."

"Were you aware of Jacob Senior being part of a group of people that wanted to make this country a monarchy instead of democracy?"

"No," he said, shaking his head. "I heard the rumor long after Jacob Senior's death, but I was never aware of anything like that at the time. I do remember, though, that he was quite worried about the establishment of the republic here, and that he wasn't sure this was the right step to take, but then he got swept along like the rest of us when the day arrived."

"Have you kept in contact with the family?"

"Yes, my wife and I often called in on the widow while she was alive. We bought a house not far from Birkihlíd, and we often popped in there when we went for walks."

"Have you been there recently?"

"Yes, I visited Jacob Junior last Monday. I was tidying up our document store here and came across some papers of Jacob Senior's that I had brought from the engineering firm at that time; they had been amongst the contracts in the safe and I hadn't checked them properly. I delivered these papers to Jacob Junior and he was very grateful."

"What papers were these?"

"There was the agreement Alfred Kieler made with the contractor who built Birkihlíd; birth certificates for the two brothers, Jacob Senior and Matthías; Alfred Kieler's will; and other documents of historical value to the family."

"Do you know Matthías?"

"No. He had moved to Berlin by the time I came back home after finishing my studies. I have only seen him twice in my life, the first time at Jacob Senior's funeral and then this last Wednesday evening."

"Was Matthías here in Iceland when Jacob Senior died?"

"Yes, he had just arrived from Germany. He came on *Esja* along with a large number of other Icelanders who had gotten trapped in Europe during the war."

"Where did you see him last Wednesday evening?"

"At Birkihlíd. I went for a walk and met him on the sidewalk by the gate."

"Are you sure it was Matthías?"

"Yes, I'm good at remembering people. He had aged by nearly thirty years and put on a good deal of weight since I saw him at the funeral, but I still recognized him immediately. I said good evening to him, but he didn't reply and went in through the gate."

"Are you sure that he was making for the house?"

"Yes, I watched him walk up the steps."

"What time do you think this was?"

"It must have been between nine thirty and ten. I watched a documentary on Africa on the television and then went out for a walk."

Diary X

February 23, 1928. My father and I have between us bought an automobile, a 1927 Pontiac. This is a good, sturdy vehicle. Hallgrímur the shop assistant will be my father's driver, whereas I shall drive myself on my rounds...

March 20, 1928. Took young Jacob for a walk. Made changes to the drawing of Elías the pharmacist's house. His wife is not happy with the day parlor. My mother is not well...

May 20, 1928. My father was summoned to the town sheriff today. My brother Matthías has been involved in some kind of difficulty. I shall deal with this tomorrow. Made certain that the newspapers were kept out of it...

May 21, 1928. Spent the whole morning talking to my father, then went to see the sheriff. The case has been settled. Matthías will be going immediately to Berlin to begin his studies at the music academy, rather than waiting until fall as had been the original plan. He sails on the Gullfoss *next week...*

May 27, 1928. Accompanied Matthías to the ship. He gave me heartfelt thanks for my help, but was somewhat miserable. Father had not spoken a word to him...

CHAPTER 40

Having concluded her interview with Yngvi Jónsson, Hrefna carried out an exhaustive, if unsuccessful, search for Elísabet. She tried the Nýi Gardur student residence, at the University of Iceland, but Elísabet was not in her room, nor did any of the students on her hall know where she might be; she also tried the university library, and the various other places on campus where students usually congregated, to no avail.

She decided to phone the number she'd been given for Kirsten when she got back to the office.

"I only need some information from her, it's nothing to worry about," Hrefna explained, after asking Kirsten if she knew of her daughter's whereabouts.

Kirsten didn't, or if she did, she wasn't telling.

So Hrefna set about transcribing the notes she had taken of her conversation with Yngvi instead. She was just finishing up when Jóhann arrived at the office clutching a cardboard box.

"This will cheer you up," he remarked, emptying the box of the things they'd retrieved from the Birkihlíd safe on her desk. He handed her the last seven diaries and then took the rest of the contents over to his desk and began examining a pile of documents, along with the ammunition they'd recovered.

Hrefna inspected the stack of books, which looked very much like the older ones, both inside and out. The entries were quite similar to the ones she had already been studying. Still, there had to be a specific reason why these particular books had been kept in a locked cabinet rather than on the shelf with the others.

She paged to the last entry, near the front of diary number nineteen. It was dated July 8, 1945, and contained only a single sentence: *Matthías arrives tomorrow.*

After that the pages were blank.

Jacob Kieler Senior had died on July 15, 1945. He had kept a diary continuously from June 30, 1910, until July 8, 1945, writing something every day, whether well or unwell, happy or sad. On the day his brother Matthías arrived home, after many years abroad, Jacob Kieler Senior stopped writing in his diary. Six days later he was shot dead. Hrefna read the last sentence one more time: *Matthías arrives tomorrow.*

Diary XI

March 13, 1930. The latest Engineering Association
magazine has a summary of the major construction
works undertaken by the state last year. Bridges
and roads feature prominently, with a budget
of just under one million krónur. The annual
number of man days worked amounts to 113,731,
a five-fold increase since 1925. I welcome the road
improvements, of course, but at the same time worry
that the continued emphasis on road works will
result in dwindling interest in the railway project...

*June 25, 1930. At noon cannon shots sounded twice
from the harbor to announce the arrival of King
Christian X and Swedish Crown Prince Gustaf Adolf
for the Althing Festival... We set off eastward at
six o'clock and arrived at the car parking area just
after nine o'clock. We found our tent immediately.
Hjörleifur had brought our equipment here yesterday
and set everything up. Young Jacob is very excited
about sleeping in a tent. There is a damp fog that
makes it dark despite the fact that the sun hardly sets
at this time of the year...*

*June 26, 1930. There are more than 4,000 tents in
the Leirar area. I dug out my college graduation
cap, and we marched to the religious service by the
Almannagjá waterfall at 9 o'clock. At half past nine
we processed up Lögberg with a brass band to the
fore. The festival was inaugurated, and the choir sang
"Ó, Gud vors lands." A thousand years have passed
since Icelanders, the earliest ones, assembled for the
first meeting here at Thingvellir by Öxará River. At
half past eleven, the session of the united Althing was
formally opened by the king. I have long held the
view that this nation needs a head of state. Our king
is most stately and gracious, but it is not enough that
he only comes here every few years, and then there*

is the fact that he does not speak the language. It is my opinion that we need our own king, even if that means severing the link with Denmark...

CHAPTER 41

Halldór found the former surveyor in a small double room in the Grund Nursing Home, resting on his bed and listening to the radio. The bed was too short, and had been extended by placing a small chest at its foot and draping it with folded blankets. The old man rose to receive his visitor; he was a giant of a man, a good six foot six despite his slight stoop. He had a neatly trimmed white beard, an aquiline nose, and sharp eyes. When they shook, Halldór felt his hand engulfed in the old man's powerful grip.

Halldór explained the purpose of his visit, and Kristján invited his guest to take a seat on the only chair in the room, as he sat down on the edge of the bed. It took Halldór a moment to decide how to begin, finally settling on the simplest question. "How did you meet engineer Jacob?"

"He asked me to be his survey assistant," Kristján replied.

"How come?"

"I had some experience with that sort of thing. I graduated from secondary school in 1912 but couldn't afford college, so I became an assistant to some people in the Danish army who were mapping Iceland. My father was a farmer in the Kjós district, and the surveyors rented horses from him, which I looked after as they traveled about."

"What surveying did you and Jacob do?"

"The first job we did together was to survey for the railroad eastward through the Threngsli Pass. After that it was whatever came our way."

"Were you fully employed by Jacob right from the start?"

"No. I did a lot of tourist guiding across the highlands, as I'd gotten to know the countryside well during my survey trips with the Danes."

"When did he offer you a full-time job?"

"That was in the spring of 1927, when it looked as if the Hydroelectric Company would be building the railroad."

"And that came to nothing?"

"That's right."

"Did you take an interest in the setting up of the railroad company?"

"Yes, of course; shares in the company made up the bulk of my salary from 1932 until 1939."

"So you must have lost a lot of money."

"Well, I made my choices."

"What did you do during these years?"

"In the summers, I selected routes and did the basic surveys for the railroad line northward along Kjölur, and in the winters, I worked on drafting."

"Was this a feasible option for a railroad?"

"Yes, definitely. Three German railroad engineers came here in the summer of 1936, and I showed them the route I'd picked. They were very pleased with it."

"Was this presented to the authorities?"

"No, it was a very sensitive matter during those years. Because we had a left-wing government, we had to keep everything involving Germany under wraps, so the Germans pretended to be geologists taking soil samples. I remember that we ended our journey back south to Reykjavik by filling some hessian sacks with stuff taken from an earth bank in Kjalarnes, and labeling them with all kinds of symbols."

"Tell me a bit more about that trip."

"We took Jacob's car and headed east. I went with the Germans on foot through the Threngsli Pass, while Jacob drove over Hellisheidi to pick us up and drive us up through Biskupstungur all the way to Lake Hvítárvatn. From there we, the Germans and I, continued northward on foot, along the Kjalvegur track and down into Blöndudalur, while Jacob turned back, drove up through Borgarfjördur, and met us in the north, where we then drove on to Akureyri."

"Wasn't it difficult to keep all this secret?"

"We were careful."

"What was the outcome of the journey?"

"The Germans were very happy with our plans, and gave positive feedback when they got back home."

"What happened then?"

"Jacob devised a way to utilize the Germans' contribution, involving an independent limited company he set up in Germany to own the trains and lease them to the company here. The trains were built in Germany so it didn't cost the Germans any foreign currency, which they were very short of during those years. Most of the Iceland Railroad Company's capital was then used to buy cross ties in Norway and rails in Germany. They were ready on the quay in Hamburg when the war broke out."

Halldór brought out the picture of the train.

"Have you seen this picture before?"

Kristján took the picture.

"Yes, Jacob showed it to me. We were very pleased about it at the time."

"Were you aware of Jacob's illness?"

"What illness?"

"Depression."

"Jacob wasn't mentally ill; he just needed to rest from time to time and think things through. Who says that he was mentally ill?"

"Thórdur."

"I might have known. Why does he have to blacken Jacob's memory after all that's happened?"

"Are you and Thórdur not on friendly terms?"

"I didn't particularly like him."

"Why was that?"

"I didn't feel he was sincere about the railroad project. He was continually trying to discourage Jacob with all sorts of pessimistic notions. He wasn't happy until he had dissolved the company after Jacob's death."

"Were you against that?"

"Yes, there was no reason for the company to cease trading, and I would never have agreed to it if Elizabeth herself hadn't asked me to sell her my stock."

"So were you then paid this twenty percent?"

"No, that would have been blood money. I *gave* Elizabeth my stock. There were others who got a lot of money, but I'm not naming names."

"Can you remember Jacob's death?"

"Yes, as if it had happened yesterday."

"Were you working for him then?"

"No. He came to the office on the morning of July tenth and told Thórdur and myself that he planned to close the business for a few days. We were to take time off. I went to visit my parents, and was busy baling hay on my parents' farm when I heard the news."

"You remember the date remarkably well."

"Yes, it was my birthday, my fiftieth. It was also really unusual. We were not in the habit of taking time off at what was our busiest time of year."

"Have you any idea who might have shot Jacob?"

"No, though hardly a day has passed these twenty-eight years when I haven't thought about it, but I have never been able to understand it."

"Did anybody benefit from Jacob's death?"

"It seems to me that Thórdur has done all right after getting the engineering firm for next to nothing."

"Have you had any contact with the family since that time?"

"No, I haven't been to Birkihlíd since he died. I met Elizabeth only once, and that was when she came to me and asked for the shares."

"You haven't met Jacob Junior either?"

"No."

Halldór got up to leave, and held out his hand for the photo.

"I wonder if it's possible to get a copy of this?" said Kristján, looking at the picture lying in his lap.

"You can probably talk to the beneficiaries about that when the investigation is over," Halldór replied, "unless they would rather keep the existence of this train quiet. You never know."

"I would really love to have a picture like this one," Kristján said, handing it back. "What irks me most," he added, "is that I have never been abroad...I have never traveled on a train."

Diary XI

September 12, 1930. We had some very tragic news today. Our motor car went off the road on Kambar Hill and overturned. My father ended up under the car and died instantly. Hallgrímur, the shop assistant, survived, but with injuries to his head and arms. The Árnessýsla County sheriff telephoned us and then the parish pastor visited us. My mother has taken to her bed...

September 13, 1930. My father's body was conveyed to Reykjavik today. I am consumed with deep and impotent fury. If only we had had the railroad, this would never have happened. This road down Kambar Hill is very dangerous...

November 21, 1930. Our little daughter was born this morning. We are so happy. Now there is joy once more in this house, which has been so silent since my father died. Such is the way of life, one person leaves and another arrives...

November 29, 1930. This evening I sat by my daughter's crib. She is a tiny little human being, and yet she looks so intelligent. When she looks us in the eye, it seems as if she is aware of something we don't know of. Young Jacob is besotted with his sister.

CHAPTER 42

The snow had been trodden down on the paved area in front of the yellow apartment block, and it was not easy to shovel. Pétur didn't seem too concerned with the job, though, as he leaned on his shovel gossiping with his friend and neighbor, Albert. Or rather, Pétur pontificated while Albert listened with interest, grinning from ear to ear, and emitting an occasional nasal laugh.

Albert was a short fellow in his seventies; he lived in the house next door and spent the better part of each day on the lookout at his kitchen window. As soon as he spotted someone familiar outside, he'd nip out for a chat. Today, he was wearing a green sheepskin coat and a fur-lined baseball cap with earmuffs, whereas a sweater seemed to be adequate for Pétur, whose snow-shoveling duties, as relaxed as they were, kept him warm.

Now and again Pétur would shift a few shovels of snow, but then he would think of a new story that he wanted to tell Albert, and the shoveling would cease again. If a resident of the house passed, the pair would give a cheery greeting and follow the person inquisitively with their eyes, while Pétur speculated as to their particular comings and goings, based on previous observation, often concluding with some juicy rumor about their subject of the moment.

When Hrefna came through the gate carrying plastic bags in both hands, Pétur instantly put down his shovel and opened the front door for her.

"Good afternoon," he said cheerfully, "any news of the murder case?"

"Good afternoon," Hrefna replied. "No, not as far as I know."

Pétur watched her as she went up the stairs, then turned back to his shovel. "She's coming home from work. She's not married," he said to Albert.

"Ehe he," Albert laughed.

"She works for the detective division, but they don't tell her anything much."

"He he."

"They're investigating this murder of Jacob Kieler in Birkihlíd."

"Ehe he he."

"Once, many years ago, I did a job for him with my jackhammer."

"He he?"

"There was a fireplace in the laundry room that had been bricked up, and he had me open it up. The guy was trying to restore the laundry room to its original state and wanted the fireplace to follow suit."

"He he."

"But could I get him to pay? I charged him a fortune, of course, because I thought that they must have a bit of money in that palace of theirs, but I didn't get a bit of it. In the end, I had to reduce the amount by half, and then he finally paid up. He threatened me with the tax authorities when I suggested I do it for cash."

"He he."

"But that's not the whole story. There was some funny business going on in that house."

"He he?"

Pétur kept Albert in suspense while he shoveled a bit more snow.

Diary XII

March 5, 1931. I have been looking for an opportunity to speak with ministers and members of parliament to press for some action on the railroad business. It seems to me that they are being evasive. Last year it was the preparations for the Althing Festival, whereas now they plead political conflicts and the financial crisis...

May 5, 1931. These are difficult times. Father's shop has not done well this winter, and I don't seem to have any other option but to close it. I have not found a buyer, and letting other people manage it clearly doesn't work. I do not feel I can deal with this. I must try and get more projects for the engineering firm. We should be poorly off financially were it not for Elizabeth's funds...

May 8, 1931. I am experiencing an odd anxiety. I try, nevertheless, not to show it, but I sense that Elizabeth is watching me. Is it possible that my work of ten years on the railroad business will come to nothing?

CHAPTER 43

As she climbed the stairs carrying the plastic bags filled with the diaries, Hrefna could hear the scrape of Pétur's shovel on the hardpack below. Those two were certainly irritating, she thought to herself; she found it very annoying, and a bit uncomfortable, to be watched every time she came and went.

Her cozy apartment was a welcome relief, after so many long days on the job. She sighed, tired from the difficult day, and knowing it was not over yet.

Elsa greeted her mother warmly, took her coat, and brought her a cup of tea in the parlor. They chatted for a little while. These quiet moments at the end of the day, when they sat down and talked with each other, were some of her most cherished. They were good friends and able to discuss everything, although Hrefna tried to avoid the topic of her work with Elsa; not because she didn't trust her daughter in confidential matters, but because it seemed of little interest to Elsa. Instead, they talked about school, music, books, relatives and friends, films, boys, sports, and just about anything else that came up.

Hrefna made her special meat stew for supper; it was a favorite of both of theirs. Still, she couldn't help thinking about the fantastic meal she'd enjoyed the previous evening and felt a tinge of inferiority at the comparison. How wonderful it would be to have time and money to cook such a feast; as they ate, she shared the experience with Elsa.

"Dig that, a servant all to yourself," Elsa said enviously. "This must be a big-time important guy."

"Yes, he is," Hrefna replied. "In some ways."

After supper, she drank two cups of coffee, before returning to the diaries. She looked again at the last entries in book number nineteen:

July 5, 1945. Went to study the route for a road to the President's mansion at Bessastadir for the Director of Highways.

July 6, 1945. Bought new black shoes for 58 krónur.

July 7, 1945. Sorted out papers in the office in the morning. Had coffee outside in the sunshine in the afternoon. Kirsten's girlfriends came for a visit.

July 8, 1945. Matthías arrives tomorrow.

It was all very mundane and ordinary, and yet the diaries stopped so abruptly. She leafed back and forth through the final few pages to try and find an explanation, but there was nothing, so she returned to where she had left off, at the beginning of diary number thirteen.

Diary XIII

February 25, 1932. I have now lost all hope that the authorities will involve themselves in the construction of the railroad. Perhaps that is for the best. Private enterprise should deal with this. I have decided to set up the Iceland Railroad Company Ltd. and dedicate all my vigor to its realization...

March 4, 1932. I have asked Kristján to design the share certificates for the railroad company and devise its trademark...

June 28, 1932. I have been touring around the farms in the Flói district today, having discussions with farmers. I am having very little success selling stock in the company. Many refuse completely, while others subscribe token sums that will not get us anywhere. The occasional one who is reasonably well off makes a larger contribution. This is going to be an uphill journey.

September 15, 1932. My wife and I held a concert in our home this evening. A string quartet from the music society played a few pieces, and a young tenor sang to piano accompaniment. I asked Magnús to stay behind when the guests left, and asked if I might put his name down for some shares in the railroad. He agreed on condition that I would assist him in the business with the king. He has told me before that he is of the opinion that Iceland should become a monarchy when we sever the connection with Denmark. He wants to look for a potential king among noble or ruling families in Europe. He must be a well-educated man, married, and the father of one or two sons. Magnús thinks that Germany may be the most likely place to find such a man, but he needs help with his search. He thinks that if a suitable candidate is found, he might be invited to visit the country and be presented to the nation. He feels the population will welcome their potential king with open arms when they see that here they have an aristocrat who is prepared to reside in the country, learn Icelandic, and live with the nation in good times and in bad. I suggested that a monarchy might be too costly for Iceland, but Magnús said that need not be the case. Some royal people are so wealthy that they could to a large extent pay their own way, and even bring capital into the country. The nation would, of course, have to build a residence for the king and contribute some initial capital expenditure, but that would also be the case were the country to become a republic under a president. Magnús does not speak foreign languages and, therefore, needs assistance with his search. I said that I would think about it...

October 23, 1932. I have decided to assist Magnús with the monarchy issue. Not because of the railroad, as he came here this morning and bought shares in the railroad company without condition, but because I can see that becoming involved in this may open up opportunities for meeting foreign investors, as I now realize that I shall never acquire sufficient capital for the enterprise here in Iceland...

CHAPTER 44

While Halldór was at Birkihlíd opening the safe, Egill and Marteinn rented a car to make the long drive to Ólafsvík. They got a relatively new Land Rover, and the man at the rental office lent them a rope and an old shovel in case they hit heavy snow.

Setting off from town just after four o'clock, Egill drove as fast as he could, stopping for coffee, just under an hour later, at a café next to the oil storage tanks in Hvalfjördur.

Marteinn was worried. "How are we going to find this guy in Ólafsvík?" he asked.

"He'll no doubt be holed up in some fish-workers' accommodation somewhere," Egill said breezily.

"Shouldn't we tell someone that we're on our way?"

"That might be a good idea," Egill agreed, after some thought.

Egill used the café's phone to ring the police officer on duty in Ólafsvík. He told him about their business there and asked him to make inquiries about Sigurdur in the meantime.

By the time they resumed their journey, it was dark and icy, slowing their progress, and the Land Rover was certainly not built for speed. Driving past Mount Hafnarfjall and up Borgarfjördur, the lights of Borgarnes, on the other side of the fjord, appeared tantalizingly close.

"They're planning to build a bridge here, apparently," Marteinn said, gazing longingly across the fjord. It took them another half hour before they'd made their way around the inlet and were buying gasoline and hot dogs in Borgarnes.

At nine o'clock they reached Fródárheidi, but the snow was falling fast and had formed deep drifts in the road.

"Let's see how this thing drives," Egill said, accelerating up the first slope.

The vehicle sloshed its way up the snow-covered road, but the drifts quickly became too deep for them to negotiate. Egill tried reversing, but the wheels just spun futilely in the deep snow.

"Better grab that shovel," Egill grumbled to Marteinn. An hour later, they had progressed a mere twenty meters, when a pair of bright lights from a large road grader appeared in the drifting snow in front of them.

"Are you the cops from Reykjavik?" the driver asked, jumping out of his rig and trudging up to the passenger window of the Land Rover.

"Yes," Marteinn replied.

"I'm glad I found you. Officer Helgi reckoned you would get into trouble when the weather got worse, and asked me to come looking for you."

He turned the grader around, which had chains firmly attached to all four wheels, and hitched a thick rope to the Land Rover.

"Right boys, let's be off," he cried.

The powerful grader pulled the vehicle across the snowdrifts of the heath like a toboggan.

It was nearly eleven o'clock when they finally arrived at the police station in Ólafsvík, and were met at the door by a plump officer.

"Welcome you two, I'm Helgi," he said cheerfully, extending his hand.

"Have you found out anything about Sigurdur's whereabouts?" Egill asked by way of a greeting.

"Yeah, he's here."

"Here?"

"Yeah, I went to the fish-workers' hostel and told him to pack his stuff, that you were coming to pick him up. He came as soon as he was ready, and he's been waiting here since."

Egill didn't believe Helgi's story at first—surely he had the wrong man—but once inside the station, Egill saw him; the young man they had met in the Old Town was sitting by the officer's desk, ready to go.

"You'll stay the night given the situation," Helgi remarked. "According to the weather forecast, it'll improve toward morning. I'll make sure the grader opens up the road over the heath for you first thing."

Egill sat down in front of Sigurdur, pulled himself up straight, and in his most serious tone said, "You probably know what we want to talk to you about."

"Nope," Sigurdur replied casually.

"Then why have you been running away?"

"I haven't been running away."

"You ran away from us the night before last, at your apartment."

"I was supposed to play at a high school gig. They'd set up all the gear and sold lots of tickets, and I didn't have time to go with you to headquarters."

"Why did you come here, then?"

"I had another gig here last night, and then I was planning to do some work in the freezing plant for a few days, but it's great that you came."

"Oh?" Egill replied, surprised.

"Yeah, I've been asked to play with a band in the city next weekend. We have to practice beforehand, so it's great to get a lift back to town," he explained. "What was it you wanted?"

"We think you may have killed a man."

"You're joking!" he exclaimed, half-smiling.

"No, we have reason to believe this is the case."

"Right, then I won't talk any more to you unless I have an attorney present."

"It's quite safe for you to answer a few questions."

"No, I know your ways. I'm not answering any questions here."

"You've obviously got something to hide," Egill said, growing perturbed.

Sigurdur turned to Helgi. "Hey, mate, where can I sleep?"

"Here, in cell one," Helgi replied. "You two can share cell two," he told Egill and Marteinn.

"I was going to go to a hotel," Egill said.

"Then you'd have to take the prisoner with you," Helgi replied awkwardly. "My shift ends at midnight and the wife is expecting me home."

Egill frowned. He knew he didn't have another option. He'd be sleeping in a cell with Marteinn tonight.

"Okay, well, I'm off to bed," Sigurdur said rather cheerfully, given the circumstances, and made his way to the cell.

Diary XIV

December 12, 1933. This morning there was a meeting of the Monarchy Society. Magnús and I have decided to sail to the continent in the summer. We intend to make careful preparations in advance and correspond with a number of people. I have already written a few letters today. It is a beautiful day and I am feeling well. When I look up from writing, I see the birch trees through the window. They stand there modestly in their winter slumber, while in the summer, they dress in leafy robes and give the house a warm glow in honor of my dear father's memory...

January 20, 1934. City council elections. My wife and I voted for the Independence Party's list of candidates...

May 1, 1934. Saw the Nationalist Party supporters marching through the town. More than 100 of them were wearing uniforms. There were standard-bearers at the front, with one Icelandic flag and two banners with swastikas. The parade stopped in front of the Midbær Primary School, where speeches were delivered. A substantial body of people congregated there, many more than for the social democrats or the communists.

June 6, 1934. On board the Brúarfoss, *heading for London. This is my first trip abroad since I came home in 1920 after my long stint overseas. This goes to show to what extent the railroad has absorbed my whole attention.*

June 12, 1934. Elizabeth and the children went to Leicester today, where they will stay for the next few weeks while I complete my business. I shall stay on here in London with Magnús for a few days, then we are off to Germany...

June 15, 1934. As I suspected, I have had little success in my dealings with English investors. They are willing to advance loans, if the interest is high enough, but they also demand substantial guarantees, preferably state guarantees. I have not found anyone willing to either buy or trade in our shares...

June 18, 1934. On board the train to Berlin. There is a great shortage of foreign currency here in Germany and they do everything they can to encourage foreigners to visit the country. Foreigners even get a good discount on railroad tickets. I am thrilled to be traveling by train again after all these years. I have become a little bit weary of Magnús. He has never traveled before and is completely helpless. I have to look after him the whole time. But he is paying the full cost of our journey...

June 19, 1934. Matthías met us at the station. He is looking well, and I sense that he feels comfortable here and is happy. He escorted us to our hotel...

*June 20, 1934. Met Helmut Klee and his brother
Björn this morning. They gave me a warm welcome.
Helmut works for Deutsche Reichsbahn. He is going
to introduce me to industrialists specializing in
railway manufacturing. Björn Klee gave me some
postage stamps with pictures of steam engines. It
pleased me very much and I asked him whether
he could get me some more of them, in return for
Icelandic stamps...*

*June 21, 1934. I am finding Magnús very tiresome.
He seems to think that we can invite ourselves to
the mansions of the aristocracy here and advertise
publicly for a potential king. I try to make him see
that circumspection and a great deal of groundwork
is needed for our enquiries...*

*June 22, 1934. Matthías introduces us to Birgir
Valdal, who has lived here over the past few years
and works for the Ministry of Education. He is
prepared to assist us in our quest for a potential king
but says he needs a good deal of time...*

*June 23, 1934. Order and discipline are the rule
everywhere here in Berlin. The public are grateful
to the National Socialist Party for having dealt with
communism. The previous situation in the city was*

such that the violence and killings perpetrated by the communists were intolerable. Nearly every citizen had at least once experienced a life-threatening situation as a result of street fighting. This plague has now been eradicated. Though the National Socialists may have placed certain limits on the people's personal freedom, the idea that it is forbidden to express criticism of the regime is pure fabrication by foreigners. Ill-feeling abroad toward the National Socialists is often based on the fact that they are considered to be too demanding on party members, who must be prepared to make sacrifices to help fellow party members suffering hardship. They are required to eat simple rather than elaborate meals on Sundays, and to donate the difference in price to a fund for the unemployed. This policy of assistance is not mentioned in foreign papers. The fact is also suppressed that the German government wants by all means to avoid war, a policy that is consistent with German public opinion...

July 4, 1934. There has been unrest here in Germany of late, but today Hitler announced that the revolt has been stamped out... We are about to go home. Our visit here has laid solid foundations for our goals, but there remains plenty of work still to do...

CHAPTER 45

Halldór had slept badly. He spent much of the night think-ing about the case he had been tasked with solving. Until now, all the clues had led down blind alleys, and he was at a loss as to what to do next. He would certainly have a further talk with Matthías and ask for an explanation for this visit to Birkihlíd last Wednesday evening, but he doubted that it would bring him any closer to solving the case. He finally fell asleep early in the morning, but was plagued by bad dreams. He dreamed he was at Birkihlíd looking for some clue, he didn't know what, as water streamed down the chimney. He was madly bailing it out through the parlor window, which for some reason was broken, and he felt it was his fault. Morning finally came, and Halldór stumbled out of bed, washed his face, shaved, got dressed, and made his way down to the kitchen and his cup of tea. *Morgunbladid* slid through the letterbox a few minutes later, and he had only just begun reading an interest-ing article on police households when the phone rang. Stefanía leapt to her feet immediately.

"Perhaps it's the minister again," she said, hurrying to answer the phone.

"He's just a bank manager now," called Halldór.

"Hello," she warbled happily into the receiver. Her smile faded almost instantly.

"It's only a long-distance call," she said disappointedly. "It's for you."

Halldór took the receiver. "Hello...hello."

Erlendur's voice came through the receiver along with a bit of static. "Hi. How's it going?"

Halldór looked at his wife, whose ears were twitching. "There's not much progress."

"Right. Well, listen, I was in Salzburg yesterday. I sent the wife and kids on up into the mountains so I could have some peace and quiet here in the city."

"Okay."

"Yeah, I went to the police station and spoke with the officer in charge, a Mr. Kirschbaum. He was very friendly, and took me to the place where Matthías lives. We talked to some of his neighbors and various things emerged."

"Really?"

"Yes, apparently, it is common knowledge in the area that Matthías and his servant Klemenz are queers who live together as a couple."

"Really?"

"Yeah, they even seem to be members of a club for men like that, here in the city. Mr. Kirschbaum found their names on a secret list the police keep of clubs of this kind and their membership. You can never be too careful with guys like this."

"No, that's true."

"Well, that was all. Mr. Kirschbaum then drove me to Zell am See, and we drank beer and Jägermeister well into the night. He's ready to lend assistance if we need any further help in this matter."

"That's good news," said Halldór, looking at the clock. "You're up early."

"Yeah, Halli woke us at dawn. He's off skiing and I'm just getting dressed."

"Right, have fun."

"Thanks, good luck."

"Bye." Halldór put the receiver down.

Diary XIV

July 20, 1934. My brother Matthías is thirty today. I dare not mention this to my mother, as she never initiates conversations about him. I thought this would change when Father died but I can see no signs to indicate this. I am writing to Matthías secretly to thank him for all his help in Berlin. I am sending him a little book of poetry...

July 26, 1934. Morgunbladid *reports clashes in Austria...*

July 31, 1934. Completed the purchase of a new automobile today. It is a Ford...

August 3, 1934. Hindenburg, President of Germany, died yesterday. The office will be amalgamated with that of chancellor, and Hitler will, consequently, become the country's next president...

January 17, 1935. I have been unsure about whether I did the right thing when I decided on one meter gauge rather than standard gauge, as the wider gauge can carry heavier railcars with large snowplows. I have, however, just heard of a new type of rotary snowplow that digs itself through the snow, with big motorized blades throwing the snow to one side. I can have a railcar with a plow like that run before the train to clear the track. Then there is little danger of cancellations on account of the weather...

March 29, 1935. I have had quite a few projects to work on this summer. I cannot see myself being able to finish them all if I am to work on the railroad as well...

April 3, 1935. Had a letter from Berlin with many beautiful railroad stamps. Björn Klee has done a good job for me exchanging the Icelandic stamps I sent him last winter for stamps from various countries with pictures of steam engines...

June 7, 1935. I have had one reply to my advertisement in the engineer's magazine for an assistant engineer. A young man, recently graduated from Copenhagen, Thórdur Thórdarson, his family from the Gnúpverjahreppur district...

June 8, 1935. I have now realized that there will be no viable basis for operating the railroad if it only goes as far as the Thjórsá River. There are, on the other hand, enormous opportunities if we take the railroad onward, north to Akureyri. Then there would be a large junction station at Ölfusá River, below Mt. Ingólfsfjall. From there the track would go via Biskupstungur on to Kjalvegur and along the existing road route north to Akureyri. The new snowplow makes this very feasible. I assume that a densely populated area will form round the junction station...

June 21, 1935. Now that there are three of us working in the engineering studio, I need to think about accommodation. The office is not large enough for all of us. Having to approach it through the parlor is also a disadvantage. Thórdur suggested I should have an extension built on the north side of the house...

August 5, 1935. Kristján is back in town after his trip north. He says there is an excellent route for the railroad from the Kjalvegur Road along Blöndudalur Valley to the populated areas in the north. There would then be a junction station near the mouth of the valley, and perhaps a branch line going to

Blönduós. The main line would continue through the Vatnsskard pass over to Skagafjördur...

September 25, 1935. We moved the drafting table and the cabinet into the extension this morning. Everything fits in very well there. The studio is very light, and will probably be an excellent place to work. I gave a small reception to mark the occasion this afternoon...

October 12, 1935. Young Jacob is ten years old today. He is an obedient and polite little boy...

December 1, 1935. My mother was suddenly taken ill during the night with severe internal pains and vomiting. This continued well into the day, before subsiding so that she was able to sleep. It is Sunday and difficult to get hold of a doctor. Sveinborg is sitting with her...

December 2, 1935. The doctor gave my mother laudanum to alleviate the pain...

December 9, 1935. My mother died this evening. She was conscious for a while this morning and asked about Matthías. He has not been mentioned in the house since he went abroad. I saw that it made her happy when I told her that he was well and that I had met him last year...

CHAPTER 46

Hrefna slept longer than she had intended, but was nevertheless lucky: when she got to the students' residence, Elísabet was still asleep in her room.

"There are some things that have emerged in the investigation of your uncle's murder that we need to find a credible explanation for. I think you may be able to help me," Hrefna explained once inside Elísabet's room.

"What do you mean?" Elísabet asked, lighting a cigarette.

"I have been tipped off that you have more than a casual relationship with Sigurdur Sigurdsson, the son of Sigurdur Jónsson."

Elísabet looked defiantly at Hrefna. "Yeah, Diddi and I are good friends."

"Why didn't you tell me when we spoke before?"

"It would probably have shocked Mom. She doesn't even know I'm going out with a guy, let alone this guy. But I can't see that it has anything to do with your investigation."

"We have firm proof that Sigurdur was in Birkihlíd on the evening Jacob was murdered."

"What proof?"

"I'm not discussing that with you."

Elísabet inhaled the smoke deeply and then blew it out forcefully. "If I tell you that the reason for his being there was completely normal and had nothing to do with the murder, would that be enough?"

"No," Hrefna replied, shaking her head.

Elísabet was quiet for a few moments.

"Okay. I'll try and explain this a bit better. When I was younger and my mom and I came for a visit to Birkihlíd, I sometimes used to read Grandpa Jacob's diaries. He died a long time before I was born, of course, but I felt I got to know him through those books. It always seemed so sad to me how he dedicated his life to that railroad, but never saw his dreams come true. He was so talented that he should have been able to make his mark in any field in the community, but instead he ends up in this blind alley. Do you know what I mean?"

"Yeah, I have also read the diaries."

"Well. I've been dabbling in writing poetry since starting college, and Diddi has written music to a few of them. He plays the guitar, you see."

"Yeah, I know."

"I wanted to write a poem that described Grandpa's destiny. It's almost ready and I asked Diddi for a song. I had to try and describe Grandpa to him, naturally, and Birkihlíd was the best place to do that. I also wanted to show him the diaries. I knew what time Sveinborg goes shopping on Wednesdays, and we were waiting outside when she went. I had my key from when I was supposed to be living there."

"So you both went in?"

"Yes, for a little while. We just went through the main rooms, and Diddi sat down at the piano and played a few chords. And then I just felt a bit weird, and we went back outside. That was all."

"Where can I find Sigurdur and get him to confirm this?"

"I don't know. He was going somewhere out into the country to play a gig, Ólafsvík, I think. Then he was planning to work in the freezing plant for a few days if there was any work available. I haven't heard anything from him since the day before yesterday."

Hrefna decided her story was implausible enough to be true. "Let me hear the poem," she said.

Elísabet bit her lip. "Okay," she replied, and then recited it confidently.

> "Awake I lie, and wintry visions
> within life's path to me appear;
> as bitter winds they blow, to weaken
> the boldness of your yesteryear.

> "You left in silence; lost forever
> in Lethe's depths your thoughts now lie.
> Bold your venture, but too heavy
> a burden: did your spirit die?

> "There are no tracks that onward gleam,
> there are no tracks to carry me
> out from dark, into the dream,
> there are no tracks that man can see.

> "There are no tracks on empty roads,
> there are no tracks—and ever more
> swift the train runs, speeding goes,
> and sweeps o'er all that lies before.

> "You nursed a hope, though no man saw
> unknown the checks that hindered you.
> Striving, dreaming, strong-willed, more,
> yet still the aim was never true."

Elísabet fell silent, awaiting Hrefna's reaction.

"I believe you," Hrefna finally said.

Elísabet sighed in relief.

"Tell me about your visits to Birkihlíd when you were a child," Hrefna asked.

"What do you mean?"

"Just anything you can remember."

Elísabet thought for a moment and then said, "At Christmas we either came south to Reykjavik or Granny and Uncle Jacob came north to us. That's how it always was until Granny died. Mom and I also visited Granny every summer for a couple of weeks or so."

"Tell me about your grandmother," Hrefna asked.

"Granny was an amazing lady. She always spoke English to us, but she understood Icelandic perfectly. Mom speaks English like a native and she often spoke it to me when I was little, so I could also understand Granny. We got on very well, even though she was very determined and wanted to control everybody."

"How was life at your grandmother's?"

"Everything was very fixed. Mealtimes, for instance, were exactly on time because Granny was a stickler for routine. She always went for a walk at the same time, and always walked the same route. Then she had a nap in the early afternoon."

"What about Jacob Junior?"

"The strange thing is I don't remember him very well. He worked in the bank and then spent evenings in his study. He had no idea how to deal with children, and I think he avoided me when I came to visit."

"Would you say he was normal?" Hrefna asked.

"What's normal? Uncle Jacob was an intelligent and well-educated man. He didn't have much in common with most people, but he was the victim of extraordinary circumstances, given the violent death of his father."

"Have you any idea why he was killed?"

"No, I don't. It actually seems completely absurd to me...and tragic. Not because I mourn him so much, but that anyone could have been driven to kill such a man."

"What were his relations with the rest of the family like?"

"Very good while Granny was alive. We all knew that he sacrificed himself for her, but after she died his eccentricity became unbearable."

"Tell me more about your grandmother. Did you feel happy in her company when you were a child?" Hrefna asked.

"Yes, I was always happy with her. Many of my first memories are from Birkihlíd."

"Tell me about them."

"They're just childhood memories," she replied. "There's one that I've always been very fond of. In Granny's little bookcase, there were a few English women's magazines that I looked through over and over again. Granny was sitting on a chair and I lay on the floor, leafing through them. I remember they all featured various cartoon strips, but because there were only single copies of this or that magazine, I had to imagine the stories before and after the installment that I had. I told Granny this, and she helped me improvise the stories. I remember one of the cartoons very well. It was about a boy and a girl who were lost in a dark enchanted forest. Suddenly, in the last picture, there was a white horse with a big horn sticking out of its forehead. In my version, the horse took the boy and the girl on his back and fought all the evil things in the forest with his horn. Then he brought them back home to their granny and grandpa. I sometimes dreamed of the white horse with the horn, and they were good dreams. If I was unhappy, all I needed was to think about the white horse with the horn...the white unicorn."

"Were you aware that your grandmother wanted to keep the home unchanged, as it had been when your grandfather was alive?" Hrefna asked.

"That's simply how it was. She didn't particularly try to, she was just happy in the house as it was and there was no need to change anything. It wasn't a compulsion like it became with Uncle Jacob later."

"Did she keep in contact with her relatives in England?"

"Yes, she did, all her life. She visited them almost every year until the final years, when she had to be careful with her money."

"Did your grandmother talk about Jacob Senior...your grandfather?"

"Yes, she often told me stories of what they did together, especially their travels. As I got older, she showed me the diaries, and I really enjoyed reading them."

"Did you read all the diaries?"

"No, not the books after 1932. They were not with the others."

"Did you ask your grandmother about them?"

"Yes, but she wouldn't show them to me."

"Do you know why that was?"

"She said that I wouldn't understand some of the things in them. I just accepted that and didn't ask anymore. I never doubted anything Granny told me. She always knew best."

"What can you tell me about your uncle Matthías?"

"About Matthías? What do you mean?"

"What was the relationship between him and the family like?"

"There was no relationship, apart from a letter at Christmas. But Grandpa Jacob often mentioned him in the diaries and seems to have really appreciated him."

"Have you met him recently?"

"No, I haven't tried to get to know him. Most of my interests lie outside the family. But I was pleased that he stood up to Uncle Jacob. Mom was getting really fed up with this compulsion of his."

"Do you know Klemenz, his manservant?"

"No. I find all that rather unpleasant. One person waiting on another for years on end doesn't fit my worldview. I'm quite a bit more radical than this family of mine."

"You said that you had begun to feel a bit weird in Birkihlíd when you went in there with Sigurdur. In what way?"

"I don't know. It's never happened before; maybe it was some kind of premonition."

Diary XV

January 14, 1936. 11 degrees of frost. Walked on the ice across Skerjafjördur from Skildinganes over to Álftanes and back. The ice is thick enough to walk on everywhere…

February 4, 1936. A letter from Helmut Klee. He has arranged for two railroad engineers to visit me this summer to examine the route and go over my plans. I shall write to him and ask him to keep this scheme quiet. This will be a sensitive issue on account of the political situation. The best way to deal with it is for the men to pretend to be geologists who are here to study Icelandic minerals…

February 10, 1936. A secret meeting of the Monarchy Society. All four were present…

*March 6, 1936. Plans are afoot for a new motor
road between Reykjavik and the southern lowlands.
The route lies through the Reykjanesskagi uplands,
Krísuvík, and Selvogur, about 115 km in total. The
only positive thing about these plans is that they are
so stupid that they may enable me to boost interest
in the railroad, should they come to fruition. Nobody
is going to travel all this way in a motor if a 60-km
railroad journey is available instead...*

June 26, 1936. Today Morgunbladid *published an
interview with a famous Danish editor who has
been staying here recently in connection with the
Royal State visit. He says: "I am convinced that it
will never be possible to achieve real progress in
developing these regions without building a railroad
from Reykjavik to the east so that this country's main
agricultural areas may enjoy truly low cost and
secure transport of freight. It is a fallacy that motor
roads can replace railroads. In order for farmers in
the southern lowlands to be competitive with their
products in foreign markets, they must have as
secure and cheap transport as, for instance, Danish
farmers have." Our perceptive visitor continues
in this vein at some length. I cut the article out
and keep it with the other material. I am going to*

translate it into German and send it abroad. It is
clear that it will be left to foreigners to make my
fellow countrymen see sense in this matter...

July 10, 1936. The Germans came with the Brúarfoss
this morning. I asked Kristján to meet them, and they
will be staying at Hotel Ísland. One of them speaks
excellent Danish; his family comes from Flensborg...

July 12, 1936. The German visitors were here with
me today going through drawings and calculations.
They are astute men and quick to understand
figures. They dined with us...

July 13, 1936. We set off early, heading east. We are
somewhat cramped in the motor as we are carrying
a considerable amount of baggage. At Kolvidarhóll,
Kristján and the Germans got out to journey on foot,
while I continue by motor and will meet up with
them further east. Kristján will show them the route
for the railroad...We took accommodation at Lake
Laugarvatn...

July 14, 1936. After a hard day, we have arrived at
Lake Hvítárvatn. Here our ways part. Kristján will
guide the visitors on foot through Kjölur. I will motor
back to meet them in the north. I dread traveling this
route on my own. It is a poor road...

CHAPTER 47

When the team met after lunch, everyone was exhausted apart from Jóhann. He had finished early the previous evening, gone to the cinema, and turned in at a reasonable hour.

Hrefna had read the diaries well into the night, and then gone to see Elísabet that morning already. Halldór did not offer any explanation for his exhaustion, but a poor night of sleep was evident by the dark circles that seemed to stretch from under his eyes down to his cheeks. And Egill and Marteinn had left Ólafsvík at seven that morning, having spent an uncomfortable night in a police cell. They had then driven to Reykjavik without stopping and taken Sigurdur Sigurdsson, who refused to utter a word, straight to the jail at Sídumúli.

After they all reported their findings, Jóhann confirmed that the parcel of documents in the safe at Birkihlíd was the one Thórdur had recently delivered to Jacob Junior.

"There is one very interesting thing about these documents," Jóhann added. "Alfred Kieler's will names his son Jacob as the sole heir. In other words, Jacob Senior inherited the house and contents, and all other property. Matthías is not even mentioned in the document."

"And yet Matthías claims to own half of Birkihlíd," Halldór remarked. "I'll have to talk some more with him today."

"Could it be they were going by a later will?" Hrefna suggested.

"Hardly," Jóhann replied. "This one was dated 1929, just a year before Alfred died."

"What about the ammunition in the safe? Have you examined that?" Halldór asked.

"Yes," Jóhann replied. "There were, in all, twenty-odd different types of ammunition for various firearms, amongst them one packet of rounds for a 38/200 Smith and Wesson."

"That's interesting," Halldór said.

Jóhann continued, "It doesn't really tell us much, because there were many types of cartridge that don't fit the firearms found in the house."

After Egill finished describing their arduous trip to Ólafsvík, Hrefna snapped, "This journey of yours was totally unnecessary. You could have sorted this matter with one phone call."

Egill bridled. "The only fingerprints from the scene of the murder belong to this guy and you would have phoned him up!" he replied angrily.

"I have been given a completely satisfactory explanation for those fingerprints," Hrefna said smugly.

Halldór turned to her. "You go and talk to the guy," he said. "Maybe you'll get something out of him. Jóhann will go with you and take a new set of prints."

Hrefna drove in silence to Sídumúli, and when the jailer admitted them, she asked if the prisoner was asleep. He told her he doubted that, as Egill had ordered he be kept handcuffed.

"Bring him out here at once," she said, clearly angered at Egill's overzealousness.

The young man whom the jailer led out into the corridor looked tired. His hands were cuffed behind his back, and he shook as Hrefna removed the manacles. Jóhann examined the prisoner's wrists, which were badly bruised, asking, "Did they keep you cuffed in the car all the way from Ólafsvík?"

The prisoner looked at them with disdain, and then nodded.

"We'll start by taking him to the ER to have this looked at," Jóhann told Hrefna. "He can get an injury release there. We don't need to bring him back here."

Out in the parking lot, the prisoner looked around, sizing up the surroundings.

"You can run if you like," Jóhann said. "But you'll do better coming with us."

Sigurdur looked Jóhann in the eye for a moment, then relaxed and climbed into the backseat of their car.

"Are you going to take a new set of prints?" Hrefna asked Jóhann on the way to the hospital.

"No. I didn't even bring the kit."

Diary XV

October 2, 1936. I have been making tentative approaches to the government as to what its reactions would be to the railroad company's initiative. I was not at all happy with the response. I feel that their policy is to strengthen the power of the state in every way, at the cost of individual freedom of enterprise. It is going to be difficult to obtain foreign exchange licenses for purchases of railroad supplies...

December 9, 1936. Thórdur and I discussed the railroad today. He is rather pessimistic about the idea, but is objective. He is careful by nature so this is understandable. Despite his tendency to discourage, he nevertheless proposes workable solutions. Kristján supports me wholeheartedly...

February 15, 1937. It distresses me how some Icelandic newspapers deprecate the regime in Germany under the swastika, often out of ignorance. Left-wing propaganda depicts the situation there as simply vile and cruel. The English present a different view. I have been reading the English newspapers that were sent to Elizabeth, and these generally report the Germans in a positive light, even considering them a model nation. The English do not consider it shameful to do justice to their political opponents. The number of people who believe in the one-sided fanatical writings of the communists is dwindling, of course. The Germans have been friendly to us Icelanders for a long time, devoting themselves to Icelandic studies and writing numerous books about the country and its nation. "Diverse our passions..."

March 20, 1937. The German Consul-General summoned me for a meeting today. Enquiries have come through from Germany about me and my company. The Consul is a pleasant and polite official. I told him of my plans and answered his questions. He said he would try to be of assistance to me...

April 14, 1937. I have now drawn up a schedule for the best procedure to carry forward the railroad business. The first section of track will be very short, only going from the harbor to Öskjuhlíd. We will also begin construction of the main railroad station. When this is ready, a locomotive and freight wagons will be shipped to Iceland. We shall be able to utilize these wagons later, for further construction works on the railroad. To begin with, the largest gravel quarry will be at Öskjuhlíd; then we shall head bit by bit east, pressing on until we reach Akureyri. I shall go north this summer to do some surveying.

May 6, 1937. Have just had a meeting with the consul. He has put together an extremely clever proposal for how the German industrialists can participate in our railroad business. A limited company called Isländische Bahn AG will be established in Germany. It will own the trains and lease them out to the Iceland Railroad Company. This way the Germans can invest funds in the project

*without incurring outlay of foreign currency. In
return, the railroad company will purchase steel
for the tracks from Germany. We both feel that
this arrangement could be very practical for both
parties...*

*June 24, 1937. Today we were surveying the
Vatnsskard Pass. Kristján knows this area very
well, and is of great assistance to me. The road from
Bólstadarhlíd in Svartárdalur no longer snakes
round in countless corners and bends, as it did the
last time I traveled here. The new motor road follows
the slopes mostly straight, after a turn by the river.
It seems to me that the railroad should go somewhat
below the road in a lengthy cutting to limit the
gradient. There is a wonderful view from the bridge,
into Svartárdalur Valley with mountains on all
sides...*

*June 25, 1937. There will be an important railroad
station at Varmahlíd. The inhabitants here welcome
me with open arms. Chatting with a farmer, I
reminisced about my trip round this region in the
year of my high school graduation, and I asked
him about the ferryman at the western lagoon who
gave me the brennivín. The farmer told me he was
known as Jón Ferryman and that he had drowned*

in the estuary in 1914. Probably drowned himself deliberately...

June 26, 1937. Carried on into Blönduhlíd. There will be no problems with the railroad here provided it is a suitable distance from the river...

August 5, 1937. Have decided to postpone my trip abroad until next summer...

CHAPTER 48

"What is this supposed to mean, dragging me out of the house like a common criminal?" Matthías snarled at Halldór when Egill brought him into the office.

"I think, sir, that you haven't been completely honest with us," Halldór replied calmly.

"In what respect?"

"We have a witness who states that you were at Birkihlíd on the evening Jacob Junior was murdered."

"I have not concealed that fact. I do not recall having been asked where I was that evening or whether I had visited Birkihlíd. If you had asked or if I had thought that was of importance to you, I would of course have mentioned it."

Halldór bit his lip; Matthías had a point. He had probably not been directly asked about his whereabouts that evening.

"What was your business with Jacob?" he asked, moving on.

"You could say it was just an ordinary courtesy call."

"Did you notice anything unusual that evening?"

"No."

"How long did you stay at Birkihlíd?"

"I arrived there at about ten o'clock and left for home about an hour later. Klemenz will confirm that I arrived home shortly after eleven."

"We'll check that later," Halldór promised. "Now to your father's will; according to it, your brother Jacob inherited the entire estate. You are not mentioned in it at all, sir. Why would that be?"

"My father was not happy that I went abroad to study music, as he did not feel it was a suitable study. When I refused to comply with his wishes in this matter, he disinherited me."

"So then how did you come to own half of Birkihlíd?"

"I see. You think that there is something strange about that. Well, it's quite simple. My brother ceded half the property to me after our father's death. The title deed was notarized accordingly."

Halldór looked at Egill. "Get hold of someone at the city magistrate's office and find out if that document exists," he said. Then, as Egill made his departure, he turned his attention back to Matthías. "Why did Jacob Senior assign half the property to you?"

"There were personal reasons. You could say that he was not happy about our father's behavior and wanted to make it up to me."

Halldór regarded Matthías silently for a long time, and then said, "Do you really expect me to believe this?"

"Yes. It is the truth, my good man."

Halldór shook his head and glanced at his notebook, where he had listed in advance a number of issues he wanted to address with Matthías. "You arrived in the country on July 9, 1945. Six days later your brother was murdered. On your arrival, he stopped keeping the diary that he had written every day since he was twenty years old. Can you explain this?"

309

"No. Naturally, my brother's death was as traumatic for me as for the rest of the family. The fact that I had only just arrived in the country was a coincidence."

"So you leave the country and don't visit again for nearly thirty years. And then on this second visit, your nephew is murdered with the same gun."

"If you are insinuating that I had anything to do with this, you are barking up the wrong tree."

"So tell me the truth about what you were doing in Birkihlíd on the evening Jacob Junior was shot."

"The truth? Oh, well. I do not mind telling you exactly what passed between us. Jacob Junior phoned me that evening and asked me to come by. He said it was about the sale of the house. I did as he asked. He had apparently come into possession of a parcel of documents that contained, among other things, my father's will. He, like you, had come to the conclusion that it threw some doubt on my ownership of half the house. I told him what I told you, that his father had ceded this half of the property to me."

"How did he react?"

"He was disappointed, of course. He had assumed that it had meant he could acquire possession at less cost to himself."

"What happened after that?"

"I reminded him that the next payment for the house was due, and went home."

Satisfied for the moment with his reply, Halldór turned to the next item on his list. "We have learned from Salzburg that everything is not all it seems in your relationship with Klemenz, your manservant. Do you have anything to say about that?"

"Our relationship is our private affair and does not concern you in any way."

"So you admit there is more to it than an ordinary relationship between master and servant?"

"I don't have to admit anything of the kind," he replied coldly. "These are inappropriate questions."

"I am simply showing that there is more than meets the eye as far as you are concerned, sir," Halldór said.

At that moment, Egill reentered the room, and Halldór paused, awaiting the detective's report.

"There was an official at the city magistrates when I called them who was able to look into this," said Egill. "The document exists, notarized and dated July 12, 1945."

"Right," said Halldór, turning back to Matthías. "That's three days after your return to Iceland and three days before Jacob was murdered. Certainly convenient for you."

"There is no connection between the reassignment and my brother's death. I can assure you of that." Matthías's face reddened and his breathing quickened.

Halldór pressed on. "In your brother's diaries there is an entry to the effect that you had been involved in some sort of disreputable activity in 1928, and that you had left the country as a consequence. What can you tell me about that?"

"Sir," Matthías said. "It is now 1973, forty-five years have passed since that time. What in heaven's name is the purpose of stirring all this up?"

"I am simply demonstrating that you cannot be trusted."

"This is inappropriate talk," Matthías declared.

Halldór ignored his protests and continued. "You told my associate that it was not true that you and your brother were involved in the so-called royal affair. We have, however, found unequivocal confirmation of this involvement in your brother's diaries."

311

Matthías was quiet for a while, and then said, "So now you know. So what? Will I be charged with treason? Hardly. The only thing that can come out of this is cheap tittle-tattle that will make money for unscrupulous gossip writers, who will distort the story and misrepresent it, and a family name that would otherwise soon disappear from history will become synonymous with some fantasy of treason and dark deeds. High ideals and the struggle to bring them to reality would be made to appear absurd and ridiculous. I think it is in our nation's interest to keep this quiet. Mark my words, mister policeman!"

Halldór sighed and then looked down at his list. There was nothing left to address, so he stood up and beckoned Egill to accompany him outside.

"What do you think?" he asked when they were out in the corridor.

"We'll have to do a search of his home. Maybe we'll find the gun," Egill replied.

"Yes, possibly."

"Let's lock him up in Sídumúli in the meantime so he can think things over. We'll talk to him again this evening and see what he's got to say then," Egill suggested.

"Do you think that's necessary?"

"It's bound to work. Guys like him start to talk when they see the inside of a jail."

Halldór mulled this over. He was very disappointed in Matthías; he had begun to like the man, and now he turns out to be nothing but a liar and a homosexual. It was impossible to distinguish truth from falsehood in his testimony. Egill was right: they had to search for the weapon in Matthías's home, and it wouldn't hurt to demonstrate the seriousness of their intentions.

"All right then, but treat him gently," Halldór warned and then added, "Take Marteinn along with you."

Diary XVI

July 14, 1938. Matthías met us on the quay here in Hamburg, and we proceeded directly to the railroad station. We are waiting to set off for Berlin...

July 15, 1938. Arrived in Berlin (Anhalter Bahnhof), early this morning. Went to the hotel and then to a meeting with Birgir Valdal. He invited us to supper in a restaurant called Die Grüne Traube on Kurfürstendamm. Birgir has arranged interviews with three aristocrats of this country, men he feels are suitable candidates for kingship...

July 16, 1938. Everything is in place regarding the setting up of Isländische Bahn AG. Helmut Klee arranged for an attorney to finalize the documents, and they are now ready for signing. Matthías, as a resident of this country, will sit on the board on my behalf. He had been planning to move to America, but I have prevailed upon him to put those plans on hold and he has agreed...

July 20, 1938. Living conditions here in Germany seem, at first glance, to have improved a great deal since the last time I was here. Mortality rates

among children and adolescents have fallen within
a short period, and are now lower than in England.
Tuberculosis and other diseases are much less
prevalent. Judges have never had so little work, and
there have never been so few prisoners in jails. It is
a pleasure seeing young people looking so sturdy and
healthy. The poor are now better dressed than ever
before and their faces reflect an attitude change...

July 21, 1938. Birgir Valdal took us to see Herr
von Kuppel. He is a high-ranking official in the
Department of the Interior and was very agreeable,
a tall and handsome man. His wife is of an Austrian
noble family and they have three children, two sons
and one daughter. He knew of our business and
received us warmly. He is prepared to go to Iceland
and introduce himself. This could happen as soon as
next summer. He invited us to a Youth League rally
tomorrow...

July 22, 1938. Herr von Kuppel escorted us to VIP
seats in the stadium. This worker youth movement
sprang up of its own accord among students, and
met with the approval of the government, which
has supported and developed it. Students must have
participated in the League's work for six months in
order to qualify for possible employment in official

posts, though in other respects such participation is largely voluntary. The rally began with a march that was drilled to a standard that fully trained soldiers would have been proud of. The bands played with great skill, with one person directing all exercises and displays. The climax of this pageantry came when the various groups flocked into the arena and arranged themselves into a series of military-style columns. Instead of weapons, they carried shovels, whose blades glinted in the sunshine as these regiments of youth paraded by. Now began a strange memorial ceremony, so simple and solemn, genuine and serious, that it mostly resembled a religious service, in the best sense of the word. Trumpets sounded and the audience stood up while hundreds of flags saluted. Then came a kind of litany and dialogue. First one person spoke, and sometimes the platoon leaders replied, at other times the whole group of workers. The main content of the speeches and songs was to encourage work and concerted effort for the fatherland, the brotherhood of all classes, magnanimity in everything, and complete trust in the Führer. It occurred to me that such a movement in Iceland would be able to tackle the building of the railroad, something that is undeniably in the interest of the whole nation...

*July 25, 1938. Met with the Mannheim Stahlwerke
representative in the Department of Commerce.
The German consul in Iceland has done a good job.
Everyone here involved in the business is completely
familiar with it. The Department of Commerce
has negotiated a loan for Isländische Bahn AG.
The mechanical engineer presented a design for the
locomotive. It is the latest type of dual-mode electro-
diesel, powered by diesel oil or electricity...*

*July 26, 1938. I have had doubts about the Hitler
regime's decision to ban other political parties, and
political discussion in the newspapers. People seem,
however, not to miss it. I have asked people whether
they do not find it dull that all the newspapers are
of one opinion. One man replied that I had clearly
not had to put up with over forty political parties
fighting to get people to buy and read their papers,
with each one of those papers claiming to report and
defend the one and only true point of view. Some
papers carried scandals and slanders about people
and businesses, for days on end, year in year out, all
more or less lies. The German nation, having had to
tolerate this, is now grateful for peace. Now people
can sit down with a newspaper without a feeling
of sinking deep into mud and mire. The difference*

*between the press before 1933 and that of today is
principally that previously the papers had license
to dehumanize and stultify their readers. Now that
license has been taken away...*

*July 30, 1938. I feel certain that the German
authorities seek peace. There are, however, some
German leaders who prefer to gain a little by conflict
rather than much by negotiation, but these men
can be stopped if other countries demonstrate some
resolve. The younger generation in Germany is
fired up by military enthusiasm, and this produces
anxiety elsewhere in the world, but it is preposterous
to presume that these young men are longing to kill
or be killed. They may kill or be killed, however, if
other nations do not conduct themselves sensibly, but
that is another story. Of course it is necessary for this
nation to arm itself now, with the ever-increasing
communist threat in the east. I am convinced that
should Stalin present a danger to Germany, the
British and the French will come to their assistance.
The proliferation of communism must be stopped
with all available means...*

CHAPTER 49

At the hospital, Hrefna, Jóhann, and Sigurdur were waiting silently to see a doctor—each lost in their own thoughts. Finally Hrefna looked up at Sigurdur and asked, "Are you tired?"

Sigurdur shot her cagey look before admitting he was.

"Elísabet told us that you had gone to Birkihlíd last Wednesday," she continued. "All you have to do is to tell us a story that matches hers. Then the two of you are in the clear."

"First I want to speak to Ella," he said soberly.

"That doesn't work. We need identical testimony without you having compared stories. Otherwise it's no good."

"How do I know that you're not bluffing?"

"Ella's story is very innocent. Confirming it shouldn't harm you in any way."

Sigurdur thought about what she had said. "Oh, well, okay. Ella had written this text and she wanted me to write a song to it. She was trying to explain what sort of geezer this granddad of hers had been. She thought I'd understand her better if we were to go to the house and have a look around. She didn't want this uncle of hers to know about it, so we went in when the old housemaid went out shopping. But then Ella began to feel a bit weird, so we hurried back out, really more or less straightaway."

318

"Do you remember touching anything in there?"

"I was just looking at things in the parlor, some stamps in a frame, and then I opened the piano and played a few chords to hear what it sounded like. It was the only thing that interested me in there."

"The poem Ella wrote, do you know it off by heart?"

Sigurdur smiled wanly. "Well, at least the first verse. I finished writing the song while I was over in Ólafsvík."

"Let's hear it."

Sigurdur pondered the request for a beat. He seemed to be singing the song in his head, but then he recited the first verse out loud.

"Awake I lie, and wintry visions
within life's path to me appear;
as bitter winds they blow, to weaken
the boldness of your yesteryear."

Although Hrefna had only heard the verse once, she knew it well enough to recognize that he had recited it correctly. "Why did you bolt when they came to pick you up for questioning last Thursday evening?"

"It's probably in the blood."

"Have you got something on your conscience?"

"No, my conscience is clear, but my experience with the police is lousy."

"How come?"

"How come! Lots of reasons. When I was growing up in the west part of town, on Brekkustígur, my family was virtually starving. My two elder brothers occasionally nicked stuff from vegetable gardens or fish sheds for us to have something to eat.

Sometimes they were spotted—they weren't exactly master criminals at twelve and thirteen. This meant that the whole lot of us
was branded as thieves, so that whenever as much as a bucket of
shit disappeared from a piss house in the west of town, the cops
came looking to us. When I was ten, my teacher gave me his old
guitar. The next time the cops came they took the guitar from me,
figuring it must have been stolen. My teacher had to go down to
the station himself to get it back for me."

Hrefna asked no more questions, and they sat in silence until
the doctor was ready to see them. He took a look at Sigurdur's hands
and decided to send him for an X-ray. Hrefna and Jóhann returned
to the waiting room. "What do we do now?" Hrefna asked.

"Go home and have a rest," Jóhann replied. "Apparently it's
Sunday today. I'll wait for the guy and drive him home. You can
take a taxi."

"Okay, I'll go home but not to a rest; I've got to keep reading
old Jacob's diaries."

Diary XVI

*September 19, 1938. I have been collecting new
foreign material about railroads in order to write an
article for* Morgunbladid. *There are a few aspects
that I intend to focus on: trains' superiority lies in
the fact that they can carry heavier loads and go
faster than automobiles; those automobiles that can
go faster than trains do so purely for the purpose of
sport, and have no practical value; the best modern
passenger motor cars only match the speed of trains*

provided that all conditions are perfect and the road is hard and as smooth as an egg...

October 2, 1938. Went to church this morning. The pastor prayed for peace in Europe. It has to be said, though, that the outlook is much improved after the Munich Agreement. Rarely has the world seen the outlook take a more rapid turn for the better. There seemed to be no room for negotiations when, suddenly, everything cleared. We have the leaders of the major nations to thank for this successful outcome, and there is no doubt that they were influenced by a public that is completely set against war...

January 10, 1939. I have had informal talks with members of the government about a foreign exchange license for railroad materials. It has been an uphill struggle, but I have made some progress. The ministers know that I am not a member of their party, which dampens their willingness to help, even if they see this as a useful project that will benefit the nation. The city mayor has agreed that I should renew the railway track from the harbor to Öskjuhlíd. It will have to be widened by ten centimeters...

February 21, 1939. I obtained a foreign exchange transfer to purchase cross ties from Norway. To simplify things, I am referring to this as timber for building. A large part of the capital stock will be used for this purchase, and I will have to rely on loans to buy the steel. I am going to test the waters in Copenhagen, as the District Heating Company did...

March 1, 1939. Today a new commercial agreement between Iceland and Germany comes into effect. It is a good deal more advantageous than in previous years. Our export to Germany of a variety of producer goods is being increased, and the frozen fish quota has been scaled up. I have no doubt that this will facilitate my plans for purchasing rails...

March 26, 1939. My struggle continues to be arduous, this time as a result of the German airline Lufthansa's request to operate a weekly service to Iceland. The government immediately announced that, given the current volatile political situation, they would not grant such a license. I have been asked if the railroad operation will be subject to the same limitations, but I naturally reply that the Iceland Railroad Company is a purely Icelandic company, in no way linked to Germany. The company's dealings with German businesses are completely normal in all respects. The communists have stirred up a great fuss about the influence and rapacity of Germans here in Iceland, and have fantasized about Nazi sympathy among Icelanders.

April 18, 1939. A new government, an all-party national coalition, came into power today. The hope is that import restrictions will be lifted and foreign exchange regulations revised. I listened to the ministers' statements, but otherwise the public gallery was half-empty...

April 25, 1939. I have still not received the import license for the steel for rails. In the meantime, I am postponing the shipping of the cross ties. There is no point in spending money on that part of it unless all the material can be brought into the country...

May 20, 1939. Visited the new German Consul-General, who arrived in Iceland earlier this month. He is very familiar with my work on the railroad and wished me well. He assured me that people's fear of confrontation because of the Danzig dispute was unnecessary...

June 20, 1939. The photograph Matthías took of our train in Hamburg arrived in the post this morning. I showed it to Thórdur and Kristján but then locked it away. Now is not the right moment to talk about this...

July 25, 1939. Whenever two people meet here in town, they talk about the omens of war. I still do not believe that it will come to that, despite all the threats. The leaders of the major nations will think twice before inflicting such horror on their peoples again. I dare not even think about the effect war would have on our work on the railroad...

September 1, 1939. Morgunbladid *today publishes Hitler's "sixteen points" regarding Danzig. The first one is that the city should be handed back to the Germans immediately and unconditionally. There are also reports that Polish soldiers have crossed the German border in Silesia and captured a radio station. I told Elizabeth that there would be war...*

September 3, 1939. News came in the early afternoon that Britain and France have declared war on Germany...

September 20, 1939. I am following the news about the confrontation in Poland. This will end in disaster. Elizabeth is very listless and fears for our future. I tell her not to worry; I shall make sure she never wants for anything...

September 26, 1939. At the shareholder meeting this morning, it was decided to put the rail enterprise on hold until after the war. All prices have rocketed, and business dealings are subject to all manner of conditions. Shipping is also treacherous. Hopefully this will only last a few months...

CHAPTER 50

Halldór had at last managed to get a search warrant from the criminal court for Matthías's home, but he needed someone to go with him. Unfortunately, everybody seemed to be busy.

The phone rang. It was Egill.

"Now we're in deep shit," he said, sounding unhinged, which was unusual for him.

"Oh?"

"Marteinn and I took the guy to Sídumúli as agreed, and that went pretty well; he seemed calm and under control on the way there. But when we were about to stick him in a cell, he freaked out and lost it completely. He screamed and howled."

"I hope you decided not to lock him up," Halldór said anxiously.

"Not lock him up?" Egill repeated. "No, was that what we should have done?"

"He could have waited here while we searched the apartment," Halldór said, exasperated.

"I didn't think of that," Egill said quietly.

"Right, so what happened then?"

"Well, it took three of us to get him into the cell and lay him down. We cuffed him before we went out and the duty officer phoned the doctor because he was shivering and shaking all over."

"What did the doctor say?" Halldór asked, uneasily.

"The doctor never came, because when we looked in on him a bit later he had puked and was unconscious, so we immediately called an ambulance. I'm at the hospital now."

"How is he doing?" Halldór asked.

"That's the deep-shit part. He's dead," Egill said.

"What! Are you telling me that the prisoner is dead?"

"Yeah, the doctor thinks he probably had a stroke."

"My god. What have you done?" Halldór groaned.

"I haven't done anything," Egill exclaimed. "It was just bloody unlucky, but we can fix this. We just quickly search his home, find the gun, and prove that the bugger shot both father and son. Then nobody can blame us."

"Egill!" Halldór cried. "You get into the office right now. I don't even want you going to the john without asking my permission. Do you understand me?"

"All right then. If that's what you want…" His voice trailed off.

Slamming the phone down, Halldór snatched the search warrant and threw it into his bottom desk drawer. He sat motionless for a long time. There was a procedure the police had to follow when a prisoner died in custody.

He picked the phone up and dialed the number for the chief of police.

Diary XVII

January 1, 1940. On this first day of the year it seems a good idea to sit down and look back at the past and think about the future. People's opinions are very divided about independence. There are voices that maintain that Icelanders are too poor and too few to take charge of their foreign affairs. Prima facie, this seems a reasonable argument, but it is not a new one. It has always been put forward against every demand that Icelanders have made on Denmark for increased liberty...

February 11, 1940. The German Consul-General called me to a meeting this morning. He asked me to assist him with the gathering of information, as the embassy has become very isolated because of the war. I asked if he was expecting me to spy on my own nation. He said he didn't mean that at all. "Embassies are supposed to monitor developments in their host countries and file reports on them. That is what they are there for," the consul said. I replied that I was much too busy, and was about to leave when he stopped me and said that my brother Matthías had been arrested in Hamburg for planning to leave the country illegally and without identification papers. The German partners in Isländische Bahn have complained to the authorities about developments in the business, and they hold Matthías responsible. The steelworks that sold us the rails have not received any payment in spite of having had a number of assurances. Naturally, I became angry on hearing these words, as it is Hitler's warmongering that has caused all this trouble. It was the onset of hostilities that stopped loans, both domestic and foreign, to the railway as well as foreign currency transfers. I told him that this disaster was going to bankrupt me. Finally, I asked him to use his influence to have Matthías released, because he was simply my representative in this matter. I also said it was essential that my relationship with the embassy does not in any way give rise to suspicion. He must understand this...

April 9, 1940. A German force is reported to have invaded Denmark today...

April 10, 1940. A parliamentary session was held overnight, and two resolutions were passed unanimously. Foreign affairs and all powers exercised by the Danish Crown in Iceland are to be assumed by the government...the Norwegians are still resisting the German invasion...

CHAPTER 51

MONDAY, JANUARY 22, 1973

Halldór was not feeling himself. *Morgunbladid* was not published on Mondays, so he couldn't even seek refuge in its pages that morning. Perhaps this would change one day, he reflected. Perhaps *Morgunbladid* would be published on Mondays and there would be television broadcast on Thursdays. To Halldór, these deviations from the rule interrupted the pleasant and predictable rhythm of life.

He sat and nibbled absentmindedly on a piece of toast, pondering whether he had become too old for this job, or had lost interest or competence in it. It wouldn't be too long now before he could retire, or maybe he could apply to be an attendant at the parliament building, as one of his old colleagues had done; that would definitely suit him nicely.

He listened to the morning news on the radio, relieved to hear no mention of a prisoner having died in police custody. If luck would have it, something else, something bigger, would occupy the headlines, then perhaps the newsmen would miss the story altogether. Matthías had, after all, actually died in the hospital, he reminded himself.

This situation was going to cause them a deal of trouble, though, that much was obvious. Solving the murder case was the only thing that would appease his superiors at this point. He closed his eyes and prayed silently to God almighty that something would fall from the sky that would give him the answer; there was certainly not much hope that the investigating team would do it anytime soon. Halldór was a believer, and he and his wife attended church services regularly, but he hardly ever prayed; on this particular occasion, he figured it wouldn't hurt, and he did feel better afterward.

His ruminations were interrupted once again by the telephone. Halldór glanced at Stefanía, but she did not look up from the travel brochures she was absorbed in. Perhaps that was a good idea—a trip, a nice, long trip.

Halldór answered the phone. It was Fridrik, the pathologist. "You're up early."

"Yeah, listen," Fridrik said, "I have a *corpus* here that you wanted me to dissect."

"Yes, the body of Matthías Kieler, who died yesterday."

"I think you should come down here and have a look at it."

Halldór was startled.

"I hope there are no injuries?" he asked anxiously. That mustn't be the case; they were in enough trouble already, but he was beginning to think that Egill was capable of anything.

"No, that's not the problem, but you should come right away," Fridrik said firmly and hung up.

Halldór had lost his appetite. He abandoned his toast, unfinished, on the plate and left the house without saying good-bye.

Diary XVII

May 9, 1940. I was informed in confidence that a telegram had arrived at the foreign affairs committee from our envoy in London, reporting that last Monday a question had been tabled in the British parliament as to whether the British government was planning to occupy Iceland. The question was withdrawn without the minister having replied to it. People are wondering what this means...

May 10, 1940. I woke at nearly three o'clock this morning when an airplane flew over the town. I was in no doubt that this was a military aircraft, as there are no planes in airworthy condition here at the moment. But what nationality was it? Sleep eluded me after that, and I got up, dressed warmly, and went out. The sky was cloudy and it was sleeting. I walked through town and down to the harbor. By then it was after four o'clock. Dawn was breaking, and between gusts of hail, you could see three warships lying just beyond the islands. Just then the British Consul arrived in his motor car along with a number of his compatriots. I asked him if these were his people, which he acknowledged. I hurried home to tell Elizabeth the news...

CHAPTER 52

Egill went to the office early, as usual. He was restless. They had not yet dealt with what he felt was a crucial part of the investigation. They needed to search Matthías's home; he felt certain the weapon would be found there. Halldór was really unnecessarily sensitive toward these people, he decided.

Marteinn arrived, greeted him, and sat down at his desk.

Egill made up his mind. He slipped into Halldór's office, scanned his desktop, then rummaged in the drawers until he found what he was looking for.

Donning his jacket, he called to Marteinn, who was absorbed in writing something, "Come with me."

"Where to?" Marteinn asked suspiciously.

"To that old geezer's home, the one who died yesterday, Matthías Kieler. The search hasn't been done yet."

"What? Who authorized that?" Marteinn asked.

"The judge, of course. I've got the warrant."

"I'm not coming."

"What do you mean?"

"I'm writing a formal complaint about your methods and requesting not to have to work under you."

"What are you driveling about?"

"You are a disgrace to the force, and I don't want to have to be part of it anymore."

"What the fuck's gotten into you? You're getting just like the girl."

Marteinn was furious. "First it was the visit to the old lady in the nursing home, then keeping that guy handcuffed all the way from Ólafsvík."

"Hey, he was a murder suspect," Egill interjected.

Ignoring him, Marteinn continued. "And finally that scene at Sídumúli yesterday. It was blindingly obvious the old man was in no state to be locked up."

"But you took part in all of this."

"Yeah, but only under orders from you. I couldn't sleep a wink last night because of it."

"You poor thing. Maybe your mommy can help," Egill taunted.

"Oh yes, and put that piece of paper back in Halldór's drawer. I saw you take it out." Marteinn turned away and returned to his report.

Egill was staggered. You couldn't trust anyone anymore. Until now, Marteinn had always stood by him, or at least pretended to. Egill slumped down at his desk, where he remained motionless, his arms crossed, scowling at Marteinn's back.

This workplace is turning into a parish meetinghouse, he thought to himself. How would they be able to solve any cases if everyone was so concerned with playing it safe and by the book? Whatever happened to taking a little risk? Oh well, it was all the same to him; he wasn't in charge.

Diary XVII

June 3, 1940. Elizabeth and I went for a meeting
with the British military command to offer the

services of my engineering firm. We were very well received. The general thought initially that I was an American who had settled in Iceland, as my English is so good. They will be contacting us on Wednesday...

June 5, 1940. I was called to a meeting with Mr. Sullivan, who is head of the British forces engineering unit. He wants me to take charge of surveying for an airfield at Vatnsmýri.

June 23, 1940. Mr. Sullivan and Mr. Freeman accepted our offer to come and dine with us at Birkihlíd. They are both well-qualified engineers of good families, and are notably polite. They were very grateful for such a feast after the constraints of military camp life. I showed them the railway designs, and they thought it quite possible that the military command would want to have the railroad built in order to facilitate military transport round Iceland...

November 3, 1940. Woke up to sustained gunfire directed at a German reconnaissance aircraft that flew over the town. It escaped to the west...

CHAPTER 53

Jóhann had woken unusually early that morning, but instead of heading directly to work he went for a swim in the Vesturbær pool. He had been in the office the previous day when the news came of Matthías's death, and had witnessed the ensuing chaos. Everyone had concentrated on covering the matter up and very little had been done to work out what had actually happened. This distressed Jóhann, and he was not keen to go in to work at all. He swam slowly back and forth for thirty minutes, and then sat in the hot tub for another half hour.

The weather was lovely—no wind, a cloudless sky, and frost. The sun hung low in the sky, and its rays shone through the steam rising from the pool.

Two old guys sat in the hot tub with him, talking about the weather.

Days such as this reminded Jóhann of his childhood home in the north, and usually made him feel happy, but today he was not thinking about home. Something was bothering him. He knew things were not as they should be. It wasn't just Matthías's death; there was something else. He didn't know what it was, but feared it would soon become clear.

He had a shower and shaved carefully. He took his time getting dressed, but as he was putting on his shoes, it occurred to him that Hrefna had probably not heard about Matthías's death yet. She would turn up at the office at eleven o'clock, and he did not trust anyone but himself to tell her the news.

Diary XVII

March 25, 1941. I have asked the authorities to try and find out about the fate of my brother Matthías. Not a day, an hour, a minute passes without my thinking about him. I blame myself completely for what has happened to him. He had planned to move to America but I asked him to stay on in Germany because of the railroad company. Perhaps I should use my connections in the British military command. They might have the means to get some information about people imprisoned by the Germans...

April 6, 1941. There is a rumor going round that the Germans are planning to blast the town to bits. I have found no grounds for this rumor, but am telling everyone in the household to be on the lookout... Mr. Freeman is worried about the drawings of the oil depot that I keep in my office. He says it would be terrible if the Germans were to get hold of this information. An aircraft carrying a single bomb that hits the exact spot could destroy the whole depot.

I tried to calm him down; I have great faith in my employees and I do not believe that there are spies in town working for the Germans. He asked me to accept a revolver for safety's sake. I told him that I was well armed, with a rifle and a shotgun, and that I could defend the house with those weapons if necessary. He thought that the revolver was a more suitable weapon, and I consented to accept it. It is a Smith & Wesson 38/200 officer's revolver, and comes with a plentiful supply of ammunition. I shall have to practice shooting with it when I get the opportunity...

CHAPTER 54

Halldór arrived at the hospital and headed straight for the laboratory. He was shown into a brightly lit room smelling strongly of antiseptics. In the center of the floor stood a long table on which a large corpse lay under a green sheet; over it shone an adjustable light, and next to the table was a cart with various pieces of equipment, assorted containers, and a selection of knives and forceps.

"Have you found the cause of death?" Halldór asked Fridrik, who was standing by the body.

"No, that was not why I called," Fridrik said, adding, "I haven't started the autopsy yet."

Halldór sensed that the pathologist was disturbed about something, and waited silently for him to continue. Putting on rubber gloves, Fridrik said, "Before you begin to dissect you have to examine the surface of the body carefully, looking for injuries."

"Did you find any?" Halldór asked apprehensively.

"No, not new ones—but take a look at this."

The doctor pulled the sheet off the lower half of the corpse, revealing snow-white legs and a prominent, hairy belly. He adjusted the light so that it shone between the legs, then, using both hands, lifted up the lower half of the torso.

Halldór moved closer for a better look. Below the belly there was dense pubic hair, as one would expect, but apart from that there was nothing there, nothing at all. There were big, ugly scars on the skin, but no genitals.

Halldór recoiled, and Fridrik let the body fall back into place.

"My god," Halldór gasped.

"Yeah, it's pretty ugly," Fridrik replied. "The genitalia have been cut off, and not very neatly either." He pulled the sheet back over the bottom half of the body.

"How the hell did that happen?"

"Not easy to say, though it's clear that it was many years ago. The wound was closed up immediately with coarse blanket stitching, but it looks as if much later a skillful surgeon restored the urethra as best he could."

"He was, simply…castrated," Halldór said.

"Yes, and more."

"Wouldn't that have affected his bodily functions?" Halldór asked.

"Yes, and I imagine it encouraged the deposit of body fat, but he must have been under medical supervision and received injections of male hormones."

Halldór went round to the other end of the table and lifted the sheet. There was more peace in Matthías's expression than one would expect, considering the manner of his death.

"It seems clear that there are one or two things we didn't know about this man," Halldór said wanly. He remembered how Matthías had knelt by his nephew Jacob's body in Birkihlíd, and automatically made a sign of the cross over the face of the corpse before pulling the sheet over it again.

Diary XVIII

*July 7, 1941. The Icelandic government called
the press to a meeting today, where the following
announcement was distributed: "The Icelandic
government and the President of the United States
have reached agreement that the United States shall
undertake military protection of Iceland for the
duration of the war between the major powers; an
American force has already arrived in Iceland. An
extraordinary session of the Althing has been called
for this coming Wednesday, the 9th of this month,
at one o'clock p.m., when the government will issue
a full statement on the matter, together with an
explanation why it was not possible to convene the
Althing any earlier...*

*July 8, 1941. Kristján arrived back in town having
completed his surveying work in Hvalfjördur. He
says that about 30 American warships sailed into the
fjord yesterday...*

*July 9, 1941. The Althing convened and approved
American military protection with a 39 to 3
majority...*

*August 16, 1941. We learned yesterday of Mr.
Churchill's impending visit to Reykjavik today.*

Elizabeth was very excited and we went down to the harbor at nine o'clock and waited there. At eleven his ship docked at the Gróf pier; on the quayside there was a unit of soldiers and a band of Scottish musicians. A large crowd had gathered, and as Mr. Churchill disembarked he received enthusiastic cheering by the Icelanders. He walked up the pier, gave a friendly greeting, and raised two fingers in the V for victory sign...

CHAPTER 55

When Hrefna arrived at the office just after eleven o'clock, Jóhann called her into the lab and told her of Matthías's demise.

"I'd rather you heard it from me than Egill. I'm not sure that he realizes the seriousness of the situation yet. That guy is completely lacking in judgment."

Hrefna was grateful. "I'd probably have hit him over the head," she said.

They sat together sipping coffee for the next hour. Neither felt like doing any work.

When Halldór arrived, he summoned Hrefna to his office and explained in private what he had found out that morning. She listened without interrupting, her thoughts on poor Matthías.

"I'm not going to share what I have told you with the others," he explained. "It's enough that you know about it for now. I do need to ask you to go see Klemenz and talk to him, though. There are still some issues that we need explanations for."

"I'll do that," Hrefna replied, "but I want to take this opportunity to give you my letter of resignation." She placed an envelope on Halldór's desk.

"Is this something to do with Matthías's death?" Halldór asked, taken aback.

"No. I've been carrying this in my bag for a few days; I just haven't got around to giving it to you. But today's a very suitable day for it; there are plenty of good reasons."

"I'm not going to try to talk you out of it," Halldór said. There was a short silence before he added, "I'm thinking of quitting myself."

I'm not going to try to talk you out of it either, Hrefna thought, but she didn't say anything.

Diary XVIII

November 1, 1942. Went ptarmigan shooting today with Jacob Junior. We drove to Kolvidarhóll and hiked up past Mt. Hengill. The weather was fine and plenty of game. Jacob is a poor shot and not very interested in hunting, but he likes to walk with me and carry the bag. He also really enjoys looking after the guns for me, cleaning them and oiling them. We practiced shooting with the revolver...

March 23, 1943. Yet again the communists were creating trouble over the drainage project. I managed to settle matters so that the work was finished by evening. Mr. Wallace thanked me especially for it...

CHAPTER 56

Hrefna opted to go on foot to see Klemenz; the weather was ideal for walking, and she needed time to think. She was used to delivering bad news in this job. Many times she had had to visit people and tell them of their loved ones' demise, and though she suffered with them, she did not shirk these tasks. Now, however, she felt unusually anxious. Someone had already phoned Klemenz the night before to tell him of Matthías's death, but she would have to ask questions about their private life, and she was not happy about it.

Half an hour later she was standing outside the apartment; she grasped the knocker and rapped on the door.

A finely dressed older woman answered. For a moment, Hrefna imagined this to be a female visitor of Klemenz's, but when the woman said "Hello," Hrefna recognized the voice immediately.

Klemenz was wearing a dark gray, two-piece suit with a pale pink silk blouse, nylon stockings, and black high-heeled shoes. His face was carefully made up and his black hair was nicely blow-dried. He had on a pair of modest earrings and a matching necklace.

"I hope my being dressed like this doesn't upset you," Klemenz said as he invited her in. "I wasn't expecting visitors, and I find it easier to cope with my grief if I am wearing my own clothes."

"Umm..." Hrefna hesitated. "I just need a bit of time to get used to it."

"The men's clothes were just an uncomfortable disguise," Klemenz explained. "Matthías preferred me to wear them in public, of course, and I complied with his wishes. Now I don't need to anymore."

He invited Hrefna into the parlor, and she couldn't help but notice how feminine his movements were. As he sat down, she said, "I should like to offer you my condolences on the death of your loved one."

"Thank you."

"The last twenty-four hours have been very difficult for you, I imagine."

"Yes, my dear, this has been difficult. Matthías and I have lived together, been a family, for over forty years. We have gone through thick and thin together, been as one. And then, when my spouse dies, I just get a phone call from the detective division to announce that he is dead and that the family will be in touch for a final salary settlement."

Hrefna bit her lip. She wished that Halldór had had the sense to let her speak to Klemenz the evening before.

"We were actually prepared for the eventuality of one of us dying before the other, and had made financial arrangements," Klemenz continued. "I do not, therefore, have to worry about being unfairly treated in that respect."

Hrefna did not write any of this down, the notebook and the pen remaining untouched in her bag. She knew that she could remember every word of this conversation if necessary, and she doubted much of it would end up in the official report anyway.

"Tell me about your relationship with Matthías," she finally asked. "If you care to do that and feel able to, that is," she added.

Klemenz thought for a moment. "It's probably good to talk at times like this. Besides, I have no secrets anymore." He paused again and then said, "I am not a homosexual man. I am a woman in a male body. There has never been any doubt in my mind. My earliest memories are of feeling confused when people talked about me as if I was boy. I knew I was a girl!

"My father was a seaman and my mother worked in a shop. I was a biddable kid and mostly looked after myself. I just always had this compulsion to swap clothes with the girls I played with."

Hrefna smiled faintly, and Klemenz went on. "When I reached puberty I only had feelings for men, there was never any doubt about that. Still, my sex life was very limited. I did not have a strong sexual drive, and my first lovers were unfortunate souls, desperate over the shame and guilt attached to their urges. I never felt guilty, just disappointed when my lovers turned out to be rather worthless characters. All that changed when I met Matthías."

Klemenz smiled at the memory and wiped a few tears from his eyes.

"I had gone to a concert at the Music Society where he was playing. Afterward there was coffee, and I noticed that he was watching me from across the room. Of course, I had often fallen for heterosexual men, and that had naturally come to nothing, but I sensed that this man might be different. And, as it transpired, Matthías was a homosexual."

Klemenz got up and paced the floor slowly.

"We got to know each other very gradually. It took me a long time to get Matthías to respond to his feelings. When he finally did, and we became lovers, I had to use all available means to counteract the shame that his upbringing had instilled in him. But we got there in the end, and we enjoyed every moment of our time together. The big upheaval came when my father caught us in my bed together. Though I was nineteen at the time, I looked young for my age, and Father regarded me as a child still. He was convinced that Matthías had seduced me, an innocent boy, and so reported him to the authorities. Old Alfred was summoned, and he immediately renounced Matthías forevermore. Jacob Senior saved whatever could be saved of the situation. He got them to agree to drop the case, provided Matthías left the country. I was not allowed to see him before he left, and that almost finished me off. I was ill for weeks, but in the end, I secretly met with Jacob and told him the full story. He understood it as much as he could, and advised me to convince my parents to let me go abroad and learn to be a waiter, which is what I did. I left Iceland in the second half of 1928. By then, Matthías was in Berlin and had started his cello studies at the music academy, which were going well, as he had learned German from his old music teacher. We met again in Berlin, and were now able to live together; I began my course, and life was wonderful. We got to know a large group of homosexual men and women, and we were able to live there in an incredibly tolerant environment. I worked while going to school, and very soon Matthías also began to earn money playing the cello. We severed all connections with Iceland, with the exception of Jacob; Matthías and Jacob kept up a correspondence."

"Did you never come back to Iceland?" Hrefna asked.

"No, we had no desire to do that."

"So how did Matthías get mixed up in the monarchy business?" Hrefna asked.

Klemenz laughed softly. "Jacob Senior was working on promoting his railroad company, and was negotiating with German companies during the years before the war. As a way to build up working capital, he became an envoy for some eccentrics who wanted to find a king for Iceland in Europe. Jacob tested the opinions of some of the aristocracy here, in confidence, but von Kuppel became rather too interested, and tried to get the support of people of influence in Germany so that he would be the only candidate for the office when the invitation arrived. Then, during the war, he became a bit confused, and began to believe that he had actually been offered the position. That was how Jacob's and Matthías's names came to be associated with this matter."

"How successful was Jacob with the railroad enterprise in Germany?"

"That's another story." He sighed. "Jacob was well received, and there were German businesses prepared to assist him with the company. But it all had to be played down in Iceland because of the political situation, so it was agreed that Mannheim Stahl-werke would build two trains and contribute these as equity in Isländische Bahn AG. That company would then lease the trains to the Iceland Railroad Company."

"Was Matthías involved in any of this?"

"Yes, unfortunately, he agreed to become his brother's agent in Germany."

"Tell me more about that."

"By 1937, homosexual people in Germany began to be perse-cuted. I wanted to emigrate, but Matthías felt he had to look after the interests of the railroad company. By the end of the year, we moved to Hamburg, where nobody knew anything of our per-sonal affairs. Matthías oversaw the building of the trains, and he had to push hard for progress on the project, as military industry had been prioritized. In the meantime, Jacob was preparing the construction of the track in Reykjavik. He wanted to build the railway from the harbor to Öskjuhlíd to begin with, because he was convinced that as soon as the Icelanders saw the trains, they would open their eyes to the value of the railroad. He was, however, not able to deliver his part of the project on time, which meant that it wasn't possible to ship the trains to Iceland when they were ready; so Matthías took a picture of one of them, parked on the quayside in Hamburg, and sent it to Jacob."

"Where were you during the war years?"

"The Germans were not happy with how things were progressing with the railroad company, and imposed travel restrictions on Matthías, confiscating his passport so that he was unable to leave the country. Of course I could not abandon him. We tried to get out of Germany secretly at the beginning of 1940, but we were betrayed and arrested on board ship at the Hamburg docks. We were imprisoned until the end of the war."

"Do you feel able to talk about that time?"

"Yes, perhaps it's time that story was told," he replied, sighing. "To begin with, we were detained in Hamburg while our case was being investigated. The conditions there were tolerable to start with, compared with other prison camps, but they would later become worse. We were lucky enough, however, that a young German woman, who worked for the Ministry of Justice as an interpreter for the Norwegian prisoners, put us on her list of clients. The Norwegian seamen's pastor in Hamburg was thus able to visit us with her, and they sometimes sneaked in vitamin pills, which probably saved our lives, because the food they gave us was little and unvaried. When the Allies began to step up the air raids on Hamburg in 1943, we were moved north of the city, to a town called Rendsburg, on the Kiel Canal."

Klemenz was silent for a moment, and then continued. "In Rendsburg we were forced to do hard labor, and our health began to deteriorate. We were, nevertheless, relieved to be there, because other inmates transferred to our camp brought terrible stories of prison camps elsewhere; names such as Dachau, Auschwitz, Buchenwald, and Sachsenhausen would come to epitomize horror to our ears. Although our guards were of varying dispositions, there were those there who tried not to treat us with unnecessary cruelty."

Klemenz paused and gazed out the window. Hrefna waited patiently, in silence, for him to continue with his story.

"On the second of December 1943, we were paid a rather unpleasant visit in prison," he began again. "Up to that point we had been detained on the basis of the escape attempt and alleged fraud to do with the railroad company. Later, actually, we learned that the German envoy in Iceland had tried, in vain, to use our imprisonment to bully Jacob Senior into spying for them. Anyway, on this atrocious day, two men arrived from Berlin with an indictment for alleged antisocial behavior and immoral acts under the so-called Paragraph 175 law. Our friends and comrades from the homosexual community in Berlin had been arrested, and, after brutal torture, had broken down and named names. These men from Berlin now wanted more names. We were interrogated in separate rooms, and I immediately told them everything I knew, whereas Matthías remained silent. The men were clearly not satisfied, having probably long since arrested all those I told them about. They took me into the cell where Matthías was being held. He was naked, and they had tied his hands and hung him from a hook high up on the wall. He had been beaten badly, and his mouth was bleeding. I was told to strip, and they tied me and hung me up, too. They kept pressing Matthías for names, but he kept as silent as the grave. Then the knives came out."

Klemenz fell silent. He looked down and put his hand to his eyes.

"You don't have to say any more," Hrefna said.

"If you think you can hear it, then I think I can continue," Klemenz replied, looking at her. She met his gaze and, after a moment, nodded.

"They told Matthías that if he didn't answer their questions, they would torture and then kill us. At that, he relented, but the names he was able to give them were no different than the ones I had already given them. The men were still not satisfied. They seemed to be looking for evidence that some high-up people in Berlin had been members of our circle. Something we had no knowledge of. They beat us and threatened us with their knives. And then, without warning, they cut my genitals off and threw them to the floor."

Hrefna felt like she had been kicked in the guts. "Off you? But Matthías, he was…are you also…" She could not finish the sentence.

"Yes, then it was his turn. But I had passed out by then." The thought seemed to send a chill through Klemenz, and he crossed his arms over his chest, his eyes closed.

There was a long silence, until Hrefna finally said, "But you survived."

"Yes, we survived. The men from Berlin left the scene, and the guards at Rendsburg took over. There was an old German doctor, long since retired, who served the camp, and with the help of some Norwegian prisoners, he was able to stop the bleeding. He also managed to preserve the urethra, though it was not neatly done. We spent months in the hospital wing, until we were moved east to Dreibergen."

"How did you feel after that?"

"I didn't really miss those organs. I should naturally have preferred the operation to be tidier, but my problems were only physical. Matthías, on the other hand, was never the same man again; his personality changed completely. Once a strong, virile man, he became very sensitive, listless, and lethargic. I had to become the strong one in our relationship for many years after."

"Where did you say they moved you to?"

"To Dreibergen. As the war drew to an end, the Germans retreated eastward from the Allied advance, taking their prison population with them. The Dreibergen prison also played an important role after the abortive attempt on Hitler's life on the twentieth of July 1944. Everyone implicated in that conspiracy was taken there and executed. We prisoners witnessed the executions that night, though we didn't know who these people were. We just saw the shadows and heard the cries of agony. Up to that point, we had believed that the Nazis would not actually put us to death, and that if we could just survive the mistreatment, we should be safe. These hopes were shattered that night, and Matthías broke down completely. Over the next months, all he wanted to do was to curl up on the floor and await his fate."

As Hrefna listened to this account, she thought about how distant these events were from her own reality. She had been five years old at the end of the war, and remembered nothing of the war years. During her life, there had always been peace. She thought about the generation that had been born in Europe before the turn of the century and had experienced two world wars. How had they managed to stay sane?

"What saved you?" she asked.

"It was the German girl from Hamburg, the one who interpreted for the Norwegian prisoners, who saved us and many others. The president of the Swedish Red Cross, Count

Folke Bernadotte, managed to negotiate with Himmler for the release of Scandinavian prisoners. A motorcade of Swedish buses traveled between prison camps in Germany to pick people up. The German girl had put us on her list. Because our names were there, we were set free. We arrived in Sweden in April 1945. We were in a sanatorium there until we managed to get to Iceland on the *Esja* that summer, arriving in Reykjavik on the ninth of July."

"And then you met Jacob Senior again."

"Yes, that's why we went to Iceland. We were in a bad state after the mutilations in Rendsburg; our urinary systems were a mess, and we urgently needed the attentions of a skillful surgeon. We knew of a clinic in Switzerland where we could have treatment, but it was expensive, and Matthías thought that Jacob might be able to help us."

"Was he able to?"

"To a very limited extent. It was a mistake for us to come home."

"Why?"

"Hearing our account proved too much for Jacob Senior. He blamed himself for what had happened to us, and he had a breakdown."

"And that was when he stopped writing his diary," Hrefna said.

"I do not know," Klemenz said.

"What happened next?"

"Jacob managed to scrape some money together for us, and made a legal transfer of half of the house to Matthías. Old Alfred had disinherited Matthías, and Jacob wanted to make amends. Jacob died a week later, as you know."

"Do you have a theory about what happened to him?"

"When I heard that Jacob Senior had been found dead, I felt certain that he had taken his own life. His reactions during our meetings over the previous days were of that nature. I recognized them from the prison camps; it was usually obvious when people were haunted by such thoughts. I discussed this with Matthías and we were both worried, regretting very much having burdened him with our troubles. At that point, we decided that this would remain our secret forever."

"But Jacob Senior was murdered."

"Yes, according to the police, Jacob was shot. For what reason I do not know, but then I was not familiar with his history here."

"What did you and Matthías do after Jacob died?"

"After attending the funeral, we left the country on the first available boat. We managed to put together enough money for our operations, and stayed on in Switzerland for a few months. Matthías was on hormone injections after that, and recovered fairly well, mentally. I, on the other hand, chose not to have hormone treatment."

"Were you told what happened to Matthías yesterday?"

"Yes, I went to the hospital and talked to the doctor who treated him. He said that he had been brought there from the prison. I cannot imagine why he was locked up in the first place, but I know he would never have been able to tolerate it, given his health condition. After the prison camp internment, he suffered from acute claustrophobia and could, for instance, never sleep in a closed room."

Klemenz had finished his account and now sat forlornly on the sofa, his head down, tears silently falling down his cheeks. Acting on an impulse, Hrefna moved over to the sofa, sat down next to him, and put her arm around his shoulders. He leaned his head on her chest and cried like a child. She hugged him and thought about this man, this human being—this woman, because she now felt in her heart that the person she held in her arms was an old, tired, grief-stricken woman. A woman who might have become a good mother and a good grandmother, had not a quirk of nature put her into the wrong body many, many years ago.

And still, fate had continued to prey upon her, right up to now. What an ordeal, to have had to conduct one's life in such deception, just to be able to live in peace with someone you love. Perhaps things will change one day, and people will be able to live the way they were created.

Hrefna recalled having held her mother like this in difficult times, when she had become ill; even the perfume smelled the same.

They remained like this for a long time, until Klemenz recovered himself and sat up.

"Thank you for being so kind to me," he said, and blew his nose into a white handkerchief.

It was dark outside when Hrefna left Klemenz. She walked through town enjoying the cool breeze. Her head felt empty, and she barely registered the displays in the shop windows she passed. When she reached Borgartún, she found the detective team gathered together in the office.

Something was wrong. Jóhann wiped a tear from his cheek and sniffed. Halldór was cleaning invisible dust from his glasses, and Egill paced the floor, his head bowed. Marteinn sat with his head down, wringing his hands.

"Has something happened?" she asked.

Jóhann looked up and nodded. Then he asked her to come into the lab with him. For the second time that day, he wanted to talk to her in private.

Diary XVIII

December 3, 1943. I dreamed about my brother Matthías last night. He was standing here in the garden, talking a lot, but there was no sound coming from his lips...

February 25, 1944. The Althing passed a unanimous resolution to sever the union with Denmark and annul the Danish-Icelandic federal treaty of 1918. There will be a national referendum at a later date...

May 21, 1944. We went to the polling station and voted for the break-up of the union with Denmark and the formation of a republic...

June 1, 1944. The results of the referendum have now come in. Separation from Denmark: 70,536 for, 365 against. Establishment of Republic of Iceland: 68,862 for, 1,064 against. Average turnout over the whole country was 98.61%. In some constituencies the turnout was 100%.

June 17, 1944. We got up at 6 o'clock this morning and drove to Thingvellir, all four of us. It rained. We were present at Lögberg when the republic was formally inaugurated. The Regent of Iceland was elected as the country's first president, a good compromise. I am, nevertheless, still of the opinion that crowning a king of Iceland would have generated an even more solemn occasion. We did not want to overnight at Thingvellir, and got home just after midnight.

August 10, 1944. This is the last entry in this diary, the eighteenth of the series. The nineteenth lies here on the table, brand new and ready to receive the record of days to come, and my thoughts on matters concerning this country and its people. With these diaries, I have sought to be honest; I thus learn more about myself and gain a perspective of the development of my life. This also means, on the other hand, that I do not want all and sundry to have access to these, my writings, and have therefore consigned them to a safe place. This particularly applies to the diaries dating from 1932, books that are to remain indefinitely closed to all persons. Yet I cannot bring myself to destroy them. My descendants may read those diaries that deal with the years before 1932, numbers 1–12, if they so wish after my death. Elizabeth is aware of this decision of mine, and will ensure it is observed. I can trust her in all matters...

CHAPTER 57

After Jóhann and Hrefna had talked together privately in the lab, he took her home in his car. They drove there silently; she felt numb and tired, and she needed to think. When Jóhann stopped the car outside her house, however, she stayed in her seat.

"I handed in my letter of resignation this morning."

"Did you have to do that?" Jóhann implored. "Not all days are as bad as these have been."

"No, I've thought this out very carefully. I've been offered a job at a law firm. I'm going to accept it and go to night classes to finish my university entrance exams; I've already completed five terms for them a few years back. Then I'm going to study law at the university."

"I'll miss you," he said sadly.

"Maybe we could meet up sometime," Hrefna suggested, climbing out of the car and then bidding him good night.

There was nobody near the house or on the stairs when she approached the building. She was relieved not to have to put Pétur off with some subterfuge.

"Elsa, love," Hrefna exclaimed, when she found her daughter in her bedroom studying Danish. "Come, let's cuddle up in bed together, there's something I need to tell you."

Elsa looked at her in surprise, but put her book away and followed her into her room.

They climbed into the old bed, and Hrefna put her arms around her daughter. "The last time you said something like this to me was when Granny died. Is it something just as bad now?"

"Yes, it's bad this time, too." Hrefna hesitated a moment, before continuing in a trembling voice. "Dear little Halli…is dead."

"Halli? Dead?"

There was a short silence while Elsa took this in.

"What happened?"

"He was hit by a train in Austria."

"No!"

"Yes, sweetheart. Apparently he went out for a walk last night, and it seems he went along a railroad track near the hotel where they were staying; and because of his low intelligence he didn't know that was a dangerous thing to do. He didn't hear the train coming from behind. The engineer wasn't able to stop in time."

"Intelligence!" exclaimed Elsa. "It's got nothing to do with intelligence; it's just that he didn't know it was dangerous because there are no trains here in Iceland. I wouldn't have known that, either."

"Maybe that's true." Hrefna was silent a while; then she continued. "When he phoned, Erlendur told us that this had been Halli's best day ever. He took the first lift of the morning up the mountain and spent all day skiing—his last run was with the patrol, who are the last ones down when the runs are closed for the day."

"I would have done that, too," Elsa sobbed.

Tears ran down Hrefna's cheeks as well. After a while Elsa asked, "What are you thinking, Mom?"

"I'm thinking about what you just said, and about the man who wrote the diaries I've had to read these past few evenings. His dream was to build railroads across Iceland; if that dream had come true, then perhaps Halli would have known about trains and their dangers."

"Do you think he was a good man, this man who wrote the diaries?" Elsa asked.

Hrefna thought for a moment before replying. "Yes, I'm sure he was a good man. He had some difficult moments and was often depressed, but he was a good man."

They lay there together for a long time until they both finally dozed off. It was well past nine o'clock when hunger woke them again.

"How was your day, my dear?" Hrefna asked.

"I was going to have a bath, but the tap wasn't working properly, and there was nothing but scalding hot water," Elsa said. "Pétur came and tried to help me. He said there was sand in the pipes."

"Was he able to fix it?"

"No, it's still not working, but Pétur was asking if I knew anything about this murder case you're investigating."

"Oh, so he's resorted to asking you now?" Hrefna laughed softly.

"Yeah, but I knew nothing, of course. Then he told me that he had once done some work in that house where it happened."

"Really?"

"Yeah. He said that he was breaking something down with his jackhammer and had found some kind of a gun."

"A gun?"

"Yeah, you know, the sort of revolver you see in the movies."

"Perhaps he was joking?"

"No, no," Elsa remarked. "He seemed pretty convinced."

A revolver in Birkihlíd. Hrefna had to check this out.

Pétur lived in an apartment on the top floor, and as Hrefna mounted the stairs, she realized she had never been upstairs, despite having lived in the building for several months. She rang the bell, and Pétur answered the door in his undershirt.

"Sorry to bother you," Hrefna apologized, "but Elsa told me that you once did a job in Birkihlíd, and that you'd found a gun there. Is that right?"

"Yes," Pétur replied. "I've been wondering whether I should mention this to someone, but it was such a long time ago that I didn't think it mattered."

"When was this?"

"Around 1960."

"What kind of gun was it?"

"Just an ordinary revolver."

"Where did you find it?"

"I was using the jackhammer to knock out a fireplace that had been bricked in, down in the basement of the house. The gun was lying at the bottom of the hearth."

"Do you know how it might have gotten there?"

"Either it was there when the fireplace got bricked in, or it fell down the chimney."

"Was there anything else there?"

"Yeah, one or two dead birds, as far as I remember. They must have flown down the chimney and got stuck."

"Anything else?"

"Well, there was some kind of cord, and then there was a weight like what they used to use on shop scales back in the old days. Apart from that there was just a lot of dirt."

"What happened to the gun?"

"Jacob, the one that's just been shot, was hovering over me, and he took it. I never saw it again."

"Did he say anything?"

"Nothing. He just said that I could go, that he would clean up the rubble himself."

"You didn't ask him about the gun later?"

"No. But he was bloody difficult when I was trying to bill him for the work. It all turned into a complete pain."

"What do you think he did with the gun?"

"Probably threw it away with the other rubbish. It seemed a bit rusty to me."

It was almost eleven o'clock when Hrefna took a taxi to Borgartún.

She began checking through the case reports, and it was not long before she found what she was looking for. "Deceased was sighted on the roof of his house on Tuesday, January 16. According to witness, he was fixing the chimney stack."

Egill had clearly typed this. Hrefna counted seven misprints.

"You weren't asleep, were you?" she asked when Jóhann answered the phone.

"No, not very."

"Come and fetch me from the office. We have to go to Birki-hlíd immediately."

Diary XIX

September 6, 1944. The bridge across the Ölfusá
River collapsed last night. One of the cables broke
under the weight of two automobiles. I had warned

363

*people that this might happen, and had banned
military vehicles from crossing more than one at a
time...*

*November 12, 1944. Everything is going very well at
the engineering studio. Thórdur is of invaluable help,
as is Kristján. Thórdur told me to take time off, and
he will complete the cross-sections...*

*November 13, 1944. I did not sleep a wink last night,
I sat downstairs and thought. I keep on getting
new ideas that will aid this nation's prosperity and
progress. Paid a few visits today...*

*November 15, 1944. The lack of respect for my
talents here in Iceland has become intolerable. I have
visited persons of authority, with good ideas and
proposals regarding a variety of matters, and they
all say that they will "look into the matter." They do
not want to listen. There is an old proverb that says,
"Many a man might have gained wisdom had he
not considered himself wise already." The editor has
stopped publishing my articles, as he says that there
is no room in the paper. I went to see the President of
Iceland with a list of good suggestions regarding his
office because, as it says in Hávamál, "Who wanders*

wide hath need of wits." The president only listened for a few minutes, and then he had a meeting to attend. He will talk with me at a later date...

November 16, 1944. Elizabeth has locked away my clothes. She says that Jónas, the doctor, has ordered that I stay at home. These people are all nonentities...I have decided to become an artist. My only worry is that I may not have time to paint enough pictures to meet the demand, like Kjarval...

CHAPTER 58

TUESDAY, JANUARY 23, 1973

It was past midnight when Jóhann arrived at Borgartún in his Cortina; Hrefna was waiting in the lobby and quickly got into the car. She had brought two large flashlights with her.

On the way to Birkihlíd, she recounted what Pétur had told her that evening. Jóhann listened to her story in silence, and then said, "I checked the fireplace in the basement. There's definitely no gun there now."

"Still, I want us to have another look," Hrefna said.

"Where is all this leading?"

"I don't know yet, but I'm sure that this gun is important. I also want to get an explanation for what Jacob was doing up on the roof by the chimney, assuming, of course, that Egill was right about that."

It was dark around the house, so they had to use the flashlights to see their way to the door. Once inside, they headed straight down to the basement.

It was just as Jóhann said, the fireplace was empty but for a bit of dirt at the bottom of the hearth.

"Can you take a look up the chimney?" Hrefna asked.

Anticipating a dirty job, Jóhann had brought his tools and a pair of coveralls from the car. He changed into the work clothes and then lay on his back, squirming his way into the fireplace until he was able to shine his flashlight up the flue.

"Can you see anything?" Hrefna asked.

"There's some sort of grill shutting it off up here," Jóhann called. He tried to reach up, but the flue was too narrow for him. "Looks like something's lying on top of the grill. At any rate, my flashlight doesn't seem to shine beyond it."

He wriggled back out again and said, "We'll have to break up the chimney to get a better look at what's up there."

"Let me try," Hrefna offered.

She was about to clamber straight into the fireplace, but changed her mind, realizing how filthy it was. "Give me your coveralls," she demanded.

She pulled them on, then rolled up the sleeves, and crawled into the hearth. She was able to squeeze her head and one shoulder up into the flue.

"Can you reach it?" he asked.

"Yes," she replied, her voice strangely distorted inside the chimney. "I can get my fingers through. There's something lying on top of the grill."

All of a sudden there was a deafening explosion. Hrefna shot from the fireplace and rolled out onto the floor, where she lay curled up, her hands covering her ears.

Jóhann was badly shaken as well. "Are you okay?" he asked, kneeling beside her.

"Shit, that was loud," Hrefna said. "It's still ringing in my ears."

"What was it?" he asked.

"The bloody gun, of course. I must have hooked my finger around the trigger."

"In that case, it was lucky you didn't shoot yourself."

"Yes." Hrefna sat up, regarding the fireplace angrily.

"Why don't we come back tomorrow and knock a hole in the chimney?" Jóhann suggested.

"No, we are going to sort this out right now," she declared.

"All right then." Jóhann crawled back into the fireplace and shone the flashlight up the chimney again. This time he took a closer look: The grill, made of steel, seemed comparatively new; it fitted closely inside the flue and was held in place by wedges pushed up between it and the sides of the flue.

"This'll be easy," he said, crawling out again. In the laundry room he found an old wooden pole that had been used to stir the washtubs, and he shoved it up the chimney and banged vigorously at the grill several times until the wedges gave way and the whole setup came crashing down onto the bed of the fireplace.

Jóhann jumped out of the way, in case the gun should go off as it fell; fortunately, it didn't. Once the dust had settled, they both focused their flashlights on what had fallen: there was the steel grill; on top of it, a heavy weight covered by a large tangle of cord; and crowning the whole pile, a gleaming revolver.

Jóhann took a screwdriver out of his bag and poked it into the barrel of the gun so that he could pick it up without handling it. He recognized the Smith & Wesson 38/200 from the picture in his manual; the cord was tied with a rough knot to the lanyard loop on its butt, and when he laid the gun down and unraveled the cord, he found that the other end was attached to the weight.

"Looks like this is the weight that was missing from the box with the distance-measuring equipment," Jóhann said.

Hrefna considered what they had found, and said, "I have a feeling that Jacob Junior was somehow responsible for his own murder. But I'm not exactly sure how yet."

"Ah, but I think I know," Jóhann said. "Father and son both shot themselves. How brilliantly clever!"

"How did they do it?"

"They stood by the fireplace in the parlor, holding the gun. The cord was threaded into the hearth and up the chimney, then over into the top of this flue, where the weight hung, pulling the cord taut. When the shot is fired, they drop the gun and the weight falls down the chimney, pulling the gun into the fireplace, up that flue, then over into this one, where it falls to the bottom here, never to be found again."

"So Jacob Senior prepared for his suicide by having this basement fireplace bricked up," Hrefna said. "Then, when the time came, he took the family to the summer house, gave the servants leave, and staged the burglary."

Jóhann nodded in agreement, adding, "His son must have worked this out when he found the gun. Then he repeated the performance."

"But why, in heaven's name?" Hrefna asked.

"Let's get Halldór here before we begin to puzzle over that one," Jóhann said. "He's going to be so relieved that we're about to solve this case."

Diary XIX

January 5, 1945. I am feeling well now. I wrote letters to the president and some of my friends, apologizing for my behavior this fall. It was inexplicable, but the doctor says it was linked to my illness. It distresses me for Elizabeth's sake...

January 10, 1945. I am planning some changes in the basement of the house. The laundry room can be made much more pleasant. There is no need for the coal storage now that we are connected to the hot water main. The large fireplace is also redundant, and I have decided to have the opening bricked up...

CHAPTER 59

While Jóhann telephoned Halldór, Hrefna went into the kitchen, switched on all the lights, and turned the radiator all the way up; the house was freezing. Then she sat down at the table and started to try to fit the pieces of this extraordinary puzzle together.

Jóhann entered a few moments later and began to make coffee. In the light of the kitchen, Hrefna could see he was pretty dirty and imagined she was probably no cleaner. Her hair felt absolutely stiff with grime.

Halldór arrived impressively fast, and Jóhann took him down to the basement to show him the setup. When they came back up, they had the gun in one plastic bag and the cord and weight in another.

They sat down at the table with Hrefna, and she ran over again what they had discovered. When it came to explaining how it had all worked, Jóhann took over. Halldór listened without saying a word; then there was a long silence while Jóhann fetched a cup of coffee and brought it back to the table. The room was finally beginning to warm up a little.

"Let's just try and figure this out," Halldór said. "Why would Jacob Senior take his own life?"

"We know that he showed symptoms of depression in the latter half of his life," Hrefna replied. "His financial situation was dire, and he was aware that all the investments in preparation for the railroad had become worthless. He had tried to work hard during the war years to pay off some of his debts. He seems to have planned in advance for this possibility, from the time he had the basement fireplace bricked up. He wouldn't have expected anybody to open it up again later."

"What was it that pushed him over the edge?" Halldór asked.

"Matthías and Klemenz arriving in the country," Hrefna surmised. "Jacob was very relieved when he learned that his brother had survived the war, and was looking forward to welcoming him home. Matthías overestimated Jacob's financial position, and, thinking that Jacob would be able to help them obtain medical treatment, told him of the mutilations they had suffered. Jacob was devastated by the thought that he had, however indirectly, brought this dreadful suffering upon Matthías and Klemenz, and as some kind of recompense, made a legal transfer of half the house to Matthías. He knew that Elizabeth would be well provided for when the life insurance was paid out, but that the conditions of the policy meant it must not appear that he killed himself, which is why he went to such lengths to cover the means of his death up."

"What about Jacob Junior? Why would he kill himself?" Halldór asked.

"Jacob Junior was probably somewhat mentally unstable, as well," Hrefna replied. "This compulsion of his regarding the family home was very morbid. He was completely consumed by his father's memory, and his life revolved around it, so it's not difficult to imagine his reaction when he found the gun and realized how it had been used. Once all his various attempts to secure the permanent preservation of the home had failed, and he had burned all his bridges financially, he must have decided to choose the same way out as his father had. He probably felt it appropriate for his own death to become an enigma as well, even a kind of homage to his father. Old Alfred's will must have been his last hope for rescuing his finances, but Matthías put an end to that when they met last Wednesday evening, the night he put his plan into practice."

"Tomorrow I'll check the gun and the weight for fingerprints," Jóhann said. "We'll need to try firing the gun to get a bullet for comparison. Then we can reinstall the whole setup and see if it works the way we think it does."

"How did they manage to set this up?" Halldór asked Jóhann.

"The first thing, I guess, was to go up onto the roof and lower the cord down the chimney into the parlor, tying one end onto something solid up there. Then they went down to the parlor and fixed the lower end in the same way. They then went back up onto the roof, detached that end of the cord, and tied it to the weight, which they lowered a little way down the basement flue, readying it for use whenever they might need it."

"An automatic gun swallower!" Hrefna said.

Jóhann continued. "We have testimony that Jacob Junior was seen up on the roof a few days ago."

"But what was the dining room chair for?" Halldór asked.

"I assume that when Jacob Junior's big moment came, he found it difficult to stand on his own two feet, and got the chair so he could do the deed sitting down," Jóhann replied.

"Perhaps this shows how different father and son actually were," Hrefna observed. "Jacob Senior stands and looks straight into the barrel of the gun as he fires. Jacob Junior sits and tries to aim for his heart, but misses; he falls off the chair and tries to crawl off to call for help. He must have been in a lot of pain, poor man."

"Well," Halldór remarked, standing. "All this is very plausible. I hope the forensics will support your conclusions. If it proves true, we need not tell the media; we're usually spared that when it's suicide."

As he reached the door, Halldór turned and asked Hrefna, "Who is this man that told you about the gun?"

"Pétur. He's the janitor in the house where I live."

"I see," Halldór said. Adding as he left, "The Almighty has his own way of answering people's prayers."

Hrefna didn't quite understand what he meant; the state of her appearance was more concerning to her at the moment. She was absolutely covered head to toe in dust and soot. It'll be great to get into a shower, she thought, but then remembered that her bath was out of commission.

She looked at Jóhann, who was examining the gun. She liked the way he furrowed his brow over it.

"It must have been fully loaded," he remarked.

She had noticed before that his gaze was gentle and intelligent, but hadn't thought anything about it at the time. She had been determined to keep her work colleagues at a suitable distance. Now, however, she had left this job, left it for good.

"Would you mind if I took a shower at your place?" she asked. "Mine isn't working at the moment."

Diary XIX

April 25, 1945. We had a telegram from the Swedish
Red Cross. My brother Matthías is alive.

CHAPTER 60

On the way home from Birkihlíd, Jóhann thought about the day to come. It would be strange to start working on another case after tonight; the investigation had lasted only five days, but he felt as if many weeks had passed since he had first examined those footsteps in the snow outside Birkihlíd. Hrefna sat in silence beside him, and he wondered what she was thinking about.

He parked the car in one of the central parking bays on Hringbraut, and they walked, against the wind, toward the house.

"You've made this very homey," Hrefna remarked, looking around his apartment.

Jóhann looked around, too. He had tried to make the apartment comfortable, but it was nice that she thought it seemed homey.

Hrefna caught sight of herself in the hallway mirror.

"Just look at me! I've got to have that shower," she said. "Can you lend me a towel and something clean to put on?"

Jóhann handed her a big towel, and while she showered, he rummaged through his wardrobe and dug out a GWU T-shirt and some cotton shorts; much too big, he thought, but they'll have to do. He slipped them inside the bathroom door.

When Hrefna came out, she had rolled up the sleeves of the T-shirt and the bottom of the shorts some.

"I've got a bottle of white wine in the fridge. How about I open it?" he offered.

"Okay, if you have some, too," she said.

"I can't. I'll have to drive you home later."

"I think you're just as much in need of refreshment as I am. Why don't I just stay over?" Hrefna suggested. "Your bed looks big enough for the two of us."

"Yes, yes, of course you can stay," Jóhann stammered. He didn't know quite what to say or do next.

"The white wine," Hrefna reminded him.

"Yes, of course," he said, smiling broadly and fetching the bottle and two glasses.

"Cheers," Hrefna said when he handed her the glass.

"Here's to a job well done," added Jóhann.

"A job done, anyway," Hrefna said. "I don't feel we can say this case had a good ending."

"That's very true."

"But it'll be good to wake up in the morning and not have to start the day trawling through those old diaries, trying to work out who might have had a motive for killing the pair of them."

Jóhann nodded. "That family will stick in our minds for some time, I imagine."

"Just think. After everything else, it was simply their own obsessions that killed them," Hrefna said. "They both got hooked on an idea that couldn't be brought to reality—the railroad for Jacob Senior and the family museum for Jacob Junior."

They were quiet for a while, and then Jóhann said, "But the path they chose is so far from being a solution. It's always those left behind that have to saddle the burdens and the pain."

"Yes," Hrefna replied. "I remember something Kirsten said to me: 'The person who killed my father also took a large part of my brother's life.' Jacob Senior definitely made many bad decisions in life, but the way he chose to end it was the worst one of all. I'm sure that Jacob Junior would have turned into a very different man had he enjoyed the guidance of his father."

Jóhann excused himself; he needed a nice hot shower as well. Afterward he put on a clean pair of pajamas and a thick robe, and they sat in the kitchen long into the night, eating a bit of smoked salmon on toast and finishing the bottle of white wine. They talked about everything except police work.

"Let's go to bed," Hrefna finally said.

They crawled into bed and she snuggled up against him. "This is good, but let's not do anything more tonight. Too much has happened today, and I need to think a bit about Matthías and dear Halli."

They fell asleep wrapped in each other's arms.

Jóhann woke up toward morning to the sound of a radio from the apartment above. He looked at the clock. It was just after six; that's weird, he thought, the state radio station didn't start broadcasting until seven o'clock, but he could clearly hear the voice of a familiar reporter.

He looked over at Hrefna and decided to stop thinking about the radio. Nothing else that might be happening in the world could spoil this moment. He kissed her gently on the cheek and fell back asleep again.

Diary XIX

July 8, 1945. Matthías arrives tomorrow.

377

AUTHOR'S NOTE

The story told here is a novel (as *Merriam-Webster* has it, "an invented prose narrative of considerable length"); no characters that appear in the story are real, nor are they based on real persons. The events as described in the novel have not actually happened.

In writing the story, however, I have consulted a large body of source material, both published and unpublished, and in a few instances have copied sentences unaltered into the narrative, for which indulgence I should like to thank their authors.

The original of the poem quoted in chapter 46 is by Adalsteinn Ásberg Sigurdsson, and was written specifically for this novel at the request of the author. It has not been published anywhere else prior to this.

Before parting with my reader, I should like to explain what lies behind the final paragraph of the novel. On the night before Tuesday, January 23, 1973, an unexpected volcanic eruption began in the Westman Islands, just off the south coast of Iceland, and what Jóhann hears indistinctly is the Icelandic State Radio reporter's account of that event.

Viktor Arnar Ingólfsson
September 1998, Reykjavik

ABOUT THE AUTHOR

Viktor Arnar Ingolfsson is the author of several books, including *Daybreak*, which was the basis for the 2008 Icelandic television series *Hunting Men*. *House of Evidence*, his third novel, was nominated for the Glass Key Award, given by the Crime Writers Association of Scandinavia, in 2001, and *The Flatey Enigma* was nominated for the same prize in 2004.

ABOUT THE TRANSLATORS

 Björg Árnadóttir is Icelandic but has lived most of her life in England; her husband Andrew Cauthery is English but fluent in Icelandic. They have worked together as translators for some years now, both English into Icelandic and Icelandic into English. Their experience includes a wide variety of subjects, including books on Icelandic nature, technical topics, and literature.

House of Evidence is their first work for AmazonCrossing.